# Gifts of Grace

Three Novellas

# Kathy McKinsey

©2021 by Kathy McKinsey

Published by Scrivenings Press LLC
15 Lucky Lane
Morrilton, Arkansas 72110
https://ScriveningsPress.com

Printed in the United States of America

All rights reserved. No part of this publication may be reproduced, stored in a retrieval system, or transmitted in any form or by any means—for example, electronic, photocopy and recording— without the prior written permission of the publisher. The only exception is brief quotation in printed reviews.

Second Edition
Paperback ISBN 978-1-64917-119-1
eBook ISBN 978-1-64917-120-7

Cover by Diane Turpin at dianeturpindesigns.com

(Note: This book was previously published in 2019 by Mantle Rock Publishing LLC and was re-published as is when Scrivenings Press acquired the publishing rights in 2021.)

Scriptures used:

Holy Bible, New International Version®, NIV® Copyright ©1973, 1978, 1984, 2011 by Biblica, Inc.® Used by permission. All rights reserved worldwide.

Revised Standard Version of the Bible, copyright © 1946, 1952, and 1971 the Division of Christian Education of the National Council of the Churches of Christ in the United States of America. Used by permission. All rights reserved.

*Holy Bible*, New Living Translation, copyright © 1996, 2004, 2015 by Tyndale House Foundation. Used by permission of Tyndale House Publishers, Inc., Carol Stream, Illinois 60188. All rights reserved.

*DEDICATION*

*To Pamela Roddy, my best friend. We have laughed together and cried together since first grade. You are precious to me, and I thank God for you.*

THANK YOU

To Mantle Rock Publishing for helping my dreams come true. To my wonderful ACFW critique partners, just thank you so. To my family, for making my life shine, for giving my life substance.

# AS WE'VE BEEN LOVED

This is love: not that we loved God, but that he loved us and sent his Son as an atoning sacrifice for our sins. Dear friends, since God so loved us, we also ought to love one another.

— 1 JOHN 4:10-11 (NIV)

## CHAPTER 1

"Grandma, you are so lucky." C.T. looked up at me, his face crumpled, ready to sleep. "You live in a house with four men." His eyes closed then opened again. "And a big dog. We'll always make sure you're safe."

My heart warmed as I bent to kiss him. "You're right. Who would dare to mess with me?"

He curled into a ball then buried his face in his arms. "Love you, Grandma. Have a good sleep."

"I love you too, baby." After tucking the covers around my seven-year-old little man, I tiptoed out of his room.

Safety was not my concern with these four men, but I did have concerns. *Lord God, help us. Especially with this new man in our home.*

At the top of the stairs, I stopped to listen. All I could hear was the television, with loud cars screeching, coming from Al's room. I sighed. Al was hard of hearing, so he kept the volume high. How would my husband and son handle that?

Not that a loud TV was my biggest worry.

My son Roland had his class tonight, but what was Karl thinking?

Pushing Al's door open a few inches, I peeked inside. "Are you all right in here?"

Al lay on his bed with a magazine in front of his face. "Sure enough, Tammy. Thank you."

Does he have to yell?

"Is the TV on too high?" He yelled louder.

Is he even watching the TV? "Maybe a little."

As I stepped farther into the room, Al picked up the remote and lowered the volume.

"Sorry about that."

"It's okay." What else could I say to this man I didn't know? "I'm taking the dog for a walk soon. Do you need anything?"

"Nah. I'm pretty much wiped out. I'm gonna take my medicine soon and go to sleep. You have a good night." He laid the magazine down. "Thank you for everything."

"Oh, sure. Of course." My voice squeaked. "Good night then." I hesitated. "Let us know if you need anything."

Closing the door, I walked across to Karl's and my room. My mouth was dry. "Honey? You okay?"

Karl lay in the middle of our double bed, a magazine in front of his face too. I swallowed and stopped from mentioning the similarity between father and son.

"I'm fine." Karl didn't lower the magazine.

I perched on the bed beside him and laid my hand on his arm. "I love you."

He stiffened under my hand. "Love you too."

He doesn't want to talk to me right now.

Squeezing my arms around my middle, I got up and headed back to the kitchen.

"Father God, how are we going to handle this?"

Before I could set the first plate in the dishwasher, the doorbell rang.

Our dog Rudy raised his head from where he lay by the back door.

"Who could that be, Rudy?"

He stood and walked with me to check it out.

Peeking through the small window by the front door, I saw a woman on the front porch. In the glow of streetlights, the way she tilted her head looked familiar.

My heart jumped.

I opened the door and stared at the young woman in front of me. "Heather? Is that, is that you?"

She raised her chin. "Yes, Mrs. Sandholz. Tammy. Yes, it's me."

It was truly Heather standing on my front porch. My son's wife. The mother of my grandson. We hadn't seen her for almost eight years.

# CHAPTER 2

With my mouth hanging open, I stood still for long seconds.

"Mrs. Sandholz?"

Shaking my head, I stood back. "Heather. Wow. Come in."

She stepped in but stopped when she saw Rudy. "That's a big dog."

Rudy had already turned and gone back to lie down in the kitchen.

"He's part Alaskan husky and the rest lazy mutt. He's harmless."

Heather blinked then glanced around.

Is she looking for someone?

"Roland's not home tonight. He has class. C.T.'s asleep. Everybody else is in bed."

Stop babbling, Tammy.

"I'm sorry. Sit down. Please." I nodded to the couch then sat in a chair close by.

Heather sat, crossed her ankles, clutched her purse, uncrossed her ankles.

She's as nervous as I am.

"There's no easy way to start this conversation, I guess." She cleared her throat, then met my eyes. "I thought you all should know that I've moved back home."

My mind spun. Almost eight years. She'd left when C.T. was three weeks old.

"I don't know what to say."

Heather took in a long breath. "Me either."

I jumped up. "Would you like a cup of coffee? Tea?" Give me something to do.

"Sure. Please. Coffee would be great." Her gaze darted around the room. "Can I help?"

"No, no. It's already made. It'll just take a minute."

Hurrying into the kitchen, I banged into a counter. *Lord, what do I do now?*

My feet couldn't move. My mind wouldn't focus.

Coffee. Mugs. Cream and sugar.

"Heather, do you take cream or sugar?" I couldn't remember.

"Just a little cream." Her voice sounded different than I remembered.

Don't forget, she's almost eight years older.

Sucking in a long breath, I steadied the mugs in my hands and walked back to the living room. We sat quiet, sipping our coffee, my eyes fixed on her bent head. What could I say? Why did you leave? Where have you been? Why did you think it was okay for you to come back to this house?

"I've moved back for good."

Although soft, her voice so surprised me that I gulped my coffee and burned my mouth. Spluttering, I hurried to set the cup down, then grabbed a tissue from the table beside me.

"I'm sorry. I didn't mean to startle you." Heather continued to talk. "Right now, I'm staying with my parents, but I plan to get my own place soon. I'm working as a social worker at Nichols Nursing Center." She caught her breath.

She said she was sorry. For startling me.

Tammy, pull yourself together.

"Good. A social worker. That sounds like a great job." Roland had planned to be a doctor. "So, college. You went to college. I mean, of course, you did. Where?"

Did I care where? Eight years and Roland was still slowly working his way through school, one or two classes at a time.

"In L.A. I lived with my aunt and uncle out there while I was in school." Her knuckles turned white as she squeezed her coffee cup. "I worked at a hospital out there for a couple years, but..."

She raised her head and caught me watching her. Her eyes widened, and she bent to set her cup down on the floor.

"So I decided to come home. And I applied for the job here, and I started this week." Her shoulders jerked. "I just thought, I thought I should let you all know."

What now?

"Okay. Thank you. Like I said, Roland isn't home right now. So..."

Heather jumped up. "I'll call him. I really should be going. Thanks for the coffee."

Before I could open my mouth or move to stand up, she'd dashed through the front door and closed it behind her.

My pulse pounded inside my head. *Dear Lord, what is this going to do to us?*

## CHAPTER 3

"Rudy, where did you get to?" I needed to take the dog for a walk. Probably more than he needed to go.

The large, black and gray and yellow and red dog meandered into the living room. Even at three years old, he was never in much of a hurry.

Picking up his leash, I stopped in front of our bedroom. "Honey," I called through the closed door.

No answer.

You're a chicken, Tammy. I texted Karl.

"Taking Rudy for a walk."

My phone buzzed as I snapped on the leash.

"Fine."

Oh my.

We turned right after leaving the house, moving toward the park a couple of blocks away.

Rudy, still in no hurry, stopped to sniff in each yard we passed.

"Father God, Heather's back. How is Roland going to handle that? What about C.T.? Poor baby."

Rudy stopped again and picked up something from the ground.

"Rudy, no. That's trash." Yanking the candy wrapper out of his mouth, I shoved it into my pocket.

"And, Lord, I'm the one who said yes to Al moving in with us. Without asking Karl first."

Rudy's ears perked up. Down the street, our neighbor Joan approached with her two poodles. As always on their walks, they strained at their leashes, running ahead of Joan, with excited yips.

"No, Rudy. Stay. Let them pass."

Standing still, I switched Rudy to my other side and waited until Joan and the loudmouths could pass us. When the poodles saw Rudy, their volume increased, if possible, and they struggled their little bodies even harder to get to him.

Joan wore earphones, her head dancing back and forth with the music. When she was eight feet from me, I could hear her music beating and whining. "Hey, Tammy," she yelled and shot me a wide smile as we nearly collided. "Nice evening, isn't it?"

Then they were gone.

"Good boy, Rudy. Good boy. Stay still." As I rested my hand on his back, his body quivered with the urge to follow them.

Once they were a house behind us, I wiggled Rudy's leash. "Come on, buddy. Let's move on."

I drew in a breath. "What could I have done, Lord? Frances said she and John couldn't take Al into their house. John's recovering from hip surgery. She's fighting her own health problems. They're both seventy-five. What could I say?"

Rudy stopped to look up at me.

Lower your voice, Tammy.

Once we made it to the park, I found my favorite bench, switched Rudy to the long leash, and fastened my end to my leg.

It was time to call Torie.

"Hi, Mom, what's up?"

Our daughter lived a five-hour drive from home. Since I couldn't stop into her apartment on a minute's notice, I used the phone to beg her for support when I needed to dump.

"Hi, sweetie. I just thought I'd let you know what's happening on the home front today."

Torie yawned. "Which highlight did you want to drop? That Heather is back in town, or that Grandfather had heart surgery and is now living at our house?"

"Whoa. You are good. I see your brother got to you before I did." My eyes opened wider. "Wait, how did he know about Heather? She just left the house ten minutes ago, and he's in class."

"What? She came to the house?" Torie perked up. "No way. Roland called me a couple of hours ago, before he went to class. After Heather's mom called him. She really came to the house? Did she see C.T.? That's crazy."

"Heather's mom called Roland today?" I hesitated. "What did you say? No, of course, I didn't let her see C.T. What did Roland say Heather's mom said? Rudy, stop that. Leave them alone."

I pulled on Rudy's leash as he circled around a couple of teens on swings. "Leave them alone, buddy, or I'll tie you down. Those kids are wearing shorts, no sweaters. What on earth do their parents teach them? It's mid-April, not June. They've gotta be freezing."

"Mother." Torie's voice blasted from the phone I'd lowered.

"Sorry, sweetie. Good boy, Rudy. Chase those squirrels instead. They can get away from you."

"Mother?"

"Yes, sorry, I'm back. So, tell me what Roland told you."

"As soon as you tell me about Heather bothering C.T. at the house."

I wiggled the leash a little and sucked in a long breath. "Okay, I'll go first. Just after C.T. went to bed, Heather came by. She had a cup of coffee, sat and talked to me about five minutes, and saw no one else in the house but me. Now you talk. What did Roland say?"

On the other end of the line, Torie banged dishes in the sink. "So, Mrs. Thomas called, said Heather had moved back, and asked if she could give her Roland's number."

"Huh. What did Roland do then?"

"What do you think? He flipped out. He hung up on her."

Grinding my teeth, I made myself wait through the noise of Torie pouring coffee and clinking a spoon into the cup.

She gulped a drink. "Then he called her back and said, okay, give Heather his number. If C.T. was my kid, I'd grab him up and leave the country."

"Oh, honey." I rubbed my eyes.

The swinging kids got up to leave, and Rudy tried to follow them out of the park. Once he pulled the leash taut, he snuffed with disgust and came back to lie at my feet.

"Good boy."

"You and Rudy are out for a walk, huh? The little woman with the big dog."

"Ha ha." I scratched behind my dog's ears. Everyone in my family, in my church, in my neighborhood, felt comfortable calling us this, my big, funny-looking dog and me. All four-foot-eleven-and- three-quarter-inches and 102 pounds of me.

Torie giggled.

## CHAPTER 4

"I don't want to go home, Rudy."

Rudy tugged at the leash. He did want to go home, lazy dog.

Torie and I had talked for close to half an hour, then I made Rudy walk three times around our block.

"You have to go home, Tammy. You've made yourself responsible for taking care of Al."

We entered the quiet house, and I released Rudy. He ran straight to his food bowl.

"Oh sure, now you show some energy."

I filled his food and water bowls then sat on a kitchen chair. "What should I do now?"

Roland was home. His car sat in the drive, so I didn't need to check on C.T.

With a deep sigh, I stood up. Get it over with.

After peeking in Al's room to make sure he was asleep, I straightened my shoulders and walked into my bedroom.

Karl sat on the edge of the bed, his head cradled in his large hands.

I closed the door and stood just inside. "Honey?"

He raised his head. His face held so much pain.

My eyes ached. "Honey, I'm sorry. I didn't know…"

"You didn't know what?" Karl sat up straight. His mouth set into a sharp line as he stared at me. Now he looked mad. "You didn't know I'd be upset that you invited my father to stay here without asking me?"

"Please lower your voice."

"Why? So he won't hear me and figure out I don't want him here? I'm pretty sure he already knows that."

Karl stood, then sat down again. He knew I felt intimidated if he stood over me when we argued. He was six-two, and I was, well, the little woman.

My heart squeezed with love that he had the kindness to care about that right now.

I gulped and dug my nails into my palms. "I tried to call you. You were in meetings all day. Aunt Frances was in a panic."

"She's his sister. She can care about him if she wants to. That doesn't mean she gets to force him on us."

My breath caught. "What else could she do? She isn't able to have him at her house. The hospital was ready to release him, and he couldn't stay by himself. What else—"

"A nursing home? Assisted living?" Karl grabbed up the magazine he'd been reading and clenched it in his hands. "Call an old girlfriend. Anything except bring him here without asking me."

Don't tell him to lower his voice again.

"He needed somewhere to go. He, he's our…"

Karl's head snapped back. "Our what? Our family?" He stood up and threw the magazine to the floor. "No, he's not. When he walked out on my mom and me, when he left me as a two-year-old, he gave up being part of my family." As he walked toward the door, I moved to the bed and sank down.

Karl turned at the door and faced me. "You feel like it's your Christian duty to take care of the sick? Fine. I'm not a part of it."

He closed the door harder than he needed to as he left the room.

~

Karl didn't come back to our room that night. When I woke in the morning, he'd already left for work, before six a.m.

In the kitchen, I started the coffee and fed Rudy. "Should I check on Al?"

Pulling out a chair, I sat at the kitchen table. "Surely he doesn't need to wake up this early." I rubbed my face and groaned. "What should I feed him?"

When Aunt Frances and her son Jack dropped Al and his TV off yesterday afternoon, she'd also given me a can of peaches and a carton of cottage cheese.

"That's all he said when I asked what he wanted to eat," she'd told me. "In the morning, I'll bring by more groceries. They've had a hard time getting him to eat much in the hospital. He certainly needs to be careful about his diet, but I'll try to find some things he'll eat."

I sighed. Last evening, Al ate a small bowl of cottage cheese and peaches. There had to be something different I could offer him for breakfast. Maybe scrambled eggs, just the whites, cooked with a tiny bit of butter for taste. "I need to be careful how much salt I give him too."

Rudy looked at me, then slapped his tail against the linoleum.

"I'm not talking about you. You've already had breakfast."

Roland walked into the room. "Are you talking to Rudy or yourself?"

He had his back to me as he got out cereal bowls and glasses for his and C.T.'s breakfast.

Show me your face, honey.

He didn't. He pulled down a box of cereal from a shelf then walked to the refrigerator for milk.

I swallowed. "How are you this morning?"

"Good. How about you?"

He still didn't look at me.

*Father, we have to get this elephant out of the room.*

"Torie told me Heather's mom called you."

He set the milk on the table. "Yeah. She told me Heather came to see you last night."

Roland was only seventeen months older than Torie, and they'd grown up as close friends. Normally, I was glad about that, but they always talked to each other about their private lives long before they said anything to me.

"She did." Now I kept my face turned away from him. "She said she's working at Nichols Retirement Center as a social worker."

"I know." He poured cereal into the bowls. "I talked to Heather last night too."

My head swung around to face him. "She already called you last night? What..." I stopped. What was I going to ask? What would he want to tell me?

Roland moved toward the door to call down to his son. "She wants to see C.T. Of course, she does." His shoulders slumped. "I told her I needed to talk to him first." He half turned back to me. "You don't need to pick him up from school today. I've asked to leave work early so I can pick him up and talk to him."

"So soon?"

He shrugged. "I'd better. Before she shows up here again when he's awake."

He went to the top of the basement stairs. "Come on, C.T. It's time for breakfast."

Lowering my face to my hands, I whispered, "Dear Lord. Oh. Please help us."

## CHAPTER 5

When I knocked on Al's door an hour later, he sat on the side of his bed, his arms wrapped around a large, red, heart-shaped pillow.

I laughed. "Did they give you that at the hospital?"

He cleared his throat. "Yeah. It's supposed to help my chest not hurt so bad when I cough."

Moving to his side, I rested my hand on his shoulder. "Do you have a cold?"

He shook his head. "Smoker's cough." He inhaled a long, shaky breath. "I've been smoking for sixty-five years. No more though."

"Why? Because of your heart?"

"Yep. The first time I saw Frances at the hospital after I had the heart attack, I told her to send somebody to my apartment and throw away every cigarette and lighter they could find." He hacked again, and his thin shoulders shook. "I've never had so much pain as this. I'll never smoke again."

"That's a smart decision. I looked at your papers from the hospital yesterday, about what you should and shouldn't eat.

Would you like some scrambled eggs? I think I can make them healthy and good."

He lifted his head and smiled. "That's nice of you, but not today. Is there still some of that cottage cheese and peaches Frances brought?"

"Yes." I stepped back. "Do you want me to bring you a bowl?"

"No." He laid the big heart pillow aside and pushed himself up. "I'll come in the kitchen if that's okay. I need to walk. They started me walking the day after surgery."

When he made it to his feet, I rested my hand on his arm. "Okay, but take it slow. You're a big man, and I'm pretty small. I don't think I could pick you up if you fell."

He laughed then stopped and pressed his hand to his chest. "Watch yourself now, young lady. You don't want to get me coughing without my pillow."

When Al was seated at the table, I set his food in front of him. "What about coffee? I don't remember if the paperwork said you could have that."

"Get me some anyway. No matter what it says, I'm not giving up coffee."

I chuckled. "So you like coffee better than cigarettes. You are a smart man." After pouring us both a cup, I sat down across from him.

His hand shook as he picked up his coffee. He let go of his spoon in the bowl of cottage cheese and grasped the mug with both hands.

When he looked across at me, a shock ran through me at how much he looked like Karl. Including the pain in his eyes.

"I heard my son yelling at you last night."

I cringed and opened my mouth.

He shook his head. "Don't say anything. Just listen." His jaw trembled. "I know how that boy feels about me. And I don't blame him." He looked down, then up again. "I don't think I have much choice but to be here with you all right now." His voice was a whisper, and a tear slid down his face. "All I can do is thank you. And promise I'll be gone the minute I'm able."

∽

"Yeah, yeah, just make sure you do what the doctor says." Aunt Frances banged Al's door shut then walked into the kitchen.

"I'll tell you, Tammy, men are worse than little kids to watch when they're sick." She shook her head and sat at the table. "He's arguing about the new medicine the doctor prescribed. Says he won't take it. It makes him constipated." She huffed. "He's as bad as John."

"How is Uncle John feeling?" The coffee pot was empty, so I filled it with water and reached for a filter. "Do you want coffee? Wait, no, you like tea, don't you?"

"If you have some, and if it's no trouble. John was back in the hospital for a day earlier this week. He got an infection at the site of the surgery."

"I'm so sorry." I stood on my step stool to look on a top shelf in the cabinet. "We have some peach tea from the last time Torie was home. She likes flavored tea."

"That sounds great. Thank you." She stood up. "Let me fix it."

I hopped down from the stool. "Aunt Frances, sit down. Rest your bones a little." After filling a cup with water, I set it in the microwave. "So he's home again? Uncle John?"

"Yes. And crabbier than he was before. The doctor said he should be fine now with antibiotics. We just need to keep an eye on the surgical site." She gave a heavy sigh. "Listen, I know this is really bad, asking you to take Al, but I just can't right now. My blood pressure is so much higher already with everything John needs from me and…"

"Frances, come on now." I placed her tea in front of her. "Of course, you can't take Al on too. You let me know if I can help you in any way. The last thing you need is to get sick yourself."

She stirred sugar into her tea. "Thank you, but what about Karl?" She took a sip then set the cup down. "I can still remember how mad he got the one time he saw Al at my house. It must've been close to a year before he talked to me again. I was afraid he never would."

My throat caught. *Oh, Father, I certainly remember that day too.*

Frances sighed. "I've always been grateful Karl let me be a part of his life after Al left. And Lucy, his mom, she was so nice to me too. You never met her, did you?"

"No. She died his senior year in high school, and I didn't meet him until a couple years after that."

I can't tell her how mad Karl is.

"We're going to be fine. And seriously." Motioning to the groceries still waiting to be put away, I gave her my meanest mom scowl. "No more buying groceries. I can handle that. I've already been looking at the hospital papers, to check out his dietary instructions. Stop it now. You can come visit him if you want, but leave everything to me."

"I know you'll do a good job. Your whole family is medical, aren't they? What did you do before the kids were born? Physical therapist or something?"

"I was a P.T. assistant." Smiling, I shook my head. "My parents are doctors, and both of my brothers. I wanted something with a whole lot less school."

"How's Roland doing with his studies? What's he want to do? Be a nurse, isn't it?"

"A nurse practitioner." Another bunch of subjects I didn't want to get into. Opening the refrigerator, I unpacked the groceries she'd brought. "How're your kids doing? We should all get together again next Christmas."

Frances talked on and on about her kids and grandkids, but I couldn't listen. My mind jumped back to my husband.

Karl's mom died of breast cancer during his senior year in high school. Then, the night of his graduation, his father showed up, after being gone for sixteen years.

"He wanted to try to make things right between us." Karl talked to me about his dad so little. Even though it'd been years ago, I could remember his exact words. "Make things right. After I'd finished school and already had a job." The bitterness on his face had scared me. "Once Mom was dead, and he didn't have to help take care of her or watch her die. He wanted to make things right."

My heart still ached from watching his pain and hearing it.

"I told him the most right thing he could do was make sure I never had to look at his face again."

*I have to stop thinking about this.*

Shaking my head to clear my mind, I sat across from Frances again. "Wait, what did you say? The youngest grandbaby is how old?"

# CHAPTER 6

Karl sent a text to say he wouldn't be home for dinner. Roland called and said since it was Friday night and there was no school tomorrow, he and C.T. were eating out and going to a movie.

Al still didn't feel like eating, but he finally agreed to half of a tuna sandwich. "You can bring it to my room this time, please."

"But you need to walk a little, don't you?"

"I will. Tomorrow. Promise." His face sagged with exhaustion.

"Okay, but please let me know if you need anything."

As I let Rudy out into the backyard, I heard Karl come in the front door and head straight into our room.

"No 'hello' or 'anybody home?' tonight, I guess."

I stayed at the back door until Rudy woofed to get back in. "Hey, buddy." When I bent down to hug him, he licked my face. "At least you love me."

After ten minutes, I forced myself to walk into our room.

My heart jumped to my throat.

"Honey, what are you doing? Where are you going?"

Karl closed the second suitcase then picked both up and

turned to face me. "Walk with me to the car. I know you won't want either of us to yell in the house."

"We're going to yell?" My voice already hit a pretty high scale. Squeezing my arms around my middle, I tried again. "Would it be better to yell in front of the neighbors?"

"Let's sit in the car and shut the doors."

I could see no choice but to follow him, with his two suitcases, out of the front door.

"What's going on?" My teeth chattered. I was so scared.

Karl leaned against his door to face me, resting one arm on the steering wheel. "I need some time." Did his voice shake too? "I'm going to stay with Randy for a while."

The wind slammed out of me. "You're what?" My voice squeaked.

Karl's other fist clenched in his lap. "I need to be somewhere I can clear my head. You letting my—" He choked. "Letting him into the house, it's knocked me off my feet."

"Honey, you were in a meeting. For hours. I tried." My whole face trembled. Tears streamed down.

He sucked in a long breath. "I hear you. I understand that. But, you let him into my house."

Who was this man? "So you're leaving me?"

"I am not leaving you." Anger filled his face. "I'm not my father."

Both of us gulped for air. Karl reached to switch on the fan.

"I need some space." His voice was softer now. "I need to figure out what has happened to us."

"To us?" Opening the glove box, I found a couple of napkins and scrubbed at my face. "What are you talking about? Honey, I know I have no idea what you went through. But it's been more than fifty years. And, he's seventy-eight, and he needs help. And, you're a Christian—"

"That is what I'm talking about." He slammed his fist on the horn, making me jump. "I'm a Christian. Yes, I am. And what are you, my spiritual mentor? My teacher? Always, you're telling me and the kids how we should live our lives as Christians. Who made you the Christian leader of all of us?"

Whoa.

He surely was yelling.

And he didn't touch me, but I felt like my head had been slammed from side to side.

Is this really happening?

"Me? I..." I closed my mouth.

Karl's eyes were wide, and his breaths were ragged. He buried his face in his hands and moaned.

Looking out the window, I saw a couple of neighbors had stepped out on their porch. The car was closed up. It must have been the horn blasting that brought them out.

"Tammy?"

I turned my gaze back to Karl.

"Honey, I'm sorry. I didn't mean to shout at you. And I didn't mean to say all that. Except..."

Except he meant it. My head spun.

He sighed. "I need to straighten out my brain. About my father. About us."

Us? I wished he'd touch me.

I have to get out of here.

Before I knew what happened, I was standing outside the car, leaning on the door. "Okay." My throat caught, and I swallowed. "Do what you need to." I closed the car door gently, waved at the neighbors, then walked to the house.

## CHAPTER 7

*A*fter locking the front door, I wanted to run to my room and curl into a ball on the bed.

But Al stood in the living room, leaning against the wall, staring at me.

My head fell back against the door. *Dear Lord, I don't think I can stand this.*

"Tammy?"

When I lifted my head, Al had moved to the chair next to the couch and sat. "Please come sit down a minute."

My stomach quaked. *Am I going to throw up?*

"Tammy."

Obeying his soft voice seemed to be the right thing to do right then. I walked to the couch and dropped down.

Al leaned forward, his elbows on his knees. "He left because of me." It wasn't a question.

"He, I…" My throat ached. My hands covered my face, and I pushed words out. "He said he needs time to, to think. About, about us."

Al reached out and pulled my hands from my face. "Please look at me."

My eyes met his.

"I am so sorry." His eyes looked old, weary, sad. A tear coursed down his cheek. "So sorry."

With my shoulders shaking, I lowered my head and wept. Al moved to the couch and wrapped his arms around me, cradling my head on his shoulder like a child. Neither of us found anything else to say. There was nothing for us to say.

AFTER CRYING for such a long time, I was able to sleep. When I woke in the morning and shuffled into the kitchen, Roland and C.T. were already at the table eating toaster waffles.

"Grandma, guess what." Excited, C.T. jumped up and knocked over his milk. "My mom's come home."

"Whoa, buddy." Roland turned his back to grab paper towels, so I couldn't see his face.

Come home, C.T. said. What did that mean to him?

"I heard that." Picking up the empty milk glass, I filled it half full. "Sit down, sweetie. Did you get milk on your shirt?"

"Just a little. Isn't that great? My mom's back. She's at Grandma Ellen's house. Daddy and I get to go see her today." He gulped down all the milk in the glass. "Isn't that great?"

His smile could not have been bigger.

I had very little idea what C.T. thought about his mother. None of us talked bad about her. Roland insisted on that. We didn't talk about her at all.

The Thompsons were good people, and Roland let C.T. visit them, as long as they promised not to let him talk to his mom without asking Roland first.

As far as I knew, Heather'd never tried to make contact. Until now.

I hugged C.T. "Wow." What should I say? "Are you finished eating? You do have a lot of milk on your shirt."

"I'll go change it right now." He jumped up again. "Then can we go, Daddy? After I get a new shirt?"

Roland turned back from the sink. "Sure. Brush your teeth too."

"I'll brush 'em good. Promise."

And he was out the door and rattling down the stairs.

Walking to my son, I took hold of his hands. "Are you okay?"

Roland slumped against the counter. "I have to be. This time had to come sooner or later. I guess." He took one of his hands from my grasp and rubbed his face.

I tipped my head to try to catch his expression, but he still kept his face turned from me. He squeezed my hands, then walked to the door. "Heather's mom has asked us for lunch. I don't know if I'll last that long. Pray for me, Mom."

"I will, sweetheart," I whispered to his retreating back.

*Father, how long has it been since Roland asked me to pray for him?*

# CHAPTER 8

"Spring cleaning. That's what I need to do."

And except for a periodic check on Al to make sure he ate something, that's what I did for the rest of that day. Vacuuming, mopping, dusting, washing windows. I stored away winter clothes and extra blankets and piled anything that might need washing on the floor of the laundry room. Anything to keep my mind from thinking. About Karl, Heather, and most of all, I didn't want to think about myself.

Al stayed in his room with his TV on, and he told me he didn't mind if I turned on music. So, except when the vacuum was on, I put the radio on high volume. Whatever I could pile on to shut my mind off.

Only because Rudy barked did I know Roland and C.T. came home.

Hurrying to flip off the radio, I looked at my boys. Roland's mouth and eyes looked pinched. C.T.'s face shone.

"Grandma, I met my mom." He spun in a circle and jumped, then spun again. "She's so pretty. Did you know that? Grandma Ellen says I look just like her."

"You do look a lot like her, son." Roland sank into a chair. "Quit jumping for a minute, or you'll make me dizzy."

Roland looked ten years older after one day.

"I'm glad you had a good day, sweetie." I sat on another chair and drew C.T. to me for a hug.

Roland held his head in his hands. "I have to get ready for work, Mom." He lifted his face. "And we're going to church with Heather and her folks in the morning. I have to work tomorrow afternoon, so Heather will bring C.T. home after lunch." He stood and walked to the stairs. "You okay, with Al here and C.T. too? Where's Dad?"

"I'm fine. We'll be fine, honey." My stomach clenched. "Just get ready for work. And call your dad."

Let Karl explain this to the kids.

AL CAME to the table for dinner, and C.T. was still moving at hyper speed.

"You're my Daddy's grandpa, right? And you had a heart attack. Can I call you Grandpa Al?"

"Please do. And what do I call you?"

"Everybody calls me C.T. I'm named after my Grandpa Chris, Christopher Thomas. He's Chris and I'm C.T."

"Makes sense. So everybody knows who everybody is."

They talked on, Al slow and steady, C.T. fast and bubbly. It was easy for me to sit between them, quiet, forcing myself to take one bite after another.

You have to eat, Tammy. To keep up your health, to take care of Al and C.T.

"You haven't met my mom yet. Her name's Heather. She's really pretty." C.T. took a long drink of juice, then burped. "Oh, excuse me, Grandma. Daddy and I are going to church with

Mommy tomorrow morning. Daddy usually doesn't go to church, and I usually go with Grandma Tammy and Grandpa Karl. But my other grandparents and Mommy go to a different church, and Daddy said he'd go with them tomorrow, so I am too. It'll be so much fun." He stuffed too much chicken in his mouth, so he couldn't talk for a minute.

He's already calling her Mommy. Should I be more shocked about that, or that Roland's going to church?

C.T. pushed his chair back from the table and sprang up. "Grandma, I'm gonna take a shower and get ready for bed. I want to be up and ready to go when it's time for us to meet Mommy at church."

It was seven o'clock. Long before C.T. usually would agree to go to bed.

"Okay, buddy. I'll come down to tuck you in after you take a shower. Do you want me to read to you if you're not sleepy yet?"

He shoved his chair in. "Not tonight. I'm pretty sleepy already. I'll read to myself if I can't fall asleep."

My heart squeezed. Am I going to lose this special time at night already?

After I'd prayed with C.T. and kissed him good night, I found Al still sitting at the table, sipping his glass of water. He definitely didn't move as fast through his evening as C.T.

"He's quite a mover. No wonder you stay so young, keeping up with him. What's your boy do for work? Frances tries to keep me up to date about everybody, but my memory is rusty."

He would be a resident by now, just finished with med school, if it hadn't been for this pretty Mommy.

Shaking my head, I pulled out a chair to sit back at the table.

Watch your mouth, Tammy, and your heart.

"Roland works at the hospital as a certified nursing assistant. He's going to school to be a registered nurse. Just a class or two at a time. He's pretty busy, working, going to school, taking care of his little boy. Eventually, he plans to be a nurse practitioner. He wanted to be a doctor, but…" I stopped and bit my lip. "Anyway, he's pretty busy. We're glad we can help."

"I'm sure you are." He didn't ask questions, and I wasn't in the mood to go into more detail right then.

## CHAPTER 9

My bedroom door squeaked open.
Whispering.
"Grandma's still asleep, buddy. Shh, let's not bother her."
"I want to tell her good-bye."
"Shh, no. Come on, let's leave for church."
"Good-bye, Grandma." A loud whisper, then the bedroom door closed again.

Was I still dreaming?

Throughout the night, I'd rolled and tossed, throwing off the covers, pulling them back. Once, not finding my pillow, I switched the lamp on to look for it. It lay on the floor beside the bed, Rudy sprawled over it. Tears stung my eyes as I reached for Karl's pillow. Karl's smell, old sweat and shampoo.

Noises I'd learned to shut out for years interrupted my sleep. Cars passing, neighbors arriving home late, the train blaring several blocks away. Did someone come in the house? Was Karl home?

When I'd drifted back to sleep, in my dreams, I walked through the house, downstairs, back up, opening every door.

Then I was outside, hurrying, panting, a long search through unfamiliar streets. Where was Karl?

And when I woke, he wasn't there, so I groaned and turned over again, and buried my head under his pillow. *I don't want that dream again.*

The bed creaked as someone sat on the side. "Tammy?" A gentle hand on my arm.

Pushing away the pillow, I opened my eyes.

Al sat beside me. "I'm sorry to bother you, but your dog wants to go out, and I'm afraid I might not be able to get him back inside if I let him out."

"What time is it?" My voice came out hoarse. The phone on the table beside the bed read 10:00 a.m. "What am I doing still in bed?"

Al stood, and I sat up, rubbing the sleep out of my eyes and swinging my feet onto the floor. "Where is Rudy?"

"Is that the dog? He's by the back door. I wasn't sure if there was any way he could get out of the yard, so I didn't send him out."

"The back yard's all closed in, but he wouldn't get out anyway." I hoisted myself out of bed. "He's such a slug."

After I let Rudy out, I looked for coffee, my head muddy, my eyes dry and achy.

Al came into the kitchen. "Roland made coffee. I saw him and the little guy before they left."

"Do you need more? Looks like there's still enough for both of us." My hands fumbled for a cup.

"I've got some still. Thank you."

I managed to fill my mug without spilling and moved to the table.

"Oh wait. Are you hungry? I'm sorry I slept so late."

"Sit down, girl. Enjoy your coffee. Roland cooked enough scrambled eggs for me too." He smiled. "He insisted on making mine without yolks. I'm not going to be able to cheat on anything, living with all you medical people." He sat in the chair across from mine. "Take it easy a minute."

Steam from the coffee refreshed my face. Closing my eyes, I took several sips, then a deep breath.

"It's Sunday morning. I figured you'd be off to church. Frances said you all always go to church."

"We usually do." I'd realized during the night I couldn't make myself go today. Not without Karl. And Roland was taking C.T. to church with Heather, so I'd cringed at the idea of going alone.

When I looked up, Al's kind eyes looked back at me.

"Anyway, I know you worked long hours cleaning the house yesterday, but I figured you probably wouldn't feel good staying in bed too long." He reached a shaky hand over to cover mine. "Always best to just get up and face the world."

My eyes grew wet, and I reached for a napkin. "You are a wise man." My throat croaked.

"I've lived a lot of years." His voice was kind too. "Lived through some pain. Caused a lot of pain. It all teaches you."

I couldn't bring myself to look into his eyes again.

∽

IT WAS after four before Heather brought C.T. home. Al and I sat in the living room, reading the newspaper when they came in the front door.

"Mommy, I love you." Tears flowed down C.T.'s cheeks. He gave her a hug, then ran downstairs.

I stood up. "Wait. C.T., what's wrong?"

"Let him go, Tammy." Heather stood just inside the front door.

My eyes widened. What...

"What did you just say to me?"

She looked over at Al. "Hi, I'm Heather." Sighing, she turned her face back to me. "He's upset. Roland and I were arguing on the phone while I drove C.T. over here. He's, upset. Just give him some time."

As if she had any idea how to take care of a little boy. I bit my lip to keep from screaming at her. "Rudy, go down and see C.T. Go on, buddy. Good boy."

Heather watched the dog as he scampered down the stairs. "That's a really big dog."

"He's an Alaskan husky. Plus a lot of other stuff."

"How old is he? Is he safe? For C.T.?"

I wanted to laugh, except that I wanted to cry. And punch her. "They're very gentle, good family dogs. Besides, even though he's just three, he's as lazy as if he was twenty." Why was I trying to reassure her? "He and C.T. are great friends."

Heather lifted her shoulders, shifted her feet, turned back to the door. "I'll go. Maybe, maybe I'll call and talk to C.T. later."

Her face crumpled. Was she going to cry?

"I'm going." She moved fast, but she was controlled. The door made a quiet click behind her.

My head spun. Now what?

# CHAPTER 10

*R*udy lay on C.T.'s bed when I came downstairs. Tears were still wet on the little boy's face, but he was asleep. His arm stretched across the dog, and their heads pressed together on the pillow.

Walking back up to the living room, I collapsed onto the couch and picked up the crossword puzzle from the paper. "I guess he cried himself to sleep."

Al took the paper from me. "Are the boy's parents married?"

He is a wise man, forcing me to talk.

"Yes." I pressed my fingers against my forehead and drew in a long breath. "They met at a party at Roland's friend Derick's house. Heather is Derick's cousin. They were seniors in high school."

*I'm not going to be able to keep from crying.*

"I home-schooled both our kids." A sad laugh. "My daughter was so mad at me back then, said it was my fault. She said I kept them away from other kids too much. Roland didn't know how to have a relationship with a girl."

Standing, I gazed around the living room then paced.

"He brought her home to meet us right away. From the

beginning, you could sense the electricity in the air. Like shots of lightning going back and forth between them. Roland told us he was going to a party at her parents' house New Year's Eve and would be there all night." Stubbing my toes against the leg of the coffee table, I blinked tears from my eyes. "They came here the next day and told us they were married. They said they were going to have a baby in July."

"Honey, sit down."

Al's voice was too tender. I couldn't look at him.

"Heather wasn't eighteen yet. The only way her parents would sign for her to get married was if the kids agreed to live with them."

My nose dripped, and I wiped at it with the back of my hand. With my back to Al, I stared without seeing out the front window and went on talking.

"Those were terrible months. We saw very little of Roland. When we did, he was happy, full of hope. He told us he would still be able to go to medical school. He'd been accepted into the six-year med-school program, right out of high school. His grades were always so good." My shoulders shook.

Al's hand rested on my arm. "Please come sit back down, little girl. I'm not strong enough to follow you around the house while you talk."

Back on the couch, I kept my head turned away from Al. "Roland wanted to be a doctor since he was ten. He worked in my brother Nick's family practice office as a teenager, answering phones, cleaning the toilets, whatever needed doing. Just so he could observe as much as possible."

Al placed tissues in my hands.

"He told us he was going to go through the hospital's Certified Nurse's Assistant training program that summer. He planned to work as many hours at the hospital as possible, even while he was going to school, to, to take care of his family. Heather was going to wait on school, staying home with the baby."

Memories flashed behind my closed eyes. They'd been so happy. Heather so pregnant at her high school graduation, laughing, so pretty. Roland with his head down by Heather's in the hospital bed, as she held the baby close to her face.

"Then she just left." My voice grated rough. "When C.T. was three weeks old, and they were still living at her folks' house, Heather disappeared."

Al's soft shaky hand lay against my cheek. "Shh, stop talking. Take a breath."

I couldn't stop. "Roland brought his baby here. I still remember how his face looked that night. You could see his broken heart in his eyes."

Al laid his arm across my shoulders. My hands squeezed so tight, the nails hurt my palms.

"He was a man all of a sudden. He asked if he could come back to live here." I choked. "Like he thought he had to ask. He said he'd finish his training, work as a CNA at the hospital like he planned, and spend as much time with his son as possible. So…" My lips quivered. "So C.T. would always know he had a parent who loved him."

Al pressed my head against his shoulder, but I went on talking.

"He said, maybe later, he'd start taking classes to be a nurse. He didn't care how long it took him. He'd do it slow, so he could be with his boy." I rubbed my face against Al's sleeve. "It's been almost eight years. And he never, never heard from her. Not until last week."

## CHAPTER 11

When Roland came home from work that night, I was waiting up for him. He walked into the kitchen then stopped. "Any coffee left?"

Standing, I poured a cup for him. "Sit down."

His head down, he wrapped his hands around his coffee. "Is C.T. okay?"

"He was crying when he came home this afternoon. He went down and fell asleep with Rudy."

Roland gave a little laugh. "Glad we have that dog."

"He got up for dinner but didn't talk much. Then he went to bed early, said he needed to rest for school." I touched my son's hand. "Rolie?"

He raised his head, his eyes exhausted, his face sagging.

He looks so much older than twenty-six.

"I shouldn't have yelled at Heather over the phone. My intention was not to fight with her around C.T." He blew air out of his lips. "I could hear him crying over the phone. 'Don't yell at each other. Mommy, Daddy, don't fight.'" Roland laid his head on his arm and closed his eyes.

Moving around the table, I circled his shoulders with my arms. "I'm so sorry."

He straightened up. "She wants to start spending time with him, just the two of them." He shook his head. "What am I going to do, Mom?"

I held him closer. *Dear God, how could we ever have been ready for this?*

Roland stood. "I've got to get to sleep. You okay? I talked to Dad…"

No, I can't add more worry to that face.

"I'm fine. We'll be fine." I hugged him again. "Go to bed now."

∼

THE NEXT MORNING I was up on time. Taking a deep breath, I got ready for the day.

You have to keep moving, Tammy. You still have people depending on you.

Al had a doctor's appointment that morning. He'd told me there was a medical transportation service he could get a ride from, but I insisted on driving him. "What else do I have to do? Besides I'd like to go with you, if I can help. I won't force you to let me go into the doctor's office with you. Karl likes me to go with him, but…"

I stopped.

Al laid his hand on mine. "I'd appreciate it if you'd come."

Al sat in my car with a pillow between him and the seatbelt. "What do you usually do during the day?"

"I offered to home-school C.T., but Roland said he wanted to send him to public school." Don't sound so bitter, Tammy. "He's the parent. He has to make the decisions."

Was Karl right? Did I try to tell him and the kids too much what to do with their lives?

"A long time ago, when Torie and Roland were in junior high, I started writing lessons and lesson plans for the homeschooling company we used. I still do that."

"I'm guessing you're good at that. Your teaching was good enough for Roland to get accepted to medical school. And what does your daughter do?"

"Torie's a physical therapist. I was just a PT assistant. She was brave enough to go all the way through school, get a doctorate. I'm not sure my teaching was the reason they did well. They're smart kids."

He tapped my knee. "I'm guessing they couldn't have done it without you."

My heart squeezed with warmth.

∼

AL'S DOCTOR recommended he sign up for the hospital's Cardiac Rehab Program, so we stopped by the clinic after his appointment. As Al was talking to the director and filling out paperwork, I sat in the waiting room and looked at a newspaper someone had left behind.

"Is it? It is. My twin."

I know that excited voice.

Before I could stand, Debra, Debbie, descended on me and wrapped me in a hug. "Tamara. It is you. You still look the same, just like I do."

Doubtful. It'd been, how long? A bunch of years.

Smothered, I squirmed to hug her back. "Dream on, girl." I pushed against my old friend. "Sit down already. You make me feel six years old."

"No, honey." Her grin was as wide as I remembered. "You do look older than that." But she sat down next to me. "What brings you, oh, Mr. Sandholz. I just met him. Are you guys related?"

"He's Karl's dad."

"Oh." She blinked, thinking that over. "Okay. So he's going to be coming for rehab here. That's great."

Turning to face her, I sat as tall as I could. "Do you work in Cardiac Rehab?"

"Nah." She shook her head. "I just tell everybody else what to do. Except Dr. Frazier, of course. I don't actually do any work." Her eyes sparkled. My friend had not changed. "I'm the director. Here he comes."

She stood up as Al walked toward us. "Mr. Sandholz. Good. Did you get through with everything?"

"Yes, ma'am. I think so. They said I could start on Thursday. Seems kind of fast to start already."

Debbie shook his hand. "No, it's good to start your rehab right away, to assure you have a healthy recovery. And I'm so glad you brought my twin." She looked back at me. "I hope I get to see you when he comes for rehab, Tamara."

"Oh yes, ma'am. I'm looking forward to it." Standing, I grinned at her. "Now that I know you'll be around, nothing could keep me away."

"Cheeky brat." She smirked at me. "I gotta go, but I'll see you all Thursday." After she walked into the clinic, she stuck her head back around the door. "Be careful, or I'll put you to work helping with the therapy."

Al sat in the chair Debbie had just left. "Did she call you her twin?"

I sat back beside him. He looked like he needed some rest before heading back out to the car. "Yes. Couldn't you tell? Neither of us is gray yet, still the same crazy curly blonds as we used to be."

"I see. Well, yes, I did notice that."

Leaning back against the chair, I laughed. "She's a physical therapist. She was my supervisor when we worked in the same nursing home. Even though I started working there six months before she did." I shook my head. "That was a million years ago."

How long ago had it been? More than twenty-five years anyway.

"Back then, we also wore the same kind of glasses, same kind of clothes. She's just above six feet tall, and I'm just below five, so everybody there, staff and residents, loved calling us the twins."

"She seems nice." He drew in a long breath and braced his hands on the arms of the chair. "Okay. For my next bout of exercise, let's head out to the car."

## CHAPTER 12

Just as I opened the car door to go pick up C.T. at school, my phone rang. "Grandma? You don't have to pick me up today," C.T. said. "I'm going home with Graham for a couple hours."

"Oh. Really?" With my back against the car door, I checked my cell phone for a text. "Your dad didn't tell me."

It was a normal enough thing for C.T. to go play with his friend after school, but usually Roland let me know before they left in the morning. I shrugged. He had a lot on his mind right now. Not a surprise if he forgot.

"Oh, uh, he met Graham's mom at school this morning and they worked it out then. She brought Graham to school this morning, but we're riding home on the bus tonight."

Smart boy. That was my next question. "Okay, sweetie. Be good. Have fun. Call me when you're ready to come home."

"Okay, bye. Gotta go."

As I walked back into the house, I sighed. It would be a good thing to cheer C.T. up, playing at Graham's house.

Almost an hour later, my phone rang again. Did he already want to come home?

It wasn't C.T.

"Tammy, I'm bringing C.T. home."

"Heather?" My heart sped up. "Why is he with you?"

Now what has she done?

"We'll be there in about twenty minutes. We'll talk then." She hung up.

What's going on? I need to call Roland.

No.

Setting my phone down, I drew in a long breath. Don't worry him yet, until you know what happened.

The dishwasher needed emptying, so I did that instead of pace or stand at the window watching for them. But when I heard car doors bang, I hurried to the front door and opened it.

C.T. ran past me and downstairs immediately.

"Honey, wait. What's wrong?"

He was crying again.

Heather came in, her face drenched with tears.

"You're crying too." I closed the door and turned to her. "What on earth is going on? Why do you have C.T.? Roland didn't tell me…"

"He took a bus and came to my job after school." Her voice sounded defensive. "I had no idea he was coming until he stood in my office door."

"He told me…" What is this craziness?

"I know what he told you. He never intended to go to Graham's house. I've called Roland. He's on the way home right now." Her face quivered. "He told me to leave before he gets here."

She opened the door, then turned back to face me.

"I know you hate me, Tammy." She struggled to hold her chin firm. "I guess I don't blame you. But the truth is, I do care about C.T. He is my son, and I love him."

Hate her?

Before I could open my mouth, she was gone.

When I got downstairs, C.T. lay face-down on his bed, his whole body shaking. Sitting on the bed, I pulled him on my lap and rocked him.

"Shh, baby. It's okay. It's going to be okay."

It wasn't okay. I wanted to scream at him. How could he lie to me? He'd run away. To Heather.

C.T. turned in my arms so he could look at me. "Do you hate my mommy?"

My chest squeezed, and I choked. "What? What are you talking about?" I stopped. "Did she tell you that?"

"No, but you never talked to me about her. Daddy didn't either. It was like she was dead or something." He scooted off my lap onto the bed, rubbing tears with his fists. "She's my mommy. I want to know her. And nobody wants me to."

"Listen, honey." What could I say? He was right. Hesitantly, I reached out my hand and stroked his back. "Baby, this is so hard. You know, you know I love you, don't you?"

He turned his head from me and didn't answer.

Roland stood next to us then. I hadn't heard him come in the front door or down the stairs. He kept his face turned from me too. "C.T., get your shoes and jacket. We're going for a ride."

C.T. stood up. "It's warm. I don't need a jacket." His mouth set in a stubborn line that reminded me of, who? Karl? Me?

"Fine." Roland sighed and rubbed his face. "Let's go then." He turned to me, his eyes deep with sadness. "I don't know when we'll be home, Mom."

"It's okay." What should I say? "I'll, I'll be praying for you."

"Yeah." He turned and followed his son up the stairs.

For a long time after I heard the front door close behind them, I sat on C.T.'s bed, and exhaustion wrapped itself around me. "Dear God, Dear God help us."

## CHAPTER 13

I sat on the porch swing for hours that evening, my heart heavy. When my phone rang, it was after nine-thirty.

Torie.

*I don't know if I can talk to her, Father.*

We hadn't talked since before Karl left, and now this with C.T.

The phone rang until it went to voice mail then rang again.

Giving in, I answered. "Hi."

"What's up with you? Are you avoiding me?" Torie always sounded so awake and full of energy, no matter the time of day.

"Of course not. How are you, sweetie?"

"Great. I know you've got a lot going on, but brace yourself. I've been selected to dump more on you."

*Oh, Father.* "Okay."

"Roland is an idiot and a wimp."

"Torie."

"He is. He asked me to tell you he and C.T. are going to move in with Heather. He didn't want to tell you himself."

"He's what?" My heart slammed against my chest.

"You heard me." A door banged shut on her end of the phone.

I shook my head. "Are you just now getting home?"

"Yep. I've been out partying. A stalker followed me home, but I beat him to the door. I hope I don't have a hangover when I go into work tomorrow morning."

Sighing, I laid my head against the back of the swing. "Thanks. Love your sense of humor."

*Lord, stop my brain spinning for a minute.* "So, Roland?"

"Mmm hmm. The idiotic wimp."

"Please just tell me, Torie."

"I guess Heather threatened… Wait, you want me to be nice. She suggested that they all get back together and try to be a family. If Roland agreed to that, she wouldn't get a lawyer and start fighting for custody."

"Ooooohh." I sank my head on my chest.

Quiet on Torie's end.

Sitting straight, I started the swing moving. "Honey?"

"Yeah?"

"Roland asked you to tell me because, because he thought I'd try to talk him out of it."

"Yeah, partly that I guess."

Grinding my teeth, I sucked in a long breath. "Your dad said I boss all of you around too much. Tell you how you should act as Christians. I've made myself the spiritual leader for everybody in the family."

"Dad's a jerk."

So, she knows about Karl leaving. "Torie!"

She chuckled. "Just sayin'." She whistled. "Fidget, come on, puppy. Let's go for a walk."

"You haven't walked that dog since before you left for work this morning?"

"I came home and walked her after work, before I went out

for the evening. Go, Fidget, run. Don't worry, Mother. I'm taking proper care of the dog God gifted me with."

"So, I do tell you what to do all the time."

"You've always been very 'righteous,' Mama."

"Great. Thanks for the loving emphasis on righteous." I kicked out too far and accidentally hit Rudy, who was lying in front of me. He rolled over and moaned. "Sorry, buddy."

I slowed the swing and thought for a minute. "Sweetie, a lot happened in our lives around the time you were born. We started going to church. Aunt Frances said we should be raising our kids in a church."

An owl called not too far away. There was only silence on Torie's end.

"Then we went with a bunch of people from church to a Carman concert, and your dad and I both decided to give our lives to Jesus at that concert."

"Yeah, *Jesus Is The Way.* '*The Champion.*' You gotta love Carman."

"He's so great." I smiled. "When my maternity leave with you was up, I didn't want to go back to work. Your dad was sweet. He told me we could make it if I wanted to stay home full time with you kids."

"Yeah, he's so sweet." Her voice growled, so I hurried on.

"My life was being a Christian wife and mom. I was so happy. And when we decided that I should home-school you guys, I thought I'd made it to Heaven."

"We were such great kids." There was a smile in her voice now.

"Right. That's what I meant." Several moments passed as I flipped through the memories. "I did a lot of Bible study. I wanted to share it with you kids, but I also loved it so much. I wanted to learn more all the time."

"You're a great teacher, Mother."

"Thanks for that." My voice caught in my throat. "Anyway,

the Bible, our family, trying to help us all grow closer to Jesus, it was everything I had in my life, all I wanted. It's, it's who I am."

"I know." Her words were soft, kind.

"I need to hang up."

"Go ahead and cry, Mama. It's good for you. A wise teacher told me that."

"I love you, precious." Sniffing, I brushed at tears.

"I love you too."

## CHAPTER 14

When Roland and C.T. got home, I was already in bed. I forced my body to stay there, to leave them alone that night.

The next morning though, I was sitting at the kitchen table with coffee when Roland came up.

"Good morning, Mom." His voice was firm, his jaw set.

"So Heather threatened to fight you for custody?" Try as I might, my voice squealed with anger.

Roland turned and closed the door to the basement, then came back and sat across from me. "She said she knew she'd done a terrible thing, leaving us."

I choked on my coffee, but Roland kept talking.

"She said she could never change that, but she wants to be a part of C.T.'s life. Of both our lives now."

He paused, but I didn't open my mouth.

"She said what she really wanted to do was to try again, with me, and with C.T. But..." He drew in a breath. "She said if I didn't want that, she was ready to ask for custody, joint, maybe even full."

My eyes sprang open wider.

"She said…" He pressed on. "She said she is his mother, and she has a more steady income than I do right now."

*I hate her, Lord.*

"We're going to give it a try, Mom. Right now." He stood up and went to get dishes for their breakfast. "C.T. got to bed late last night. I already called school to say he's not coming today." He dropped bread into the toaster. "I don't work today, and Heather arranged it so she doesn't go in till this afternoon. She's got a few apartments she's already checked out, and we're all going to look at some this morning."

"You said right now." My voice scratched.

"Yes." He retrieved butter and milk from the refrigerator. "I know this is a bad time to walk out on you." He pressed his lips together. "Since Dad did, and Al's here."

I jumped up. "Your dad didn't walk out on me."

"Whatever." He walked toward the basement door. "Anyway, I'm sorry. But this is what I need to do for my family."

"Okay, honey." I gulped. "I'll be okay. I'm, I'm doing fine with Al."

He looked back at me. "I know. You like him. I do too." He opened the basement door again. "Come on up, buddy. Let's eat and get on the road."

I liked Al?

*I do like him, Lord, but oh, forgive me. I really do hate Heather.*

∾

AFTER ROLAND AND C.T. LEFT, my mind and body shook with jitters.

*Lord, I need to run. I need to get out of the house.*

Standing still in the middle of the kitchen, I pressed my hand to my heart.

"I have to talk to Karl."

When I opened Al's door, he sat on the side of the bed, a Bible open in front of him. I'd noticed him reading it before. It looked well-worn.

"I need to go out for a bit. Are you okay alone?"

He waved his hand at me. "Go. I'm fine. The package I got yesterday was one of those medical alarm bracelets." He met my eyes and grinned. "Don't worry so much, young lady."

"Right." Like that would happen.

On the drive to Karl's office, I tried without success to slow my crazy thoughts.

My husband moved out on me.

My son and grandson are moving in with the woman who left them.

My father-in-law.

I hate Heather.

Workers at the dealership said hello as I walked through the showroom to Karl's door, but I couldn't talk to anyone. Pushing his office door open, I stepped inside. "Honey, I'm so sorry, but…"

I stopped, blinked, bit my lip.

Karl sat at his desk, and a woman sat across from him, filling out a form.

"I'm sorry. I didn't mean to interrupt." I backed out the door.

"Tammy." Karl stood up. What did his face show? Surprise? Confusion? Happiness? "Tammy, wait."

He turned to the woman at his desk. "Destiny, would you mind finishing this out in the main area?" He shook his head, took a breath. "This is my wife Tammy. Tammy, this is Destiny. She just started working here today."

Destiny stood up, gathering her papers. "Nice to meet you, Tammy. Thank you, Mr. Sandholz."

"Call me Karl." He walked around his desk and laid his hand on my arm. "We'll finish up everything later. Joe will meet with you and show you around."

"No problem." She was in a hurry to get out the door. Did I look that scary?

When the door closed, I turned toward Karl and grabbed his shirt with both hands. "Honey, I'm so sorry, I messed up, I need you."

## CHAPTER 15

Karl sat me in a chair and knelt in front of me. My breaths came in gasps, and my body shook.

"Shh, shh." He held my face in his hands. "Take a breath."

Pushing back, I coughed and choked. "You were right. I act like I'm such a great Christian. I'm always telling you and the kids what to do." I sucked in a long breath and held it, trying to calm myself. "I'm such a phony." My voice squeaked.

He wrapped my hands in his. "Just sit a minute. Take it easy. I'm here. I'm not going anywhere."

My tongue twisted as I talked on. "I hate Heather. I hate her. Jesus said that's like I've murdered her." I clutched his hands in mine and squeezed. "I need your help. Please help me."

Karl sat back on his heels, holding my gaze for a minute. Then he stood up and walked to the refrigerator in the corner of his office. He got a bottle of water and brought it to me, wrapping my hands around it. "Drink."

While I took a long drink, he pulled up another chair beside mine and sat close, bumping up against me.

I lowered the drink and opened my mouth, but he shook his

head and touched the bottle to my lips again. "Take another drink."

After a minute, my breathing came back to normal, and I no longer heard my heart pounding in my head. Karl circled an arm around me and held me tight against him. "Are you okay?"

Nodding, I rested my head on his shoulder. "I had to come to you. I need you."

"I know. I'm glad you came."

We sat in silence for a few minutes, then Karl nudged me to raise my head. "Tell me."

I scrubbed my palms against my eyes then covered my face with my hands. "Roland and C.T. are moving into an apartment with Heather."

"He told me they might."

Something in his voice made me lower my hands. His mouth twitched, and his eyes held deep pain.

"Rolie told me he was going to do everything he could to hold his family together. He said our family history of men deserting their wives and kids would end with him."

My head snapped back. "What?"

"I talked to Torie a couple days ago. She said, 'You're a jerk, Dad.'"

Moaning, I reached to grasp his hand. "Honey, I'm, I'm so sorry. They're, they're just upset."

"They're right." He kept his eyes fixed on mine. "I did desert you. I, I'm disgusted with myself. I do feel like I'm doing the same thing I blame my father for doing."

"It's not, no…"

He rested his fingers on my lips. "I can't help it, Tammy." He swallowed. "The idea of living in the same house with him, it's like a rock wall. I can't penetrate it. I think about going home, and a weight pushes against my chest. My breath hurts."

What could I say? I understood, and yet I hurt so much. Why couldn't he come home and be with me? I needed him.

Karl leaned his head against mine. "Father God, help us." His voice sounded thick with tears. "We can't do any of this without Your help. Our marriage. Helping our children. Forgiving ... my father, Heather. We cannot do it. We beg You to help us. We feel so low, so broken. Help us. Please, help us."

## CHAPTER 16

After I left Karl's office, I wanted to drive for hours. But I needed to get home to Al.

"Rolie's right, Lord. I do like Al. I don't resent needing to help him." I parked the car in our driveway. "I know I didn't go through what Karl did with him." Rubbing my forehead with my fingers, I sighed. "Help Karl, Lord. Help me forgive him for not coming home. Please. Help us both."

Al sat on the couch with Rudy leaning against his knee. "You see I've been up walking since you've been gone." His eyes twinkled.

"You have." I nodded. "That's a lot of exercise. And I see you're trying to steal my dog from me. Did you eat anything for breakfast?"

"Yes, Mommy. I had a banana. If you wanted to make coffee, though, I'd walk some more and follow you into the kitchen."

"Coming up. I went to see Karl at work." Why did I tell him that?

He came into the kitchen and pulled out a chair. "Tell me about his work. Frances has told me some. I came to see him when he was eighteen. He worked at the Ford dealership then."

"We're almost out of filters." I swallowed and took in a breath. "He started working there when he was seventeen, in the gas station that's connected." Flipping the coffee maker button on, I sat down across from him. "After he'd worked there eight years and the owner retired, he offered Karl the opportunity to buy the whole business."

"And now he owns two shops?"

"Three, in locations spread throughout the city. He's an excellent businessman."

"I guess so." He was quiet, his eyes turning inward to a place and time I didn't know. "I'm proud of him." He shook his head. "Do I even have the right to be proud of him?"

My breath caught. "Of, of course," I whispered. I wanted to say, "He's your son," but I didn't. Maybe that was what he questioned, if he had the right to claim Karl as his son.

Neither of us spoke for a minute. Al's eyes looked into the distance still, and I wanted to reach my hand across and lay it on his.

When the coffeepot growled its last, I stood up. Rudy, lying next to Al, raised his head, sniffed, then laid it down again and moaned.

"You want some coffee, buddy?" I stooped down to rub his ears.

Al wrapped his hands around the cup I set in front of him but didn't look up. "I was worthless to Karl and his mama from day one." His voice rasped. "I was almost always drunk, never could hold a job. My buddy asked me to travel the road with him. He was single, and he wanted to see California. I figured I'd be doing them a favor to get out of their lives."

A tear rolled down his cheek, and I pressed a napkin into his hand.

He raised his face to look at me, blinked, then turned his head away. "I parted company with my friend. I'm not sure why. And I just kept on traveling. I lived in Texas for a while. Found jobs, lost them, moved on. Then one night, I was drunk, and it was raining. I couldn't see anything, never should have been driving."

His lips trembled, and my stomach clenched.

"I slammed my truck head-on into a little car with a lady and her baby inside. They were both killed."

My throat jerked. Reaching across the table, I covered his shaking hands with mine.

"In prison, I met another fella who'd been driving drunk. He didn't hit a car. He rolled his car again and again down a slick embankment. He wasn't alone though. His wife and little girl were in the car with him."

*Dear Father.*

"He was almost killed. He said, 'I wish I was.'" Al took a drink of coffee. "He woke up in the car to see his wife and child, smashed and bloodied and dead."

He raised his eyes to meet mine. "That man, Jim was his name, he told me to stop feeling sorry for myself. He said I couldn't pay for all the wrong I'd done by kicking myself over and over. He said the only thing I could do was move forward, try to make good come out of the rest of my life."

Al leaned back in his chair, clasping his hands against his chest.

"Jim told me about Jesus. He said Jesus loved him even the sorry mess he was, and he said Jesus loved me too."

The refrigerator turned on.

What could I say?

"I started going to Bible study with him. They gave me that Bible you've seen me with. I've kept it all these years.

"After I got out of prison, got hooked up with AA and a church, was able to hold down a job for six months straight, I came to see Karl."

He wasn't crying any more, but I was.

"Frances told me my wife died of cancer. Karl was a young

man, taking care of himself. He said if I wanted to do anything for him, I should never show him my face again." He picked up his coffee. "I felt like I should honor that. The time I saw all of you at Frances's house, when your kids were still babies, I didn't mean to barge in on you. Frances hadn't told me you were there. As soon as I saw Karl's face, I turned around and walked out." His hands squeezed the cup. "I've never tried to see him since. I figured I owed him that." His eyes met mine, pleading. "And now this. I'm so sorry, Tammy."

Circling the table, I wrapped my arms around Al's shoulders. *Father, I love this man.*

## CHAPTER 17

The next day, Roland and C.T. moved out.

Standing on the front porch as they carried boxes to Roland's car, I twisted the hem of my T-shirt in my fingers. "Sweetie, why such a hurry?"

Roland stopped in front of me and wiped sweat from his forehead. "Mom, this just makes the most sense. Why put it off?"

C.T. walked his bicycle around the side of the house. "Come on, Dad, help me tie this to the top. Let's go."

My grandson was in a hurry to leave.

I raised my chin and smiled at my son. "Okay, honey. I love you. Call me. C.T., come up here and give me a hug."

He ran up the stairs and gave me a quick squeeze. "Bye, Grandma. Come on, Dad. Mommy's waiting."

Roland gave me a longer hug then shook his head. "I'll call you later, Mom."

On Thursday, Al and I went to the cardiac rehab clinic at the hospital.

Debbie met us as soon as we walked in. "Tamara, I hoped I'd see you."

"Tamara?" Al raised his eyebrows.

"No one calls me that but Debbie." I turned on her with my best scowl. "And that's not because I allow it."

Debbie gave me a tight hug. "She loves me. Don't listen to her."

"Not like anybody ever does," I grumbled then grinned.

"Mr. Sandholz, let me introduce you to Jake. He's one of our nurse practitioners, and he'll make sure we have all your paperwork, then tell you about everything we do here."

"That's fine, but call me Al. Especially since you're a friend of Tammy's."

She smiled. "Okay, Al. You can also join one of our meetings today. It's a small group of other folks who are going through the same thing you are." She turned to me. "I can take an early lunch. Come with me and we can catch up."

"I was going to sit in with Al."

"Go." He tapped my shoulder. "I'm a big boy. Have fun with your buddy."

"I like this man." Debbie gave me a huge grin then led Al into an office.

∼

"How long can you take for lunch?" I asked.

"As long as I want. I'm the director." She took me across the street to a coffee and bagel shop and bought me a cinnamon bagel slathered with cream cheese. "You look like you need to eat more."

"I'll never be able to eat all that." Shaking my head, I picked up the bagel. "So, how'd you get to be the director of the coronary rehab center? And where have you been for twenty years?"

"It's only been seventeen years since I've seen you. The second husband moved us to Florida." She shook her head. "Don't ask."

"But then you said you were pregnant, and I never heard from you again. Didn't you like the gift I sent you?" Drawing in a long sniff of the cinnamon bagel, I took a bite. "This is pretty yummy."

"I had twins, come on." She dumped sugar into her coffee. "And I had work. And my marriage … we'll talk about that later. Anyway, after the second divorce, I moved the boys and myself back here to live with Mom. About a year ago. You've heard my dad died?"

"I didn't. I'm sorry." I reached across the table and squeezed her hand.

"Yeah, and Mom was pretty much in shock mode. I felt like home was a good place for us right then." She took a big bite of her bagel, onion, toasted, no cream cheese. "This job had just come open." She mumbled around her mouthful. "And I'd worked at a similar clinic in Florida for ten years."

"Don't choke yourself." I took another bite. Two divorces. Twins. Her dad died, and her mom needed help. What was safe for me to ask about? "So, you like this work?"

She swallowed coffee. "I do. It's a great clinic, super people to work with. Say, we could use another PTA. Do you have a job? You're kids are all grown, right?"

I coughed and grabbed a napkin to wipe my mouth. "Debbie, I haven't worked in twenty-five years."

"Seriously?" She raised her eyebrows. "That's right, I remember, you were a stay-at-home mommy. But surely, they're grown now."

"They are, but…" I drew in a breath. "We have a lot of catching up to do."

After half an hour, Debbie knew about the latest mess in my life, but all I knew was that her boys were fourteen and were just finishing eighth grade.

"So, your son has moved out finally, and you're taking care of your father-in-law. He won't be with you for long. Come on, work for me again. It'll be fun."

"That's all you have to say?"

"What do you want me to say? Neither of us wants to talk about our husbands right now. You need a fresh start for your life."

Did I?

"Karl hasn't left me. Not really."

"Okay, if you say so. But even if he does move back, you've got no kids to take care of. Work with me. It'll be a blast. Hold your hats and look out for the twins."

"A blast." There was no doubt about that. "Debbie, I didn't keep my license up to date."

Her eyes grew wider still. "You, you're, you..." She stood, picked up her water, and splashed it on top of my head. "You what?"

## CHAPTER 18

"Why did you come back from lunch all soaked?" Al asked on the drive home.

Glancing over at him, I grinned. "Debbie threw her water at me."

"Hmm. She does seem like a character."

"She surely is. How was your time in the clinic?"

"Good. They have kind of a self-help, let's-all-talk-about-our-problems-group, so I met a few folks. They seem like a fun bunch. They have classes on diet, exercise, medication, and physical and occupational therapy. They recommend I come in three times a week to start, then work down to twice a week for a while."

"Do you think you want to keep going?" We pulled into our drive.

"Sure. I think I'm gonna get some weights to use at home too. They said lifting weights is a good exercise for me."

"Yeah?" I stretched my mind back to my years as a physical therapy assistant. "I knew that."

"Mm hmm." He opened his door. "Plus, they said I need to start walking more than just back and forth to my bedroom." His lips twitched. "I could probably start taking short walks with you and your dog, if you don't go too fast."

I snorted. "That dog might be big, and, yeah, he's only three years old, but he's the laziest animal you'll ever meet. You might have to encourage him to not lie down in the middle of our walk every couple minutes."

∾

DEBBIE CALLED me later that night.

"Okay, you're safe. I'm not in the same house with you. Why on earth didn't you keep your license active?" Try as she might to keep her voice level, it did raise a couple octaves by the time she finished.

With the phone to my ear, I flopped onto my bed. "I had two babies to raise. My goal at that point in my life was to stay at home with them forever. To be honest, it didn't occur to me for years to work on continuing ed credits."

"Honey, you're only fifty-one years old, and your kids are out of the house. You've got a lot of years left. What were you thinking?"

"I wasn't. I had diapers, meals, ear infections and strep throat, kids to play with, then home-schooling and sports and music lessons, and then a grandson to help raise."

"Right." Surely she shook her head at me with impatience. "And? What are you going to do now?"

"I never thought about now. I, I still can't figure out now. A lot of stuff just happened in my life."

"I understand." Her voice gentled. "I'll help you."

My eyes teared. "All I wanted was to be a wife and mama. Now, nobody's here. They don't need me anymore." I gulped.

"They still need you. Just in a different way. But you have to figure out a new identity for yourself. You're not a mommy with a houseful of kids anymore."

My nose dripped, and I swallowed. "I don't know how to do anything else."

"I seem to remember you being an excellent PTA."

Sitting up, I sighed. "Debbie, stop it. I don't have a license."

"I did a little homework this afternoon." Now her voice was brisk. "All you have to do is take the certification test again."

I barked out a laugh.

"I am not joking."

By now, my belly shook with laughter.

"Tamara, stop it. I am deadly serious."

Gasping, I wiped at my eyes and collapsed on the bed again. "Give me a minute." I drew in a long breath. "Debbie, Debbie, Debbie."

"You know you're the only one I allow to call me Debbie."

"We are such good friends."

"Yes, we are. That's why I'm going to help you get ready for the test."

After another deep inhale, I pushed myself to a sitting position again. "Listen. I haven't worked for 25 years. I've forgotten so much. I can't even begin to remember what I've forgotten. There must be so much new information I didn't study, new technology I was never introduced to."

"So, you'll start by volunteering at my clinic. I said I'd hire you, but maybe that's not the best idea. Mostly, we both need a good friend, and that might not work so good, for my employees to see me hire my friend. But you can volunteer. We'll teach you all the new stuff. And I've got all the books you need to refresh your mind about physiology, anatomy, kinesthetics—"

"Ooooohh," I moaned, pressing my face against my knees.

"Slowly. A little at a time. No hurry. We can do this."

"I'm feeling really dizzy right now."

"One step at a time. You can do it, sweetie. Think about it. You loved working in the nursing home before. You're great with old people. Look how comfortable you are with your father-in-law. Wouldn't you love to work in a nursing home again? You'd be great at it. Come on, baby."

My mouth opened, then closed again, and I straightened up. "Tamara?"

"Working in a nursing home again, huh?"

"There you go." She had a smile in her voice. "Listen to yourself. I think you just took your first baby step."

## CHAPTER 19

Saturday morning, I sat at the kitchen table with an empty coffee cup and a half-eaten raisin bagel and blinked at the cartoon page of the newspaper. "What am I going to do with myself today?"

Maybe I should search for some of my old PTA school books.

My phone rang. Karl?

"Honey, will you have lunch with me?"

My heart squeezed.

When I arrived at the dealership, Karl walked out into the main room to greet me. "Could I help you find the best new car for you, young lady?"

Wrapping my arms around him, I buried my face in his shirt. Who cared if people were watching? "I miss you so much."

He tipped my face and rubbed at a couple tears, then held me close. "I miss you too," he whispered in my ear. "Let's go."

We settled at a table in our favorite Mexican restaurant. Since it was near Karl's work, I'd often picked him up for lunch or met him there.

"How are you doing?" Karl reached his hand across the table and covered mine.

"Okay, I guess. Terrible. I don't know."

He stood up and came around to my side of the booth. "Scoot over." When he sat beside me, he snuggled his arms around me again. "I'm so sorry, baby. I love you so much. I'm sorry for hurting you."

Drawing in a breath, I raised my face to look at him. "You're not mad at me anymore, for letting Al come to our house?"

"No." His voice croaked. "I'm not mad at you. I'm mad at me, I'm confused, I'm messed up."

After we gave our orders, I gave his arm a gentle shove. "Sit across from me again, so I can see your face without hurting my neck."

"Shorty." He squeezed my shoulder and moved to the other side. Once he was settled, he reached for my hand again. "Will you go to church with me tomorrow?"

My eyes fell, then rose to his. "Yes, thank you. I couldn't go last week, by myself."

He shook his head. "I didn't want to go. I've been doing my best to avoid God."

Twisting my lips, I snorted. "Good luck with that one."

Our food arrived, and we spent a couple of minutes arranging our plates. After a few bites, Karl set his fork down. "I haven't been sleeping well. When I do, I keep having dreams about my mom." He picked up his fork and poked at his rice and beans. "I thought about what you said, you know? About how this has been over fifty years. How Al is a sick old man now."

"Karl, wait—"

"No, honey, listen." He laid his hand on mine and squeezed. "When he left my mom and me, Al was Roland's age. Just a kid." He lifted his eyes to mine. "Roland is still a kid to me, even though he's been walking like a man for years. Moving in with Heather now, I know he says it's for C.T., but…" He shook his head. "He stopped by the office yesterday, and I looked into his face. His eyes, they have the same bright, hopeful look in them they had when he was first dating her." He scooted his fork around his plate. "Full of dreams. He's taken on a man's responsibility for years, but he's still a kid."

My eyes blurred, and I picked up a napkin and clenched it between my hands.

"What I'm trying to say is, that's the age my…" He swallowed. "Al was when he left. Still just a kid really, nothing but stupid living behind him, not able to take care of the family he started. No idea how to handle that load."

I wanted to say, "He's a different man now. Someone you might be able to like." But I didn't open my mouth.

"Fifty-two years is a long time." Karl finally took another bite. "A long time for him and a long time for me. And my mom, she's been gone for over 30 years." He rubbed his face with his hand. "I've hated him for my mom's sake, and she's been gone for over 30 years."

"Yes. Hate. I know, I know what you feel." My voice rasped. "That's what I feel for Heather, and it's so ugly. It makes my stomach sick, my heart hurt." I pressed my fingers against my cheeks. "I want to beg God to help me, and I don't feel like I deserve to, and I feel … so, so without hope."

Karl rested his hand on mine. "Dear God, we don't feel like we deserve to come to You, but where else can we go? Only You can help us. Please God. We are begging You."

## CHAPTER 20

Karl met me outside our church building the next morning. "Aren't we a couple of brave sinners?" He gave me a small smile and linked his fingers in mine. "I'll go in if you will."

Worship service had already started when we walked in, and we found seats in the back. Neither of us was in a mood to mingle or talk to friends today.

Jared, our pastor, started off with a couple of jokes that went right over my head.

*Father God, I'm here with Karl. Thank You for that.*

Karl still held my hand. Looking down, I found my open Bible upside down. *Why am I so teary these days?*

*Why wouldn't I be?*

"This is Jesus' command for us, from John chapter thirteen." I picked up on what Jared was saying. "Let me say it again. 'A new command I give you: Love one another. As I have loved you, so you must love one another.'"

When I looked up, Jared smiled and shook his head. "Pretty hard order, don't you think? Love people as Jesus has loved us. In this book as well as in the first letter of John, He explains that

God showed us His love by sending His son to die for us. That's not new news for most of us here."

It wasn't. Jesus died for my sin. I knew that.

"Jesus says we should love others the same way. What do you think?"

In my mind, the word hate, which Karl and I had both spoken with such ease yesterday, pounded louder and louder. I shook my head and worked to focus on what Jared was saying.

His voice grew softer as he went on. "Let's look at what it says in 1 John chapter three. 'See what great love the Father has lavished on us, that we should be called children of God!' And, 'But we know that when Christ appears we shall be like him.' Whoa." Jared walked halfway down the aisle, turned and went back up front, then faced us again. "God's love is to make us his children. When Jesus appears, I'm going to be like him?" He spread his hands out in front of him, palms up. "That all sure sounds like something I'm not going to be able to do on my own."

Karl shifted beside me, and I turned my gaze on him. His face was almost white. Al's old eyes looked out at me.

Reaching for his hand again, I held it tight in mine.

Jared was going on. "Listen to this verse from Zephaniah. Listen, people. 'The Lord your God is with you, the Mighty Warrior who saves. He will take great delight in you; in his love he will no longer rebuke you, but will rejoice over you with singing.'"

My gaze moved to Jared.

"People, do you hear what your father who loves you says?"

*Father, You love me, You rejoice over me, but I...*

My throat clogged.

When I looked back at Karl, tears shone on his cheeks.

I didn't hear much more of what Jared said, and Karl and I slipped out during the closing prayer.

He walked me to my car. "I need to go." His movements

were jerky, and he kept looking into the distance. He needed to be by himself.

"Okay. I love you, honey." I squeezed his hand and let him go.

~

"I need to bake some cookies." After Al and I finished lunch, I stood up, then turned in a circle. "I'm antsy."

Al wrinkled his forehead. "You going to make me smell them and then not give me any?"

"No, no. You can have one. I don't know what I'll do with the rest. Maybe I'll take them when we go to the hospital tomorrow and give them to Debbie for her kids. Teenage boys need cookies."

"What kind you gonna make?"

I rested my hand on my chin. "What kind do you like?"

"Oatmeal raisin."

"I can do that." My lips quirked into a grin. "They're almost healthy, actually."

"Right. Remember that when you think about giving me just one."

The first pan was ready to come out of the oven when I heard the front door open and close.

"Who's that? Roland?" With the oven mitts still on my hands, I hurried into the living room.

"It's me, Grandma." C.T. knelt on the floor beside Rudy, hugging the dog, his face hidden in Rudy's fur.

My heart skipped a beat. "C.T. Honey. Where is, what are you doing here?"

He didn't lift his head or speak.

Dropping to the floor beside him, I gave him a tight hug. "Sweetie, tell me what's happening. How did you get here? Where's your mom?"

He raised his head and pulled away from me. "She's asleep at the apartment. I took the bus here." His stubborn chin set just like Roland's, and only then did I see dried tracks of tears on his face.

*What on earth should I do now, Lord?*

I swallowed then pushed myself to my feet. "I'm baking cookies. You want to come sit with Grandpa Al and have some? With milk?"

"Yes."

Before I put the next pan of cookies in the oven, I texted Roland to let him know C.T. was with me. Al and C.T. sat across from each other with cookies and two percent milk. "It's a healthy snack," Al explained.

"Okay." The little boy kept his face down.

Pulling out a chair, I sat next to him and raised his chin. "Honey, tell me why you left your mom."

His lip trembled. "Mommy and Dad aren't happy. Daddy doesn't sleep in the bedroom with her. They fight a lot, and I can hear her crying at night." He rubbed his nose with the back of his hand. "I just wanted to have a family with both my mom and dad." He gulped. "What's wrong with that, Grandma?"

I pulled him onto my lap and rocked him. His shoulders shook, and he gasped and choked hard little boy sobs.

## CHAPTER 21

C.T. cried himself to sleep on my lap. I laid him on the couch then checked my phone. A text from Roland said, "Call Heather."

Gritting my teeth, I pressed in her number.

"Tammy?" Her voice sounded groggy.

"C.T. is at my house. He took the bus here."

"What? Where? C.T.?" The noise of banging doors and footsteps came across the phone.

"Heather." I raised my voice. "He's not there. He really is here."

The phone banged on the floor, more muffled noises, then she came back on the line. "Tammy?"

"Calm down. You surely don't need to have an accident driving over here." Taking even breaths, I strained not to have my tone filled with disgust. "Don't worry. He's safe. He's asleep. Please be careful."

The dishes were done and Al had returned to his room, when a soft knock sounded on the door.

Heather ran past me and straight to the couch to kneel beside C.T. Before she buried her face in the child's hair, I saw that her cheeks were drenched.

"I'm so sorry, sweetheart." Her voice croaked. "So sorry."

C.T. wiggled in his sleep, but he didn't wake up. After a minute, she lifted her head and turned to me. "I told him I was going to take a nap after lunch. I'd done that before. I didn't think, oh, I didn't think."

Of course not. What do you know about being a mother?

I kept my lips pressed tight. Yes, I'd taken naps before when I was alone with C.T., but not while he was going through such hard circumstances.

Heather sat on the floor, hugging her knees. She still gazed straight at me. "I don't know if you can believe this, but I love him so much. I do."

She turned back to C.T. and rested her hand on his back. Her lips moved, and more tears fell. Was she praying?

She sat up on the couch then and pulled C.T. onto her lap, wrapping her arms around him. He raised his head and mumbled, "Mom, mmm, Mommy." Then he laid his head back down, asleep again.

My heart twinged. So soon he'd let her into his heart.

As I watched Heather, with her cheek resting on this child I loved, I had a surprising memory.

The day after C.T. was born, as they were getting ready to leave the hospital. Heather sat on her bed, holding her tiny baby close, leaning her face right next to his. Her eyes had been filled with fear, yes, but they were bright was something else too. Hope. Excitement. Joy.

It was the face of a mother. She had no idea what was ahead of her, but she wanted it. She loved her child.

Now, I sucked in a breath then turned back to the kitchen.

Why had she left? *Father, how can I ever believe she can be a good mother to my, to this precious child?*

∽

C.T. WAS STILL groggy when they left, but he gave me a hug. "Love you, Grandma."

Rubbing hair from his forehead, I smiled, then kissed his nose. "I love you, my young man."

After I saw their car turn the corner, I grabbed Rudy's leash. "Come on, lazy dog, I need a walk."

*Father, You want me to love as You've loved me. Too bad I didn't listen more to what Jared had to say this morning, for that is surely not something I can do without Your help.*

Most of the neighbors were out on this beautiful spring afternoon. Parents pushed babies in strollers. Bicycles whizzed past me. Kids laughed and tumbled in yards. Maybe people said hi to me, but I couldn't think to respond.

Rudy pulled me wherever he wanted to go, sniffing at fresh flowers, skittering trash, lunging at a ball that bounced toward the street.

"What? Wait, no." I tugged on the leash. "No, Rudy. Not the street." He snuffed and found another candy wrapper.

What place did I have in my grandson's life? My son's? They'd needed me for so long, but now?

What was happening between me and my husband?

Should I, could I, go back to work?

*Oh, Father.*

When Rudy brought me home, Al sat in a rocker on the front porch.

Rubbing my face, I forced a smile. "Look how far you've walked today."

He grinned and gave the chair a gentle rock. "I'll be walking with you and Rudy before you know it. Sit here with me." He nodded at the swing across from him.

I put Rudy on a long leash so he could sniff around our yard, then eased onto the swing.

"I used to flop on the swing," I told Al. "Until it spilled me onto the floor one time."

He chuckled.

We were both quiet for long minutes.

"I don't know how to forgive my daughter-in-law." My own voice surprised me.

Al turned from watching Rudy to face me. "I can feel myself connected to that young woman."

I blinked.

"We both left our young families." Al's rocker creaked. "She was really still a child though. I didn't have that excuse."

My jaw set hard. "She decided she was grown up enough to have a child and be married."

"Not a decision a child can really make. She must have been terrified."

My mouth opened then closed. I rested my face in my hands and wondered why I found it easier to forgive this man than Heather.

## CHAPTER 22

*D*ebbie found me where I sat watching Al lift weights at the rehab clinic Monday morning. She pulled on my arm. "Come into my office."

"Are you sure that's good for him?" I asked, nodding at Al.

"Oh, honey, you've been away from PT too long." She slipped her arm through mine. "I've got some fun things to show you."

"Oh yeah?" Somehow, I doubted it.

She led me into her office and pointed to a chair stacked with books and brochures. "Take a look at those. You can take them home to study. I have to meet with my boss for a minute."

"I thought you were the boss."

"Dr. Frazier from Cardiology is my boss. Everybody has a boss." She wiggled her fingers at me then closed the door behind her.

Kneeling by the chair Debbie'd indicated, I started looking through the books. They were textbooks. Anatomy and physiology. Kinesiology. Biomechanics. Neuroscience. Clinical pathology. "Whoa. Did I used to know this stuff?"

A couple of brochures were about upcoming local continuing

ed classes. "The Use of Physical Agents and Electrotherapy: Ultrasound and Electrical Stimulation." "Explanation and Demonstration of Manual Therapy and Exercise Management for Cervicogenic Dizziness."

"No way." I shook my head.

The office door opened. "I'm back." Debbie lifted her shoulders, then dropped some papers on the desk. "He's such a space case." She turned to me. "So, what do you think? I've got bookmarks on pages I think you should focus on, and I'll email you the website with sample questions for the test. I think you can be ready in a couple weeks, don't you?"

My mouth fell open, and I pushed to my feet. "Are you crazy? This is all like a foreign language to me." I flicked my finger at one of the brochures. "Cervicogenic dizziness? You are out of your mind."

"Oh come on. I'll study with you. It'll be a good time. And I think you should go with me to one of these classes. I know you can't actually use the continuing ed credits yet, but just listening to the lectures, meeting with other PTs and PTAs, will help your mind switch back into the work mode. It'll be fun."

"I don't know about your idea of fun," I muttered as I reached to pick up the stack of books.

"Leave those for now. Come on out to the clinic. I want you to walk with Mrs. Manski. You'll love her."

"Walk? What do you mean?"

She led me out to a white haired lady who was inching around the track, holding to the rail as if it were a lifeline. Debbie laid her hand on the old lady's shoulder. "Mrs. Manski, this is my friend Tamara. She's a PT assistant. She'll walk around with you."

Mrs. Manski turned her eyes on me, and her smile was huge. "I'd appreciate that, dear."

I made a face at Debbie then joined Mrs. Manski. "I think we're going to be best friends, ma'am. We're the same height."

She laughed. "Please call me Louise. My backbone has shrunk some, but I used to be five foot and one-half inch."

"I think it's legal for you to still claim that. I always claim four feet eleven and three-quarter inch." It was work to keep to her slow pace, but I caught on.

"Are you new here, Tamara?"

She would remember my full name. "I'm not actually working here. Debbie, Debra, thought I could do some volunteering. I've been a stay-at-home mom for a long time."

"Good for you. Not enough people do that anymore."

"Do you mind if I ask how old you are?"

"Not at all. I'll be eighty-three in August. And I'm going to move back into my own house." She straightened her shoulders and raised her chin. "The kids made me move in with my daughter after my surgery, but I'm doing fine. I will move home again."

"I think that's great."

She nodded and walked on. "Tell me about your kids, and I'll tell you about mine. I have three daughters, seven grandchildren and four greats."

"I have a daughter and a son, and one grandson." I swallowed. *Father, help them.* "That must be so fun, having great grandchildren."

"By the time my kids moved out of the house, I felt so old." Could her smile get any bigger? "But by the time the grands and then the greats came along, I was a young girl again."

We talked and laughed, and without her even noticing it, I believe, she picked up her speed.

*Father, I really do love this. I remember how much I enjoyed working with the people in the nursing home.*

Could it be Debbie had a good idea after all?

## CHAPTER 23

The next afternoon, Al took a walk with Rudy and me. "I've never had a dog, so I don't know. Do they all walk like this, or are you slowing him down for my sake?"

Jiggling Rudy's leash, I snorted. "No, and no. We've had dogs before that I had to all but run to keep up with. Rudy's just a lazy lump. Plus, he loves to sniff absolutely every inch along the way. I think that is a pretty common dog trait though." Looking over at Al, I grinned. "You do walk faster than Mrs. Manski. I'll give you credit for that."

"I'm four years younger than she is."

"Oh, excuse me. I guess at your age, that's a big deal."

"Watch it, young lady. I'm still on the good side of eighty."

"Yes, sir. So sorry."

We were quiet as we walked in the fresh air of an early May afternoon. Rudy found a squashed rubber ball to chew, and I drew in a long breath of spring flowers. "This is a beautiful day."

When Al nodded and smiled, I realized I'd spoken out loud.

"Sure is." He lifted his gaze to watch a bird land on the tree we were passing under. "Spring really is a reminder from God of new starts. New chances. I thank Him for that."

Rudy stopped, so I did too. And thought about what Al just said. "You're right. Oh, you're right." My chest swelled. "Fresh starts. New chances. A new day." I reached my hand over to squeeze his arm. "Thank you for reminding me."

"Sure enough." He moved a step closer to Rudy. "Uh-oh. You did bring a doggy bag, didn't you?"

Laughter bubbled out of me as I knelt beside my dog. "Oh yeah. Several. I know this guy."

*Thank You, Lord, for a good day.*

∽

My alarm wouldn't shut off, even after I'd punched it multiple times. I rolled over and pushed up on my elbow, trying to shake the sleep away.

Was that the phone?

It rang again.

"Hello?"

"Mom? Are you okay?" It was Roland's voice, but it was coming out of the wrong end of the phone.

I swung my feet over the side of the bed and turned my phone to the correct position. "Rolie? Is that you?"

"Yes, Mom. I'm sorry. I knew I'd wake you, but I'm just finishing my shift and leaving for home. And, and I needed to talk to you."

Now my brain was awake and clear.

"It's okay, honey. How are you?"

"I'm a mess. I know you didn't want me to move in with Heather. I know you don't like her. But, but I need to talk to you."

"Roland. Are you driving?"

"Yes. I'm okay. Don't worry."

Right.

"Look, honey, I don't dislike, it's not that I don't like

Heather. Don't think that." Why do you think he thinks that, Tammy? I ground my teeth. "Please, just tell me what's on your mind."

"I love her." His voice was soft and filled with pain. "I always have. I never stopped."

The line was quiet.

*Oh, Father, what can I say?*

"I know she wants to make things right, for C.T., for the two of us. I know she does. But…" His horn blared.

"Roland?"

"Everything's fine, Mother. The street's all but empty. I'm blowing off steam. And I'm in a commercial area, so I'm not waking anybody up."

"Honey, please, you need to be calm to drive. Do you want to come over here to talk?"

"No. I'm driving safe." He exhaled a long sigh. "I'm trying, Mom. I really am, with Heather. I don't know how to do this. Heather's always crying. C.T. is always crying." He blared the horn again. "I had a talk with him. About how running away is not an option. He can call you. He can call Heather's mom, if he needs to get away from us, but running away is not an option. He promised, but, but he's just seven. I don't know. And Heather, her eyes always look hopeless. I don't know how to do this. I still hurt, you know? But I want to show her, I want to show both of them that I love her, that we're going to make this family thing happen. But, but, oh, Mom, I feel like I'm going to explode."

I reached inside myself to find the hate I'd had for Heather, to shove all the blame for this on her. But I couldn't do it. Instead, I remembered her joy as she gazed at her newborn in the hospital. And the love and heartache she'd shown on Sunday when she'd fallen asleep and her son ran to me.

"Rolie, are you really driving okay? Do you need to stop somewhere and wait for me to come meet you?"

"No." He drew in another breath. "I'm okay. Seriously. I actually feel a little better. I guess I needed to get all that out." He laughed. "Thanks, Mother. Honestly, I'm okay." He tooted the horn softer this time. "I know you're going to pray for us. And I know you're thinking that if I'd come close to God again, He'd help me. You'll be happy to know that Heather believes that now. She's fully given her life to Jesus."

Oh really? I wonder. I pinched myself. Stop it, Tammy.

"Good. Then you'll come back again soon too."

"You think?"

"I do."

Neither of us spoke for a minute.

"All right, I'm home. I guess I'd better go in and try to sleep." He hesitated. "If we invite you over for dinner sometime soon, will you come?"

"In a flash."

"Thanks, Mom. I love you."

"I love you too."

After setting the phone back on the table, I fell face down on the bed. "Dear Lord, thank You. Thank You that he called me."

## CHAPTER 24

No way would I sleep again right then. Sitting up, I checked the time on my phone. One thirty-three a.m.

With a snap of my fingers at Rudy, already awake next to my bed, I moved with quiet steps toward the front porch. Before opening the door I hesitated, then went back to my room to grab the church bulletin from last Sunday out of my Bible.

Outside, Rudy ignored the long leash I clipped to his collar and settled on the floor beside me as I eased onto the swing. "Okay, God, let's talk."

Soft rain tapped the rooftop, and one car splashed by on the street. I pushed my foot to start the swing moving. "Roland did sound better at the end of the call. Thank You, Father. I know I didn't say anything to help him."

With the light on my phone, I found the Bible verses for the sermon Jared had listed in the bulletin. From John 13, "A new command I give you: Love one another. As I have loved you, so you must love one another."

"I should love Heather as You have loved me, God. Wow."

I gave the swing a few more shoves.

"That's what You want me to do. I surely need Your help. I can't do it on my own. No way. I know that."

I looked back at the verses and read out loud from 1 John. "See what great love the Father has lavished on us, that we should be called children of God! And that is what we are! … This is how we know what love is: Jesus Christ laid down his life for us. And we ought to lay down our lives for our brothers and sisters."

Tears dripped off my chin, and I swiped at my runny nose.

"It's not good enough, Lord, for me to say I can't measure up to what Jesus did. I already know that. Help me know what You want me to do as Your child."

And the words from Zephaniah 3, "The Lord your God is with you, the Mighty Warrior who saves. He will take great delight in you; in his love he will no longer rebuke you, but will rejoice over you with singing."

"Father God, how can You rejoice over me?" I left the tears alone now. The swing moved back and forth. Rudy lifted his nose and sniffed at my toes.

"Father God, You know the ugliness in me. You know how I've hated that young woman. That child." My heart squeezed. "And You know how pride is such a wicked thing in me. I've always said all I ever wanted is to be a good Christian wife and mother, to devote myself to the Bible and to helping my family grow closer to You. You see when that is pride in me, and You forgive me. You help me and love me when I make baby steps toward doing better."

Rudy stood and rubbed his nose against my hand. He hates to hear me cry. It made me cry harder.

"How have You loved me, Father? You forgive me. You gave me the life I longed for, a Christian husband, children to cherish and love and teach. And even now, You've sent Debbie to show me new things You might have for my life." Lowering my head, I cried onto Rudy's back. "How should I love Heather?" I sniffed. "I know, Father. Forgive, sure. I know I need to forgive her. Please, please help me find a way to do that. Lord…" My breath caught. "Help her have the life she longs for." I squeezed my eyes. "Show me, show me how to help her have the life she longs for."

With my arms around Rudy and my face in his fur, I didn't notice that somebody else came onto the porch. Someone sat on the swing beside me, and arms wrapped around my shoulders. "Oh, honey, don't cry." Tears sounded in Karl's voice too. "Tammy, baby, please don't cry so hard."

I pushed myself to a sitting position and looked into my husband's face. "Roland. Me. Now you? This family isn't sleeping tonight."

## CHAPTER 25

We rocked on the swing for long moments, neither of us speaking, Karl's arms around me as I continued to cry. When I lifted my head and looked around, I noticed his suitcases sitting on the porch.

My chest pounded. "You're, you're coming home?"

Karl rubbed and patted my back as I coughed and choked. "Shh. Take a breath. Yes, baby. Yes. I'm home."

After a few more gasps, I was able to stop choking and look at the time on my phone. "It's barely two in the morning. Why are you here now?"

"Where else should I be?" His warm fingers rubbed the tears on my face. "Where should I have always been?"

With my hand to my mouth, I stared at him. What should I say? Biting my lip, I struggled not to cry again.

"Come on, honey." Karl took hold of my hands and lifted me to my feet. "You need to sleep. We both do. We can talk in the morning."

To my surprise, I was able to sleep. And when I woke in the morning, Karl sat on the side of our bed.

I sniffed the wonderful scent and rubbed my eyes. "Are you making coffee?"

"No. It wasn't me." He turned his face, and I saw fear in his eyes. "I had to come home, because I've never been able to do anything, nothing worthwhile, without you." His voice grated. "Will you come with me now, so I can talk to my father?"

"All I do these days is cry." My arms wrapped around him, and I pressed my face against his. "Of course, I'll come with you."

Al sat at the dining room table, one hand holding a mug of coffee, the other stroking Rudy. "I let him out already. I fed him too. I probably gave him more than you do. He said you don't feed him enough."

When I didn't answer, Al raised his gaze from the dog. Something like awe flashed over his face when he saw Karl, and he stood up.

"No. Sit down." Karl cleared his throat. "I know you're not well."

Al's lips moved without sound for a minute, then he shook his head. "I'm much better. Thank you. I'm fine, but I'll sit." Grasping the edge of the table, he lowered himself back into the seat.

Karl pulled out the chair across from him. After I topped off Al's coffee, I filled two more mugs and sat next to Karl.

Watching these two men, I realized why Al had become so special to me.

*They are so much alike, Father.*

And they were. The way they held their shoulders, the firm set of their jaws, the depth of sadness in their eyes. But it was more than their appearance.

Without sharing the last fifty years together, both had grown into the same kind of man. Strong. Serious. Kind. Both willing to fight for what was important.

Karl allowed his eyes to meet his father's. "I almost feel like we need to introduce ourselves to each other." His jaw twitched, but he kept his gaze steady. "I'm certainly not the person you knew before you left, and probably you're far from the man you were then too."

"For most of the last 52 years, I've struggled not to be that man." Al's mug shook in his hands, but his gaze never left Karl's.

Karl drew in a breath. "It struck me, the last couple of days, just how foolish I've been. For years, I've hung on to blaming you. For everything. And all I've really managed to do is hurt myself. And everybody else."

Al shook his head. "No, you're a good man … son." His voice croaked. "I'm proud of you."

Karl flinched. "That's not how I feel."

Al gave a short laugh. "I know all about regrets. I know how you feel."

My teeth bit into my lip. *Father God, thank You for letting me have the chance to sit at this table today with these two men I love.*

But there was something else I needed to do.

## CHAPTER 26

After Karl left for work, I drove Al to the rehab clinic. "I'm not staying today. There's somewhere I need to go, so I'll see you at lunchtime."

He grinned at me. "You're just afraid Debra will test you on some of those books you took home."

I moaned. "I didn't even start on them. Don't rat on me."

"You've got my word."

After picking up coffee and doughnuts, I drove to the nursing home and walked into Heather's office.

Her eyes were fixed on the computer, so she didn't notice me until I set the cup of coffee beside her. She jerked up her head. "Tammy. What are you…" She hurried to stand. "Hello."

"Hi." After resting the box of doughnuts on her desk, I stepped back a little. How to start?

My mouth was dry. "I came because, I owe you an apology."

"You, you…" She sat back down and clasped her hands on the desk in front of her. "I don't understand." Her gaze flicked around the room then back to me. "Please sit down."

Pulling a chair up to the side of her desk, I sat on the edge and also looked around at everything except her face. On the front of her desk sat a recent picture of C.T., seated on his bicycle, smiling.

"Tammy?"

I brought my eyes back to her. "I never accepted you as a part of my family." My voice trembled. "Not when you and Roland got married. And not now that you've come back. I'm so sorry."

*Father, I don't want to cry.*

Heather blinked then opened her mouth.

Before she could speak, I went on. "I never tried to make you feel welcome. Never tried to find out how I could help you. I always pushed you away. I've been so wrong."

Tears shone in Heather's eyes. "Stop. Please. Thank you for saying that, but that's enough now." She sniffed and reached for a tissue. "I hurt your son. Now that I have, now that I'm getting closer to my son, I think, I understand better how you felt." She nudged the tissue box toward me.

Grabbing a couple, I swiped at my face.

*What else can I say right now, Father?*

Heather leaned back in her chair. "We can work through this together. I believe that. Roland told me about your talk last night, that he told you how important Jesus is to me now."

I nodded. So he'd admitted to her that he called me. That was good. They were talking.

"I'm a Christian, Tammy, and so are you. We're both going to pray, and we're going to do our best to work things out for our family, and God will help us."

"I think your faith is stronger than mine right now. Please pray for me." I grabbed more tissues.

She managed a smile. "You'll be fine. I know how much your faith means to you. God knows how important He is to you."

We were both quiet for a minute then she reached for the doughnuts. "Now, eat one of these with me, so I don't feel like a pig."

## CHAPTER 27

*K*arl joined Rudy and me on our late-night walk. We sat together on my bench at the park as Rudy sniffed bushes and candy wrappers that had been dropped by the swings.

"Honey?" I reached over and clasped Karl's hand.

He kept his face turned away from me, but in the streetlights, I saw his shoulders slump.

"I don't know what to say to you." His voice quivered. "I am so sorry for walking out on you."

"Ooohh." My chest squeezed, and I pressed even closer to him. "Please look at me."

He turned toward me.

"Heather taught me something this morning."

"Yeah?" He wrapped my hand with both of his.

Sucking in a long breath, I straightened my shoulders. "She said that there's a point when we need to stop saying I'm sorry."

He didn't speak.

"You've told me that, and you don't need to anymore."

Rudy came back and lay at our feet.

"God's been with us on this. I never really felt like you

walked out on me. I was upset. Don't give me too much credit. But I knew you were struggling, and I knew you'd come back."

Karl placed my hand on his cheek so I could feel the tears there. "I love you so much." His voice scratched.

I pressed against his chest, and he folded his arms around me.

He cleared his throat. "Friday morning, I'm taking off from work and going with my father to the rehab center. I need to do that." He paused. "You want me to ask Debra when she'd like to get together to study with you?"

Groaning, I squeezed him, then looked up. "You were right, you know. We need each other to do things right. We don't do so well alone."

He chuckled and pulled me to my feet. "Amen to that, my love. Come on. Let's take this lazy animal home while he's still willing to wake up and walk tonight."

Reaching up, I pulled him down to kiss me. "I'm still awake. Let's get this dog home."

## THE END

# GIFTS OF GRACE

## CHAPTER 1

My chest squeezed as we drove up the driveway and stopped in front of the house. It'd been almost twelve years.

Kailey shut off the engine and turned to me. "Someone's here."

Danny stood on the front porch, his arms crossed, his face stern.

"It's my brother." I shrank lower into the seat. "I shouldn't be here. I want to leave."

"No." She reached across me and opened my door. "You don't. Let's go. Straighten your shoulders and hold your head high."

As we got out of the car, Danny came down the stairs and moved to meet us. "I see you made good time." He held out his hand to Kailey. "You must be Steven's sister Kailey. He told me you were bringing Judy today."

She grasped his hand. "Yes. And you're Dan. I recognize you from the picture Judy's been showing off to all her single girl-friends for years." She winked. "Right before she tells them you're already married."

Danny cracked a smile then turned to me. "Hey, Jude."

Clenching my fists, I raised my chin. I'm not going to be a sniveling eight-year-old. "I'm here, Danny. Like it or not. You sent me the paperwork yourself. Dad left this place to me as much as to you." I gulped. "My baby died, and I don't want to be with my husband right now. For now, I'm here."

Silence. Then a cow mooed not far away.

Kailey cleared her throat. "Here I stand. Your best friend and sister of the husband you don't want to be around." She moved to the back of the car. "I'm going to carry in your stuff. You guys go along and talk."

∽

"You remind me of the day you got in a fight on the playground when you were in first grade." We'd moved inside, and Danny sat at the opposite end of the couch from me, leaning his back against the arm. "I found you crying on the school bus that afternoon. You told me a big bully made fun of your new glasses, so you punched him. He cried, so you laughed at him. He hit you back and broke your glasses, so you hit him again, and both of you had to go to the principal's office, and you didn't care if Daddy was mad at you." He shook his head. "That's what you looked like outside just now."

Maybe I was going to snivel after all. With my head lowered I sucked in a long breath. "I'm sorry. I need..." I looked up and found him with a slight grin. "Danny?"

He straightened in the seat. "You don't have to tell me right now why you don't want to be with Steven." His face was back to serious. "But you should be grateful he let me know you were coming. No one has lived in this house for six months. I turned on the furnace, and Helen did a little cleaning, made sure you had fresh sheets and towels."

When I opened my mouth, he raised a hand. "I'm almost

done. We're going to need to talk, but not today. You need to rest."

He leaned closer. "I'm sorry about your baby. Brenda told me."

I flinched. "Okay."

Our older sister Brenda was the only one I'd kept in touch with over the years.

"Brenda also told Aunt Jeannie you were coming, so she sent you a present." He stood. "I've left a few phone numbers on the kitchen table for you. Mine, Helen's, Brenda's, and Jeannie's. In case you don't have them. Call if you need us. For now, come see what's waiting for you out here."

He led me through the kitchen to the back porch, which had been screened in sometime since I'd been home. A huge white dog stood tied to a table leg on one side of the porch, his head raised and eyes bright as he watched us. "Meet Flash."

As we drew near, the dog banged his tail against the table leg and opened his mouth in a huge smile. Or was it a snarl?

No time like the present to find out.

"Flash?" Lowering myself to my knees, I held the big head in both my hands. "Hey, buddy."

"He's big, but he moves quick." Danny got on his knees beside me and ruffled the dog's ears. "Jeannie adopted this mess as a pup, and when she moved to the retirement home last summer, he moved into our house. When Brenda told Jeannie you were coming, she ordered me to bring him over for you."

"Mmm hmm." Flash licked my face. "Why's he tied up?"

"To keep him from running you over to say hello." He stood and unhooked the leash. "He turned one a month or so ago, so hopefully, he won't get any bigger. The backyard fence is in good shape, so you can let him run around." He brushed one hand against the other. "And you can let him inside. He's house-broken and pretty much over his puppy-chewing-everything stage."

"Pretty much over it, huh?" Standing, I glanced at the dog and snapped my fingers. "Come on, Flash. Let's go inside where it's warm." I turned to Danny and straightened my shoulders. "Thank you, for the gift, for turning the furnace on, and thank Helen for cleaning up." My throat choked. "And please do come by soon. So we can talk."

"How long is your friend staying?"

"She has to leave tomorrow, to get back to her husband and kids. She's going into town tonight to buy me groceries." With my hand on Flash's head, I moved toward the back door. "I'll be able to drive again in two weeks, then they're going to bring my car here. I'll be fine. I'm not going to be a burden on you guys."

His eyes widened. "Judy, wait…" He stepped toward me, but I went inside and closed the door.

I dropped to my knees and buried my face against Flash's. "Danny, I am so sorry. Thank you for being so nice to me. I'm gonna try. I promise."

## CHAPTER 2

Flash followed me into the kitchen, through to the living room, sniffing everything along the way.

"I doubt there's anything to eat down there for you, buddy. It's been a while since anybody ate here."

From one of the bedrooms down the hall came the sound of Kailey closing drawers and moving things around.

I'm not ready to talk to her.

Walking straight to the fireplace, I lifted my parents' wedding picture off the mantle then sat down in Dad's easy chair. "So."

My throat tightened as I stared at their faces. "Here I am. Home again. What do you guys have to say to me?"

Clenching my jaw, I fought to hold tears back. "You wanted me to stay at home, Daddy, didn't you? It only took me twelve years."

Flash sat beside me and laid his head on my knee. I scratched his ears. "Thanks, boy. I'm glad you're the comforting type."

He knocked his tail against the floor.

"And what about you, Mom? You didn't stick around long enough to help me with anything. You decided when I was ten days old, you could leave me with someone else and drive into a snowstorm." I swiped at my face. "So what am I supposed to do now?"

Kailey stood beside me then, resting her hand on my arm. "Oh, honey, please look at me."

"No. I want to feel sorry for myself."

She lowered her head and looked straight into my eyes. "You've done that. I guess if you want to keep on for a little longer, that's okay. But it's time to start healing now."

∼

THE NEXT MORNING, Kailey found her pity for me again. "I wish I could stay longer." She set a bowl of oatmeal in front of me. "I could probably stay a couple more days." She chewed her lip.

"No, no, no." I shook my head. "Your family needs you, and I need to start healing, remember?"

"Judy." She sighed and sat across the table from me. "Tell me about your mom. You've talked a lot about your dad, but what can you tell me about your mom?"

"I don't know anything about her. She was killed driving on an icy road when I was ten days old."

"Yes, she left you with your older sister and went out in a dangerous storm to go shopping. What else?"

Sniffing, I took a swallow of coffee. "I guess I do sound pretty sorry for myself, don't I?"

She nodded and grinned as she bit into her toast.

"When I was little, Danny told me Mom was a brazen wench. She was forty and Dad was fifty when she asked him to marry her. He'd never been married, and her first husband had been dead for a year."

"And they were neighbors, right?"

"Mmm hmm. Mom and her first husband and Dad had been neighbors and friends for years. Mom's older kids were close to Dad. They grew up hanging around here on his farm as much as their own. Then Mom's first husband died when my half-brother and sister, Wayne and Brenda, were 17 and 16. But Danny was only two, and Mom wanted him to have a father." I moved my spoon around the bowl without eating. "So she asked Dad to marry her and raise Danny as his son. She was a good mother, I guess."

Kailey reached across the table to still my hand. "Probably she was."

We were quiet for a few minutes then I pushed back my chair. "Eat your breakfast and get ready to go." As I carried my dishes to the sink, I inhaled a deep breath. "You've already had to take care of me for the two weeks since I left the hospital. You need to get back to your family."

Kailey joined me at the sink. "And my brother. He needs checking in on too."

My stomach clenched. I couldn't look at her. "Yeah. Him too."

She wrapped her arm around my shoulders. "Don't hate him. He loves you so much."

My hands jerked, and a plate crashed into the sink. "I don't... Oh, I broke the plate."

She pushed me back from the sink. "I'll get it. Sit down."

Kailey cleaned the glass from the sink while I hunched over my coffee at the table, tears dripping into my cup.

She walked back to me but didn't sit down again. "I am going to leave now. I'll call you later." She shook my shoulder. "Look at me a minute."

I raised my head and turned to her.

"I didn't mean to upset you. But Steven does love you. He's always only wanted to do what's best for you. No." She raised a hand when I opened my mouth. "You've told me for two weeks what you think of him. And I haven't gotten mad at you, because I love you. You were my sister long before you were my sister-in-law."

She moved toward the hall. "But he is my brother, and I love him too. Maybe I was harsh, saying you hate him. But I need to tell you this. You're being unfair to him. You'll know that when you've had more time to think." She turned to walk to her bedroom then looked back over her shoulder at me. "He hurts right now too. A terrible hurt."

## CHAPTER 3

"And don't forget to talk to God about all of this." Kailey turned to me from the front door. "He's waiting to hear from you." She walked out.

My throat choked, and my body shivered. *How can I talk to You, God?* I'd pushed Him away.

As I stood at the front window watching Kailey's car pull onto the road, Flash nudged my hand with his wet nose. "Guess it's just you and me, buddy." His mouth opened wide when I glanced down at his huge, sparkling eyes. "Are you smiling at me, you goof?"

I couldn't help but laugh. "Maybe you're right. We'll be better off without her. She thinks too heavy."

No, I wasn't going to remember who started all the dreary thinking.

"Follow me into the kitchen, dog, and I'll get you some food. And you just keep making me laugh."

Flash raced me to the large metal container holding his kibble. "Yes, sir. Here I come. Now you eat how much of this twice a day? Half of the can?"

Someone knocked on the back door.

"You better come with me. Protection."

Two boys with flaming red hair stood on the other side of the door.

"Whoa, you guys have to be related to Helen."

"She's our mom." The youngest handed me a basket of eggs. "She sent some stuff for you."

"I see that."

The other boy held two full paper bags.

I stepped back. "Come on in and set all that on the table."

The one who'd spoken dropped down to hug Flash while his brother moved past me with the sacks.

Taking a breath, I followed him. "You guys are Danny and Helen's kids?"

The older boy turned to me. "Yeah. I'm Brett, he's Aaron." His face looked as serious as my brother's.

"Wow. Brett. Last time I saw you..." My throat stuck. I inhaled. "You were just eight months old?"

"Then you went away and never came back."

"Right." I swallowed. What should I say to these two nephews who didn't know me? "So, your mom sent some food? Are those eggs from your own chickens?"

"Yep." Aaron stood up from hugging the dog and moved over to the table. "She usually charges a dollar a dozen, but she said you didn't have to pay." He pulled a jar out of one bag. "She sent you some stuff we canned from our garden last year. Tomatoes, green beans, pickles." Soon the bags were empty, and the table held a scattering of home-canned jars of food, a loaf of homemade bread, a couple of other baked items, and what must be meat in paper-wrapped packages. "There's peaches here, blackberry jelly, corn." Aaron smiled up at me. "You should have enough to eat for a couple of days."

"Or more." I shook my head. "And to think my friend bothered to go to the store in town last night."

Brett picked up the packages of meat. "Mom wrote on these

what they are, hamburger and roast. They need to go right back in the freezer." He moved to the refrigerator. He wasn't smiling yet.

It's going to take me some time to make up with him.

But Aaron's face couldn't be brighter. "So, you're our Aunt Judy. Can I call you Jude, like Daddy does?"

Danny must not hate me that much, if he'd used my nickname around the boys.

"Please do." I wanted to hug him. "I know Brett is twelve. How old are you, Aaron?"

"Nine. Our sister isn't even four yet, so she couldn't come today. Mom says it's still too cold for her to be out. But next week is March, so she'll be over with us soon."

"You have a sister?" For something to do with my hands, I picked up jars and placed them in the cabinet. "There's three of you, huh?"

"Yep." Aaron brought more jars to me. "Mom says that's plenty. Our sister is Elena."

Brett stood by the back door, shuffling from foot to foot and staring down at his hands.

I don't blame him for wanting to leave.

"Thanks for all the food, you guys. I bet you have chores to do at home. Do you have a 4-H project, Brett?"

He turned his gaze to mine, his eyes brightening. "I'm getting a pig to feed up. From a neighbor. He said it'll be ready to wean next week."

"That's great." Taking no chance on spooking him, I didn't move any closer. "I raised a pig for 4-H a couple of years. I hope I can meet yours sometime."

"Don't see why not. Let's go, squirt." He opened the door.

Aaron patted the bags of baked goods. "Mom sent you some pumpkin bread and oatmeal cookies. Don't forget to eat 'em. Dad says you're sick, and cookies always make me feel better when I'm sick."

"I will. Thank you."

Maybe next time I'd take a risk and hug Aaron at least.

∽

To my surprise, Danny came by that afternoon.

"I thought you were going to avoid me. Just send your kids."

Biting my lip, I looked away. Danny, why am I being so mean to you? You're the one who should be mad at me.

He walked past me and eased a heavy sack next to the dog-food holder. "I wanted to fill this up for you. I imagine you're not supposed to lift anything very heavy."

How much did that bag hold, fifty pounds? "Nothing like that, that's for sure." I gulped. "If my baby had lived, that would have been the heaviest weight I could lift for a while."

My eyes burned, and I turned my back to him. Stop it, Judy.

Behind me, Danny opened the container's lid and poured more food in. "I'm not leaving this bag here. Mr. Flash would have no qualms about tearing it open, but this should keep you for a while. Don't give him more than three cups a day. He weighs a hundred and twenty, and he could probably gain more if given the chance."

The lid slammed back on, and Danny's steps moved across the room till he stood behind me. He rested his hand on my shoulder. "Come on, little bit. We've got twelve years of talking to do. May as well get started."

## CHAPTER 4

"Now tell me what's going on with you." Danny pointed me to the couch and settled in Dad's recliner.

Daddy's newspaper reading chair. It has to be more than twenty years old.

Taking one of the couch cushions, I hugged it against me. "You mean since I stormed out when I was eighteen and never came back?" My mouth tasted bitter. "And how the one time you called me, I told you to never call again and hung up on you?"

Danny picked up the remote control from the table beside him and flipped it between his fingers. "We don't need to go into all that." He drew in a long breath and let out each word with care. "Since you kept in touch with Brenda, I know a little. Tell me about your baby. You couldn't come to see Dad in the hospital before he died because you were on bed rest with your pregnancy. What happened?"

Bile burned my throat, and I squeezed my eyes shut.

"You have to. You need to talk about it, and I need to know, so we can move on together." His voice came to me from a distance. "Judy."

Resting my head between my knees, I drew in long breaths. Danny knelt beside me then, his hands on my shoulders.

After a time, my eyes cleared, and I could sit up. Danny went into the kitchen for a glass of water. With gentle hands, he wrapped my fingers around the glass then sat back in the recliner.

After a few sips, I brought my gaze to meet his. "I had three miscarriages." My throat rasped and I coughed.

I took another swallow. "I wanted so much to be a mother, but I had constant trouble with the pregnancies. My blood pressure always spiked too high." Pushing myself to a more erect position, I set the glass of water on the end table. "After the second miscarriage, the doctor recommended I not try anymore. After the third…"

Am I being too personal? Danny and I always talked straight with each other.

He kept his gaze directed at me, not asking any questions.

"After the third miscarriage, Steven begged me to stop. He said he'd get a vasectomy." Flash pressed himself against my legs, and I focused my gaze on him. "I pleaded with him not to, just in case, someday…" I took a gulp of water. "I promised to be faithful with the pill. But sometimes, I wasn't."

My lips trembled and tears rained down my cheeks, but I wanted to tell the whole story.

Danny leaned toward me. "Honey, it's okay. You don't have to go on now."

"Yes, I do. You're right. How else can we live together unless I get it all out? I've closed myself away from you for so long."

We were quiet for a minute. A board creaked somewhere in the house. The furnace turned on.

"When we found out I was pregnant again, Steven was kind to me. He supported my attempt to make it work this time. At five months, I'd gone nearly twice as long as I'd ever made it before. The doctor ordered me to start bedrest. At seven months, my blood pressure was so high, she checked me into the hospital."

Pushing myself to my feet, I walked into the kitchen. "I need coffee."

Danny followed.

"I didn't mind bedrest, or even having to go to the hospital. We were having a baby this time. We'd seen the image, heard the heartbeat. It was a girl. We named her Alicia." My eyes were dry now. "But she barely moved. She wasn't growing right. My body..."

My hands fumbled with doors and drawers, searching for coffee and filters. "Where…"

"Stop." Danny eased me to a chair at the table. "I'll make coffee."

As he worked around the kitchen, I went on. "In the eighth month, just three weeks after Daddy died, they couldn't find a heartbeat." My eyes fogged. "And I was bleeding."

Danny took a seat across from me, but I didn't see his face.

In my mind, I saw Steven standing beside my bed that night, his face white. "They have to take the baby now. A C-section. The doctor said you should have your tubes tied at the same time. Please say yes. I need you to live."

Danny's face came back into focus.

"I said yes, but I told him I hated him, that I didn't want to see him anymore." I locked Danny's gaze with mine. "Sound familiar?"

## CHAPTER 5

Flash made me smile as he ran around the back yard, chasing imaginary squirrels up the trees. He found a patch of remaining snow against the shed and flopped into it.

I rested my forehead against the porch screen. "It's not even March yet, buddy. You'll probably still get some more snow."

In my mind, I saw my father leaning against the tree on the other side of the yard fence, gazing up at the sky, across meadows and fields. "O Lord, Thou art my God; I will exalt Thee, I will praise Thy name; for Thou hast done wonderful things."

Dad did not often use many words. But the Bible memory verses he'd learned as a child from his mother, the hymns, as well as the awe of and faith in God she lived into him, those things he never forgot. I often heard him murmuring verses and prayers as he worked around the farm, as he gazed at Danny and me, as he stood by my mother's grave. "For Thou, Lord, art good, and ready to forgive; and plenteous in mercy unto all them that call upon Thee."

"Will you go with us to church tomorrow?" Danny had asked before he left that afternoon.

How I wanted to say no.

But I kept remembering Kailey saying, "And don't forget to talk to God."

I'd often tried to run from God, but He always found me.

"What time will you pick me up?" I'd asked Danny.

Now, as I let Flash into the house, I heard Dad's soft voice singing "Amazing Grace" as we drove to church on a Sunday morning.

"Daddy, I wish you could go with me tomorrow."

## CHAPTER 6

The lovely old stone church building still stood, but with many changes. Wings had been added to both sides, and a ramp curved around to the side door. But it sure sounded like the same old organ playing "When We All Get to Heaven" as Danny opened the door for us to enter.

"Is that still Irene on the organ?" I asked Danny.

"Yep."

Is he grinning at me?

As we walked inside the back of the sanctuary, I could see why he might be grinning. "What?" I stopped and stared.

Irene Mantle did still sit behind the organ, tiny but erect, her hair even whiter than I remembered. But along with her on the stage were a handful of teens. One with a drum and another with a guitar. A girl blew on a trumpet while a boy with a crewcut said, "Test, test" into a microphone.

Turning to Danny's wife Helen, I asked, "Are you sure this is Adams Creek Church?"

Her face lit up. "It truly is."

When the pastor came out to lead in prayer and with a sermon, my eyes popped open.

That's Jonathan.

Jonathan Cooke was my first crush. His sister Marilyn and I grew up as neighbors and school friends. Jonathan and Danny were four years older than Marilyn and me, friends from informal games of softball up through high school baseball.

We spent hours giggling and dreaming of being double sisters-in-law. Neither match came about, but I smiled now, remembering.

∼

"It is you, isn't it? Stop." A voice came from behind me, then someone clasped my shoulders and turned me around. "You look twelve years older."

Marilyn stood in front of me, looking the same as I'd seen her last at eighteen in her cap and gown. Smiling, shy, brave.

"You don't." I accepted the hands she held out to me. "I don't think you're any older."

She found me after I'd wandered into the newer parts of the church building, telling Danny and Helen I wanted to check out the changes.

"I thought it was you." She gave me a hug. "Are you trying to hide?"

"Maybe. Is there a side door where I can sneak out?"

After daydreaming during his sermon, I knew I would have blushed if I'd had to go out the front door and shake hands with Jonathan and his pretty wife.

"You bet." Marilyn linked her arm with mine. "How long are you home for?"

Home.

A lump formed in my throat. "I, I'm gonna be here for a while."

## CHAPTER 7

"*Are* you awake?" My sister Brenda's voice on the phone. "Yeah." Rubbing my face with one hand, I pushed myself up in bed. "I am now. What time is it?"

"Ten o'clock, Judy. You need to be up."

I need pain medicine. "Why? Is there something I should be doing?" My voice sounded groggy. I shook my head to clear it. "What's up?"

"Jeannie and I will be over in about an hour. We'll see you then."

"But..."

Did she just hang up on me?

My half-sister Brenda, eighteen years older than me. And my Aunt Jeannie, the woman who had raised me since I was two weeks old.

"Flash? Where are you, boy? I need your support. More people for me to face."

∼

"Oh good, you do have Flash. I told Dan to bring him to you."

Jeannie stooped down to hug the dog the minute she walked into the house. Brenda gave me a hug.

"Look at you, sis. Too pale and skinny. I'm glad you came home."

Squeezing her tight, I hid my face against her shoulder. Where should I start with these precious ladies?

Jeannie stood up and rested her hand on my arm. "I don't know what to say to you, girl, after not seeing you for twelve years."

Could they be as unsure how to handle this as I am?

Stepping forward, I wrapped my arms around her neck. "I love you, Jeannie."

When we were seated around the kitchen table with sub sandwiches and hot chocolate, Flash planted himself close to Jeannie's feet.

"He loves you." I smiled at her.

Jeannie dropped a large bite of sandwich on the floor, and Flash snapped it up. "I got him from the same guy I always got our dogs from when you were growing up."

I scrunched my face, trying to remember. "Roger, Roger something. Your friend who raises purebred dogs."

"Who tries to raise purebred dogs." Jeannie threw down another bite. "He's always giving away ones who get mixed up with some stray. Flash is partly Great Pyrenees and partly country mutt. He was a precious puppy."

She sat up from scratching Flash's ears and turned to face me. "I didn't know who to be madder at, you or my stubborn brother, when you ran away on your graduation night." Jeannie never minced words.

You may as well have slapped me, Jeannie. "Me either."

She held my gaze, then smiled. "I'm glad you kept in touch with Brenda. At least we knew you were okay. And heard bits about what you were up to."

Lowering my head, I inhaled a long breath then took a bite of sandwich. What to say?

"Are you feeling all right, kiddo?" Brenda to the rescue. "Are you okay staying alone?"

"I am." As I lifted my head, I caught a glance between the two women across from me. "I'm really okay. It's been more than two weeks now since…" My heart flinched. "Since I lost the baby." Another deep breath. "Mostly, I need to take it easy." I managed a smile. "And I've got good drugs."

"Why are you here?"

Of course, Jeannie would come right out and ask.

"Things, things are hard between my husband and me right now. I need some alone time."

Jeannie shook her head. "That sounds all wrong from the get-go."

I couldn't meet her eyes. "Let's talk about something else for now."

Jeannie picked up her sandwich. "What about work? You're a nurse, right?"

Letting out a breath, I nodded. "I'm an advice-line nurse, for a medical insurance company. I work from home. People who call and have a question the operators think would be best for a nurse get switched to me."

Jeannie snorted. "Bet you get some funny ones."

It was good to be able to smile. "I do."

## CHAPTER 8

An unseasonably warm day for the first week in March drew me outside. Flash walked with me down toward a large oak tree where Dad had strung up a tire swing for me when I was twelve. "Flash, look. It's still here."

After tugging on the rope, I stepped through and sat. "It still feels safe, buddy. Daddy must have reinforced it for grandchildren." I pushed the swing into a gentle motion. "Come over here and sit, dog. I'll swing a little."

Flash eyed me, glanced around for any better prospects, then lay on the ground beside me.

"Thank you for this swing, Daddy. I spent a lot of time out here."

Branches creaked as I pushed my feet to start the swing moving.

"You were always good to me. Why did I forget that?"

One day, soon after he'd hung the swing, I saw dad smiling at me from down by the chicken house. "Every good gift and every perfect gift is from above, and cometh down from the Father of lights, with whom is no variableness, neither shadow of turning."

That day I'd just laughed at him and kicked my feet to go higher. What gift were you thinking of that day, Daddy? The gift of a swing? Or were you thanking God for me?

He would never have said words like that to my face, but I knew he loved me. Mom asked Dad to marry her so Danny would have a father. She was forty and Daddy was fifty. I doubted they'd expected to have a child together. "You were a huge surprise," Daddy sometimes told me.

He'd had a bunch of surprises at fifty. A wife, a son, and then a baby girl. And ten days after that surprise baby, Mom decided the winter storm would wait long enough for her to go into town and grocery shop.

"You knew the weather around here, Mom. You should've known you couldn't predict a storm like that. Look at what you piled on Daddy, after just one year of marriage."

"Your aunt Jeannie is a good mama to you both," Daddy told Danny and me. "Be sure you're good to her."

Daddy's sister Jeannie, thirteen years younger, a widow, working as a manager at the small-town grocery store, left her job and moved in with us when Mom died.

Danny lost his birth father when he was two and his birth mother before he turned four. "I don't remember either one of them," he'd told me years later. "Jeannie and Dad are my parents."

I reached a hand down to ruffle Flash's ears. "Jeannie always asked us to call her Jeannie, not Mommy. I wonder why."

"You had a mama who loved you," Jeannie had told me the day she and Brenda visited. "Your daddy planned to give this to you after you graduated from high school." She handed me a thick, faded spiral notebook. "Course, you didn't give him the chance."

The notebook lay in my lap now as I sat in the swing. Swallowing, I turned back the cover.

Evelyn Wolfe, my mother's name with her first husband, scrawled across the top of the page. April 3.

"Yesterday was Jake's funeral. Today, I need to move on. Wayne and Brenda are almost grown. They won't need me much longer. But Danny is barely two. Heavenly Father, how are we going to make it?"

My lips trembled, and I closed the book. "I can't read this."

Growing up, I'd hardened my heart against my mother. She hadn't cared enough about me to stick around. If I read her journal, would I have to let my heart soften toward her?

My teeth ground. You are a hardhearted woman, Judy Park.

My father's voice came to me, as it had every morning at breakfast. "Dear God, give us the strength to do everything we need to do today."

Cold wind blew in my face. Maybe it wasn't warm enough yet for me to sit out after all.

"God." My voice cracked. "Mom and Dad trusted You to help them. I haven't let You close to me recently. For years, is the truth. Kailey said I should talk to You again. Maybe I'll try. Will You help me?"

"Hey, Jude," Danny shouted.

My head jerked up. Since the trees were still bare, I could see all the way to his house, less than a ten-minute walk. He was already closer to my house than his.

"No wonder Daddy and the Wolfe family were such good friends. It's almost like neighbors on the same street in the city."

Stepping out of the swing, I snapped my fingers at Flash. We walked to meet Danny on the path between the two houses.

## CHAPTER 9

"I saw you sitting on that swing." Danny reached me first and swatted me on the back. "Is this a healthy thing for you to be doing, sitting out in the cold? Twirling in that old tire swing?"

"I wasn't twirling." I realized I was comfortable talking to Danny. "And don't forget, I'm the nurse. I know what's healthy."

"Huh."

With a hand on my shoulder, he turned me toward the back door and fell into step beside me.

As we walked into the kitchen, I slipped off my coat. "I already made coffee. Want some?"

"Would never say no to coffee. Helen sent you some more food." He set a bulging sack on the counter.

"Tell her thanks, but I really can cook for myself. And, also thanks to her, I have lots of groceries."

"Feeding people is her joy and ministry. Don't knock it." He pulled microwave containers and foil wrapped surprises out of the bag. "Some of this you can freeze, but what would you like me to leave out for dinner? Meatloaf? Lasagna? Vegetable beef soup? Homemade mac and cheese with chicken?"

"Stop, stop." My mouth watered, and I wrapped my arms around my stomach. "I don't knock it, but whew. Tell her to slow down a bit."

After we loaded the refrigerator and freezer, I poured our coffee, and we sat at the table.

"I hear Brenda and Jeannie stopped by the other day." He got to his feet. "Do you have creamer for this coffee?"

"Wimp." I sipped from my own cup. "I do have some flavored stuff in the fridge Kailey got for me, to share with people who aren't strong enough for regular good, black brew."

"Mm hmm." He poured creamer into his cup. "So what did Jeannie have to say to you?"

"She said it was good to see me after so many years, but she was still irked at me for running away. Why does she live in assisted living? Did she move there after Dad had to go to the nursing home?"

"She's not in assisted living. Not yet anyway. The retirement center has three levels, apartments for people who don't need any care, assisted living, and a nursing home. She moved the same time Dad did." He unwrapped one of the foil packages. "Will you share your applesauce bread with me? Helen is a great baker."

Nodding, I reached for napkins. "Why didn't Jeannie stay living here? Surely, she knew this would always be her home."

He brought a knife to the table and cut thick slices of the bread. "We had to talk her into moving. She wanted to stay on, but she's had heart trouble. Not as bad as Dad's, but Brenda and Wayne and I told her we'd be more comfortable if she lived in town. She's closer to Brenda there, and to the doctor and clinic. Plus, with the apartment, she has less to care for than this big house and yard."

"She's had problems with her heart? Brenda never told me that. Is she okay?"

"She is. She's had one stint put in, takes medicine." He tapped my hand with his finger. "She's fine, little bit."

Danny cut another slice of bread. "And she keeps busy as always. She volunteers with Meals on Wheels and the library." He took a large bite of bread and took a moment to swallow it. "She teaches arts and crafts at the nursing home, and she's joined a quilting club. She also decided to attend church in town rather than drive to the one out here. It just takes less time and energy. It took us some time to talk her into it, but she's happy now, I think."

"Good." I drew in a long breath. "I'll have my car back the end of next week. I'll visit her then."

"I usually go shopping in town on Saturdays and stop by to see her. You're welcome to ride along."

"I'd like that."

He laid his hand on the notebook I'd carried in with me. "Jeannie gave you one of Mom's journals, huh?"

My head snapped up. "She had more?"

"A lot. After I graduated from high school, Dad gave me an armload." He paused. "Oh yeah, I remember. The ones he gave me ended right before my birth father died. He said he was saving the last one for you."

My lips twisted. "Yeah, Jeannie told me I stole his chance to give it to me."

Neither of us spoke for a minute.

Danny leaned back in his chair. "When you're done with that one, could I look at it? You can see the ones I have too."

I scooted the book toward him. "Take it now. I haven't really started it yet."

Danny shook his head and pushed the book back to me. "How long you planning to stay here?"

Ugh. Thanks for the gentle touch, bro.

Shoving back my chair, I walked to look out the window with my back to him. "Tired of me already?"

He didn't answer.

I turned around. "I don't know yet. You said Dad left the house and this farm jointly to both of us, right? I know you work both this farm and Mom's old one, but would you mind if I lived in the house?"

"Of course not." He tipped his chair back. "But what about your home with Steven?" He narrowed his eyes. "What about Steven?"

My stomach clenched. "I don't know." What had I done to my marriage?

Danny stood up. "Be careful, little bit. Don't rush to build up dividing walls again."

## CHAPTER 10

*A* knock on the front door.

I clicked my tongue at Flash, lying in front of the couch. "Who's here now, buddy?"

He pricked his ears then went back to sleep.

When I opened the door, Marilyn stood on the front porch with a smile and holding a casserole dish. "Howdy. I hope you don't mind, I didn't call first."

"No, but..." Stepping back I shook my head. "Everybody keeps bringing me food. It's not like..." I clamped my mouth shut. Yes, somebody had died.

I turned my back and hurried to the kitchen. "Of course, I'm glad you came. And I love all the food gifts. I'm getting stronger, but..." Does she know I lost a baby?

Marilyn followed me into the kitchen and set down her dish. "So, you have been sick. I was afraid of that. You didn't look very strong the other day at church." She stood in front of me and took hold of my arm to keep me from turning. "What's wrong?"

My throat tightened, but I held her gaze. "I lost a baby. She was born...before she was born, she..."

I couldn't say the word.

Marilyn's eyes widened then she grasped my hands. "Oh, honey. Come sit down."

She led me to the table and pulled out chairs for both of us. "I didn't know. I'm sorry."

I wanted to bury my head in my arms and sob. Couldn't she please go away?

No. Straightening my shoulders, I inhaled a long breath. "I, I didn't know if word had gotten around. You said you'd heard I was back."

Come on, Judy, be fair. Your family hasn't been gossiping about you. Swallowing, I lifted my chin. "I'm sorry. Let me start over." Surely, the more times I explained my pregnancy, my marriage, to people, the easier it would become.

Marilyn listened, covering my hand with hers. "I'm so sorry, Jude. I know you always wanted a big family."

Yes. She'd been my best friend growing up. She knew. Guilt stabbed me. "I'm sorry I haven't kept in touch for so long. I should have. You—"

She shook my shoulder. "Shh. Don't upset yourself over that. I worried about you, but I, I trusted you. I figured you had good reason."

"Ha. Good reason." Pushing back my chair, I walked to the coffeepot. "I need some caffeine. You?"

"You bet."

With shaking hands, I readied the coffee and turned it on. Where to start? "You were my best friend. I shouldn't have just left without talking to you." My eyes pricked.

"Come and sit down." Her voice was calm but firm. "You can tell me if you want. Or not. It's been twelve years, and I'm sure it's painful. I don't want to make things harder for you."

I gave her a hug and sat back at the table with her. "I've missed you so much."

It was true. Even if I hadn't realized it until that moment, it was true.

Marilyn stood up. "Let me put this casserole in the fridge." She opened the door. "You're not kidding. You do have a lot of food in here. Oh hey." She turned back to me with a plastic wrapped bundle. "Is this Helen's caramel coffeecake? Whoa."

I sniffed and rubbed my face. "Yes, let me get some plates."

"Sit. I'll get them and the coffee. I love Helen's caramel cake."

When we were both seated again with coffee and sweets, I met her eyes. "Let me just explain, get it out."

She folded her hands around her cup. "Okay."

"I ran away the same night as our graduation. Dad and I had a terrible fight."

Marilyn didn't push. She gave me time.

My feet jerked under the table. I wanted to get up and pace, but I forced myself to stay seated. "I'd told you I got the full scholarship for the nursing program at the university, right?"

She nodded.

"I didn't tell Dad until we came home that night and Jeannie got out my graduation cake. I knew he didn't want me to go away for college."

Shouting voices pressed against my mind, trying to bring the memories to the forefront. Shaking my head, I went on.

"Dad wanted me to stay on the farm. He said I could get a nursing license going to the tech college in town." My face quivered. "We screamed at each other. Dad banged on the table. Jeannie cried. I threw my plate of cake on the floor."

Tears again. Not like me. Must be a post-pregnancy thing.

"Daddy told me if I left for college, I never needed to come home again."

My shoulders scrunched, and I didn't try to stop crying. "I said fine with me. I packed everything I could think of in the back of my old pickup and left before another hour passed." My voice croaked. "I never came home again until last week."

## CHAPTER 11

Saturday morning, I rode into town with Danny.
"Do you need to go with me to the grocery store, or do you want me to just drop you off at Jeannie's?"

I spluttered a laugh. "Not hardly. I've written down four things, I think, for you to pick up for me. Leave me at Jeannie's while you run around, so I'll have more time with her."

We called Jeannie to let her know I was coming, and she met us out on the sidewalk. She laid an arm on my shoulders. "I'm glad you came. Now we'll have time to talk, just the two of us."

What might that mean?

"This looks nice." Moving around Jeannie's apartment, I found pieces from the farmhouse. Jeannie's bedroom furniture, a china cabinet, a rocking chair. Besides knickknacks and wall hangings, I recognized the high-backed stools pushed up against her breakfast bar and the bookcase standing next to her loveseat. "It's really, well, tiny. Do you like that?"

One room served as a living-dining-kitchen area, with two doors opening to the bedroom and bathroom. They were small rooms, too, though they seemed to have everything she'd need.

"It took some getting used to." Walking to the kitchen area, she picked up a teakettle from the narrow stovetop. "I don't have any coffee, but will you drink tea with me?"

"Sure."

She filled the kettle at the sink and turned on a burner. "I have a microwave, but I still like hot tea best with boiled water from the stove. Have a seat on the couch."

It wasn't long before she'd set the tea tray on the end table between her rocking chair and the loveseat and sat down.

"You look good." I touched my cup with a careful finger. It needed to sit for a few minutes. "Danny said you've had some trouble with your heart."

Her face scrunched with irritation. "Not that big a deal. But the kids insisted I shouldn't live alone out on the farm."

Lifting my hand, I covered a grin. She'd always included Brenda and Wayne as part of "the kids," even though they'd been grown when Mom died.

Jeannie went on. "It was a big change for me, but I'm settling in. I'm still going through things at the house. Throwing most stuff out and giving some away. You might look around while you're there, see if there's anything you'd like to claim before I get rid of it."

That sounded like Jeannie. I'd better hurry to look around. But then, did I deserve to take anything?

Shaking my head, I pushed those doubts away. "Okay. Thanks. Come out and see me anytime you want. Or do you still drive?"

"Hmph. Of course, I still drive. I'm only sixty-seven, remember. I'm not ready for the undertaker." She stopped, and her face took on softness. "I'm sorry. That wasn't kind."

My brain cried. No more talking about death right now. Taking a tiny sip from the cup, I searched for a different topic. "I'm starting back to work on Monday. I'll be getting nursing calls again then."

"Good. That's good." The tone of her voice said she was as

eager as I was to talk about something else. "Have you checked the internet connection? Dan joined us to their satellite link a few years ago." She snorted. "Not that your dad would ever consider using it, of course. 'Ridiculous modern technology foolishness.'" She imitated Dad's growl so well, I giggled.

"Yes, I checked. And it works. I do a lot of online searching to answer patients' questions." I picked up my cup again. "How about you? Do you go online?"

"I do." Her smile, which she used only for good reason, spread. "I started as soon as Dan set us up. I do emails and check the news. I like 'good clean funnies,' sports sites, knitting and quilting groups. It's amazing."

Staring at this lively woman, it struck me what I'd missed over the past twelve years.

Jeannie, I'm sorry. Even growing up, I never really let myself get to know you.

## CHAPTER 12

My first couple of days back to work exhausted me.

Only five calls came in over the two days, and I took them sitting in Dad's recliner. But I had been away too long from listening to other people's problems. Or trying to help them understand what was happening in their bodies.

Especially the call from the lady who was on bedrest during her pregnancy and wanted tips on keeping her baby healthy.

After hanging up from that call, I covered my face with my hands. "Why did I think I could come back to this job so soon?"

Late Tuesday afternoon, a knock at the back door rescued me from my dark thoughts. Several simultaneous knocks.

"What on earth?"

Flash and I walked to the door. Brett and Aaron stood on the porch, and Elena.

"Well, hey."

"Mommy said I could come bring you some eggs and milk." Danny's daughter smiled up at me with bright eyes and something smeared all around her mouth.

"Thank you so much." I'd met Elena on rides to church, but I'd spoken very little to her. Never touched her.

Covering her tiny hands, I lifted the heavy basket from her.

"Come in. All of you." I made what I hoped was a teasing face at the boys. "You didn't make your little sister carry this big basket all the way over here, did you?"

"No." Brett and I still had to learn to like each other. His frown was not teasing. "I just gave it to her after we knocked."

Aaron, on the other hand, was my friend. He hugged me and hurried into the kitchen. "Mom sent some gingersnaps. Mm mmm. Can we have some now?"

"You bet. Brett, will you get milk out of the refrigerator? I'll get glasses."

"We brought milk with us, remember?"

How can I get the frown off this boy's face?

"You're right. Silly me." What I really wanted to do was tell him to mind his manners, but we weren't to that point in our relationship.

Elena sat at the table with a polite smile and crossed her hands. "I want three cookies, please."

My chest pinched. "Yes. And how old are you, Lanie? Is that what you like to be called?" Picking up a napkin, I wiped at the cookie already on her face. They must have sneaked some out on the way over.

"Yep." She nodded. "I'll be four on May four."

"What fun is that? Let's start with one cookie and a glass of milk, then see if you're still hungry, okay?"

How am I going to make it through this visit?

Brett already stood at the back door, in a hurry to leave. Soon, I would start hugging that boy every time I saw him, mad eyes or not.

Aaron opened Flash's container of food. "I'll just give Flash a little treat, not too much. We don't want him getting fat."

AFTER THE KIDS LEFT, I collapsed on the couch and dialed Kailey's number. "You told me I should start talking to God again. How do I do that?"

Kailey was my roommate when I moved into the freshman dorm. Since I slammed out of Dad's house on graduation night, I decided to start during the summer semester.

I had no intention of going to church, because I decided to be just as mad at God as I was at everybody else. But as soon as I walked into our room, Kailey asked me to join her at a campus ministry welcome she'd heard was happening that night.

Over the years, she was the one to keep me from straying too far from God. But when I started losing all those babies...

Her voice was calm now. "Tell me what's wrong."

"Danny's kids were just here. All three of them, so sweet, the little girl." I groaned. "I feel, like I've been hit by a truck."

"God is there with you, Jude." Her voice came across soft, strong, knowing, sure. "He always has been."

I was too beaten down to argue. Out loud anyway.

Why did God let my baby die then, knowing my lifelong dream was to be a mother? The kind of mother I never had.

But Kailey knew me. "He does love you. He wants good for you." She paused. "Talk to Him. Tell Him you're mad at Him. He doesn't mind."

After a pause, Kailey asked, "Are you still there?"

"Yes." What else could I say?

But Kailey wasn't finished talking to me. "Ryan can't come with me after all on Thursday to bring your car. Something came up at work."

My head jerked up. "So you can't come?"

"I'm coming. Steven is coming with me."

SINCE IT WAS sunny the next morning, I put on a light coat and snapped my fingers at Flash. "Let's go swing."

Resting my arms on top of the tire, I pushed my feet to start the swing moving. My mind swirled with memories from my call with Kailey yesterday evening. When I whimpered, Flash raised his head to lay it on my knee, his large eyes giving me a kind look.

I rubbed his head and squeezed my eyes. "God, I'm talking to You. How can I face my husband tomorrow?"

## CHAPTER 13

*I* fought to get out of bed. Flash lay on the floor next to me, but he didn't pressure me to let him outside. Nothing would turn off the memory in my head.

After they'd taken the baby, the doctor's voice came to me. "I'm so sorry. She didn't make it."

No, no, no, no.

The words pulsed in my mind as I swam in and out of a fog.

When my mind cleared, Steven stood beside my bed, holding a little bundle.

"You have to look at her."

I turned my head away. No, no, no.

"Judy."

Without my wanting it to, my head turned back to him. He set the blanket-wrapped bundle beside me.

"I know you hate me. But you need to look at our baby." His face was covered with tears. "You can hate me forever, but I don't want you to hate yourself someday because you didn't touch our baby."

He pulled the blanket back, and I saw her. A head with a tiny bit of blond fuzz. Her crumpled face. Ten fingers and ten toes.

Picking her up I pressed my face against her body. "Baby Alicia, I am so sorry. I, I love you. So, so sorry."

∼

"Judy." Steven's voice again.

He climbed out of my car at the farmhouse, moved a few steps toward me, then stopped. From the sorrow in his eyes, I knew he was remembering the same thing I had earlier this morning. The last time we'd seen each other, after the baby died, in the hospital.

I'd turned away when he'd tried to reach for me then. Now, I wished I could rush into his arms. But something like cement kept my feet from moving.

Kailey climbed out of her car, carrying several grocery bags. "We picked up a few things at the store in town, so you don't have to worry about shopping for a little while."

My lips twitched. "No worries." My voice croaked, and I cleared my throat. "Thanks."

Steven walked closer but stopped before he could touch me. "I brought a few more of your things from home too. Just some clothes and books I thought you might like to have. Do you want me to bring them in?"

Forcing my gaze to his, I stepped back. "No. I'll get them later."

He shuffled his feet. "Let me unload. You probably aren't supposed to be carrying anything too heavy yet."

"Right." My eyes moved between Steven and Kailey. Their father was Korean, born in the United States. Their mother was all-American. Kailey looked Korean, small and dark, but Steven was six-foot two, broad shouldered, with blond hair and blue eyes like their mom.

We laughed when people asked how we'd come by the

Korean name Park. Steven always answered, "Honestly, I promise."

Kailey walked to me and bumped my shoulder. "Let him do the heavy work. Come into the kitchen with me and show me where to put your groceries."

After she'd set the bags on the table, Kailey wrapped her arms around me. "We won't stay long. I'm not going to lecture you about how to treat my brother today."

"Not today." A chuckle escaped me.

She stepped back. "Exactly." Her smile couldn't have been brighter.

We stood on the back porch while Steven brought things in the front and dropped them in the living room. He joined us, followed by Flash.

Of course, dog, you would go straight to Steven. What kind of a friend are you anyway?

"It's not bad outside." Steven rubbed Flash's ribs then slipped his arms into the sleeves of his jacket. "Will you show me a little bit around your place?"

Of course. He had never been here.

Before I could open my mouth to say no, Kailey turned back to the kitchen door. "Good idea. I'll do you one more favor today and wash your dishes, clean up for you a little."

And she was gone.

Steven touched my shoulder. "Come on."

I turned my head to the side so he couldn't see the tears that sprang to my eyes.

Not knowing what to say, I led Steven, with Flash running ahead, past my tire swing, around the old chicken house, uphill toward the barn.

Finally, Steven spoke. "I wonder if the trees bloom earlier here than in the city, or if I just notice it more."

Following his gaze, I saw a few buds showing up on trees.

"Look, there's a cardinal." He took my hand and pointed to

the top of one tree. "It's beautiful out here. Just like you always said."

"Yes."

"Where are the cows?" He still held my hand.

"I think they're all at Danny's place." My heart pounded in my chest. My throat caught, and I coughed. "He and his family live in the house where Mom lived with her first husband and the older kids."

"Where is that?"

I turned my head and nodded to where we could just see Danny's house. "When Daddy was alive, and Danny's birth father, too, the older kids walked between the two houses all the time. They were all good friends. It's only a few minutes for kids to run back and forth."

Stop babbling, Judy.

Steven pulled me to a stop and stepped to face me. "Sweetheart, look at me."

I froze.

"How long are you staying here?"

My shoulders jerked, and I pulled away from him.

"Judy, please. Are you coming home?" His voice was strained.

When I focused on his face, the sadness there was overwhelming. My lips moved then I stopped.

This is the man who made sure I will never bear another child.

My jaw quivered, and I turned back to the house. "Kailey is probably ready to leave by now." My heart was aching, confused, so alone.

## CHAPTER 14

Fifteen minutes after Kailey and Steven left, the back door crashed against the wall.

"You sent him away." Danny's voice was loud, angry. His face held a storm.

"What?" The cup of food I was scooping for Flash slipped from my hand and scattered over the floor. Flash made a dash to scarf it up.

"Oh no. That was too much. I was trying..." I reached to gather some, but Danny stopped my hands.

"Let it go." He snapped the lid shut on the food container. "Can't you do anything right?"

My eyes widened, and I snatched my hands back. "What is wrong with you? Are you twelve again?"

"Look who's talking." His voice was calmer but just as angry.

Turning, I walked into the living room. In a minute, Danny and Flash followed me. Flash lay at my feet by the couch, and Danny sat himself on the arm of Dad's chair.

"You are so good at throwing away the people who love you." His voice came out rough, between long, slow breaths.

I couldn't look at him.

"Your stubborn pride robbed you of Dad's last twelve years. You showed no appreciation or concern for Jeannie, who raised you like her own daughter. And what about me?" His voice cracked.

I raised my face to look at him then.

"We were best friends. You're the one I came to for advice when I wanted to ask Helen to marry me."

He stood and paced across the room then back again.

"You're the first one I told when we found out we were going to have a baby. You came over to the house and stayed up nights with Brett when he was sick and crying for hours, so Helen and I could get some sleep."

He banged his fist against the back of Dad's chair. "I listened to all your complaints, all your hopes, your fears. I stood between you and Dad as a referee so many times." He drew in a jagged breath. "Then you just left. You said nothing to me. For twelve years." He turned his back to me.

Was he crying?

He paced again. "The only way we knew you were still alive is that you kept in touch a little with Brenda.

"And then you got married. To a really nice guy. I liked him a lot when I met him at the VA hospital. The one time you finally bothered to see Dad again."

He stopped at the front door. "Look at me."

I met his eyes.

There were tears on his cheeks. "And now you're pushing him away, too, just because he cared enough to try and save your life."

He opened the front door, took a step to leave then stopped. "It's a good thing you're not a parent."

He might as well have struck me with a truck.

Breath exploded from my body, and my head snapped back.

Hours later, I still sat on the couch. My phone read 9:00 p.m. Flash nuzzled my hand and whined.

You need to let the dog out, Judy.

Walking as though through mud, I opened the front door. Flash raced outside.

I waited.

What was I supposed to do next?

Cold air came through the open door. Should I close it?

Flash ran back in, shaking and wagging his tail. He licked my hand where it rested on the doorknob.

Yes. Close the door.

"Flash?" My voice was hoarse. Had I been screaming? "Oh, what do I do next?"

## CHAPTER 15

Flash woke me in the morning too. Maybe God was still watching over me. Without the dog to prod me, I could have stayed in bed unmoving for who knows how long.

After breakfast, I sat at the kitchen table with my computer and phone, hoping to get work calls to numb my mind.

Yes, God was with me still. For several hours, I searched the internet and was able to answer callers' questions about strep throat, hemorrhoids, infections and tubes in the ears, broken knees, heart rehab.

In the afternoon, Flash and I took a walk past the barn.

"God?" My voice quavered. "Is he right? Is it a good thing I'm not a parent?"

Wind lifted my hair. Flash nosed at some old leaves on the ground. My face ached.

"Oh, God, I wouldn't have been a good parent."

∼

THE NEXT DAY WAS SATURDAY. Should I go visit Jeannie again today, since I have my car now?

Danny pulled his truck in front of the house, and a cold wave fell over me.

He walked around to the back door and came into the kitchen.

Lowering myself into a chair, I stared at him, silent.

Danny reached for two cups, filled them with coffee, and set them on the table. "Have a drink." He pushed one of the cups to me then got creamer from the refrigerator for his.

He moved a chair right next to me, sat, and touched his knee to mine. "I am so sorry."

My stomach sank, and breaths shuttered from my mouth.

Danny wrapped both arms around me and pulled me against his shoulder.

Was it minutes or hours that I leaned against him and sobbed?

My head pounded, and when I tried to talk, my voice was raw.

"Shh." With gentle hands, Danny sat me upright in my own chair then went to get fresh coffee.

"This morning, I noticed one of the memory verses Helen has taped up around the house."

He sat back beside me and directed his gaze straight at mine.

"It's from Philippians chapter 2." His Adam's apple bobbed as he swallowed. "I'm pretty sure I've got it down. 'Do nothing out of selfish ambition or vain conceit. Rather, in humility value others above yourselves, not looking to your own interests but each of you to the interests of the others.'"

He drew in a long breath. "Honey, yesterday, I was surely thinking of my own interests, not yours."

My head swam. I opened my mouth, but he pressed his fingers against my lips.

"I am so, so sorry."

So I wouldn't start sobbing again, I inhaled a long breath too.

## CHAPTER 16

*D*anny stood from the table. "Come with me and visit with Jeannie while I take care of things in town. You need to get out of the house."

Chewing my lip, I rubbed my eyes. "I don't know if I'm ready for that."

He wrapped my hands in his. "Wash your face and let's go. Please."

"Stop a minute." Jeannie set her hand on my shoulder and gazed into my face before I could enter her door. "What's the matter?"

My face trembled. No, Judy, don't start crying again.

"Come on in." She closed the door and walked with me to the couch. "Sit down. I'll bring you some tea."

After Jeannie sat in her chair and we'd both spent a minute sipping tea, she directed her eyes to me again.

"You don't have to talk to me if you don't want to. I'm not

trying to stick my nose into your business." She lifted her chin. "But I love you. And I'm here if you want."

How had I missed the wonderful lady who had brought me up? My eyes pricked, and my nose ached. I fought back tears.

Jeannie picked up her newspaper. "You should order the local paper to be delivered to you at the house. It comes out on Tuesdays, and if you ordered it, the mailman would bring it on Wednesday."

Thank you, Jeannie. Swallowing, I nodded. "Thank you. I'll call them on Monday."

She flipped some pages. "Lot of people in here you'd remember."

Setting my cup on the table, I clasped my hands tight in my lap. "Jeannie?"

"Hmm?" She kept her eyes on the paper.

"You, you did so much for me. I…" My stomach clenched. "I never knew my, my natural mother." My breath caught. "I always wanted to be a mother. To have my own children." My fingernails dug into my palms. "I had three miscarriages, and then Alicia, she only made it to, to eight months…"

I guess I'm going to cry after all.

Jeannie moved to the couch beside me and pressed my head against her shoulder.

∼

The next morning, I rode to church again in the van with the family. No need to worry about awkwardness between Danny and me. Aaron and Elena talked nonstop.

Brett sat next to me, stared straight ahead, and spoke little.

Does this kid hate me? Is he depressed? I shook my head. We are going to be friends. Edging my face to gaze straight into his, I grinned.

His lips twitched before he turned his head away.

A gentle touch pressed on my arm. "Aunt Judy?"

I turned to Elena who sat in the child car seat on my other side. "Yes, sweetie."

"I was telling you what I had for breakfast." Her face puckered into a pout.

"Yes, you were. I'm sorry if I wasn't listening. Go ahead."

She smiled big. "Waffles. With lots of syrup. And I ate it all by myself."

Aaron patted my shoulder from behind. When I turned to look at him, his face scrunched into a wink. "She had syrup all over her hands and face and clothes and the table."

"Did not, did not, did not." Elena pounded her hands against the car seat and kicked. "You take it back. Take it baaaaaack."

"Enough." Helen shot a look back at them from the front seat then turned to her husband. "Dan, I told you."

"I'll have another talk with him."

Was there a laugh hidden in Danny's voice?

## CHAPTER 17

"Hey." Marilyn met me as soon as I got out of the van. "Want to sit with us?"

Marilyn's husband Kent was a guy who'd been a year ahead of Marilyn and me in school.

"Howdy, Judy." He squeezed my hand.

When we were seated, I leaned to whisper in Marilyn's ear. "He's a lot cuter now than he was back in school."

Her lips twitched.

Again, the same older lady I remembered from twelve years ago sat at the organ, accompanying a young band. She smiled and chatted with the others on the platform, laughing and enjoying herself. I shook my head. Who'd have guessed these two ages and styles could so happily co-exist?

Kailey would tell me I needed to expect better from the church.

After the service, as Marilyn dragged me to join the line waiting to shake Jonathan's hand, she asked, "I wondered if you would like to help with our after-school program."

"What?"

"Mornin', Jonathan, how are you? Remember Judy?"

My old crush squeezed both my hands. "Hey, Jude. I heard you were back."

I wanted to kick Marilyn. "Yes. Hey, Jon, look at you, preacher at the old church."

"Just like I always promised. This is my wife Lorie."

A pretty lady with curly dark hair smiled at me. "I've heard a lot about you from Marilyn and Jon."

"Uh-oh." I forced a smile. "Hopefully that's a good thing." Was she grinning at me? "I promise."

As soon as we were outside the door, I elbowed Marilyn in the side. "You are a crazy one."

She giggled. "So, what about after school?"

Across the parking lot, I could see Danny's family packing into the van. "Could you call me later and talk to me about it?"

"I could." She hesitated. "Or I could come by this afternoon. I promise not to bring any food."

I chuckled. "I wouldn't mind if you wanted to bring something. I remember you're a good baker."

∼

THE DAY WAS WARMING, so after lunch, Flash and I took a short walk. I peeked inside the empty chicken house and the cluttered machine shop and grain bins, then ended up back on the front porch. My face hurt from smiling. "Flash, this is all so familiar."

Jeannie's porch swing was still there. Sitting down, I released Flash from his leash. "Go run around if you want."

He looked out at the yard then turned his happy eyes back to me.

"No thanks, I'm not gonna join you this time. I'm staying here." I pushed my feet against the porch. "That old church may have a lot of new stuff, but they still have an organ, and they still pass out a paper bulletin."

Flash thumped his tail then jumped down the stairs onto the winter grass.

"God, this morning Jonathan talked about how You want to give us a full life."

Pulling the bulletin out of my pocket, I smoothed it across my lap.

We'd read from the book of John. I slid my finger along the sheet until I came to this verse. "John 10:10: The thief comes only to steal and kill and destroy; I have come that they may have life and have it to the full."

My heart pinched. "That was one of Daddy's favorite verses." I found the King James Version on my phone and went to John 10. "The thief cometh not, ... I am come ... they might have it more abundantly."

"I can hear Daddy repeating that verse." My hand wiped tears from my cheeks. "He'd say, 'Abundantly. God wants us to have an abundant life.'

"Daddy didn't graduate from high school, but he was a smart man. He loved to read. He knew what abundant meant."

Flash rolled in the winter grass stubble in front of the porch, making happy growling noises. Across the field, more spring birds appeared on the trees, twittering, building nests.

"And, God, Daddy had a hard life. He lost his wife. He had to raise two surprise kids late in life." My voice croaked, and I covered my face with my palms. "But he believed You gave him an abundant life."

## CHAPTER 18

Marilyn came back that afternoon with triple chocolate brownies.

"You are definitely my new favorite person." We walked into the kitchen. "Do you want milk or coffee?"

She set the plate on the table. "Just a glass of water for me. My mouth is way too sweet for any more brownies or milk." She pulled out a chair.

"Hope you don't mind if I dig in." Pulling back the foil, I licked my lips. "Mm mm mm. Yummy."

After getting her a glass of water from the jug in the refrigerator, I poured myself a cup of coffee. "So what's this deal about an after-school program?"

"Jonathan started it."

I snorted. "Of course, he did."

"Come on. He's done a lot to get our old church to spark with new life."

"Okay. I'm listening."

She took a drink of water. "It's partly for families who don't have someone at home when kids get off school, but we really want to give students assistance with their homework."

155

"Mm hmm."

"We mostly have younger kids, kindergarten up to sixth grade, but we get a few junior high and high school students. Some are there because their parents insist they come to keep them out of trouble, but some really want help with their schoolwork."

Resting my chin on my hand, I waited a minute, then asked, "And what do you want me to do?"

"Oh, I'm sure we could find a lot of jobs for you." She gave a shy smile. "Work with kids on homework, of course. And it wouldn't hurt to have a nurse around."

"Uh huh."

She shook her head. "We don't have a lot of sickness or accidents, but it could happen. Jon's certified in first aid and CPR. So am I." She hesitated. "And maybe it would be good for you."

I blinked. "Maybe it would." After biting my lip, I answered. "Okay. When do I start?"

"Tomorrow?"

"You don't mess around."

"Are you well enough?"

"I am. It's been more than a month since…" I swallowed. "I'm fine."

We were both quiet. Taking a deep breath, I managed a smile. "So, how long have you and Kent been married? I don't remember you dating in high school."

"We didn't." She reached to pick up a brownie from the plate and ignored my smirk.

"Kent stayed home after school to work with his dad on the farm. I moved to town to go to tech school. I wanted out of the house, and I got a scholarship that covered my rent."

"I remember. You were going to study bookkeeping."

She nodded. "We didn't see each other for a couple of years. Kent married Gina Spencer."

"Whoa. Really."

"Yep."

She took a bite and reached for a napkin. "I got engaged to, to a guy I met at school."

Her face clouded.

Oh no.

Sucking in a breath, she went on. "Jake, my fiancé, was killed in a motorcycle accident."

Reaching over, I laid my hands on hers.

She turned her hands to squeeze mine and went on before I could say anything. "Gina and Kent had a baby boy. Ron. Then Gina took the baby and left Kent when Ronny was not quite two years old."

And you think you have it hard, Judy girl.

"She divorced him?" Obviously, Brainiac.

Marilyn nodded. "She moved to California and got married again. Ronny's nine now. He visits us once a year in the summer."

"I am so sorry."

Marilyn took another swallow of water. "Kent and I ran into each other, not quite five years ago. I was working for an insurance company, and he came in to update the policy on their farm."

"Okay."

"We took things slow. We've been married four years now."

"Ha. Slow, yeah."

Her smile was still shy.

I had to ask. "And kids?"

"We're trying." She turned the glass in her hands. "We've been trying for a long time."

*But, God, You let me get pregnant. Four times. Wasn't it understandable I thought I was going to get to have my own baby? My own flesh and blood?*

## CHAPTER 19

"Flash? Is that snow outside?" I rubbed frost from the kitchen window. "Okay, it's just the middle of March, and I know this isn't that unusual, but seriously?"

Flash whined and licked my hand.

"Oh right, you probably want to go out and roll in it."

Sure enough, as soon as I opened the back door, he raced into the middle of the yard, yipping and rolling from side to side.

"It's only a couple inches." Danny joined me on the porch. "But there's probably enough if you want to make snow angels."

I smirked. "More likely throw snowballs."

He laid his hand on my shoulder. "Are we still friends?"

My throat choked. "You bet, if you forgive me."

"Oh, Jude." He wrapped his arms around me and held me close.

After a minute I pushed back. "Last thing we need is for me to start crying again."

"Or me." His voice came out rough. "Let's have coffee. And?" He held up a paper bag. "Some of Helen's homemade doughnuts."

"How do you deserve her?" Turning, I led the way back into the kitchen.

"I don't. She's an absolutely undeserved gift from God." He propped the outside door to the porch open with a folding chair.

"We're not going to tell Flash to come in yet?"

"Nah. He'll want to play for a while."

As I pulled cups and plates from the cabinet, I made a decision. "Can I ask you a personal question?"

He removed a doughnut and took a bite. "Go for it."

"Is Brett okay?" Forgetting about the plates, I also took out a doughnut and sat. "Oh, my goodness. These are still warm."

Danny brought our cups of coffee and sat across from me. "What do you mean? Brett's fine."

"He always seems so angry. Or is that just with me?"

He shrugged. "He's coming up on thirteen years old. What do you expect?"

"So it's not just me."

"Ev-ry-bod-y." He licked his fingers. "Except Elena."

I grinned. "She's got him wrapped around her finger, huh?"

"All of us."

"I think I'll have two of these." I reached inside the bag. "Tell Helen she's going to make me fat."

"You need a little weight."

My mouth grew dry, and I grabbed a sip of coffee. "I didn't gain much. With the baby."

Without words, he reached across and laid his hand over mine. I drew in a long breath. "So, you sure there's nothing wrong with Brett?"

"Not so far as I know." He shook his head. "But then, what do I know? I'm just the parent." He squeezed my hand. "He's okay."

MARILYN PICKED me up later for the after-school session at church.

"Ready?" She smiled across at me from the driver's seat.

"And willing. Not so sure about able."

She reached over and shook my knee. "You'll do fine."

At least forty kids, maybe six to sixteen, ran around the basement fellowship hall when we arrived.

"Whoa. Do all these kids go to this church?"

"No. News of us has spread around the area." She elbowed me. "Another good thing Jonathan has done in the community."

Before I could think of a comeback, Jon walked over to greet us. "Hey, Judy. Thank you so much."

Shaking my head, I gave a little chuckle. "Don't thank me yet."

An African-American girl about seven ran up to Jon and threw her arms around his waist. "Daddy, Daddy, Daddy."

Oh, Judy, don't you dare gasp.

"Hey, pumpkin." Jon picked her up and squeezed her. "How was school?"

She giggled and made a long raspberry with her lips.

Jon squeezed harder. "Miss Judy, this is my daughter, Angie. She's in first grade, and she's the best spitter in the world." He tickled her.

Now, I laughed out loud. "I am so proud of you, Angie."

Angie turned shy and buried her face in her dad's shoulder.

"Come with me to the kitchen." Marilyn grabbed my arm then kissed Angie's head. "Hey, sweet girl."

Angie turned her face to peek. "Hi, Aunt Marilyn."

In the kitchen, Marilyn pulled me into a corner. Her grin was wide. "So, go ahead and say it."

"I know Jon's wife isn't Black."

"They adopted Angie when she was three days old."

No, I'm not going to ask why they needed to adopt. "How does the church accept her?"

She hooted. "They love her. We've got another family who has adopted kids from China. People adore them."

"I never would've imagined."

She patted my shoulder. "Old prejudices can still stick their heads up here, but people are growing. And God is wise enough to know kids can soften hearts."

## CHAPTER 20

Soon, a mob of kids surrounded Marilyn, hugged her, and sent questioning looks my way.

Now what?

Most of the next two hours I spent with Pamela.

"She came to us as Pammy," Marilyn told me. "But right away Jon called her Pamela, to help her feel like a bigger kid."

Pamela was thirteen, just starting to show curves, her red hair cut like a boy's.

"You are new here, Ju-dee?" Her speech was slow with only a slight impairment.

"I grew up here. On a farm. Now I'm back to visit for a while."

"Oh, I live on a farm." Her head bobbed. "Do you have family here?"

"Yes. Dan and Helen Heitzmann."

She clapped her hands. "I love Dan's family. Aaron is my best friend."

Yes, I could believe that of that boy. "Danny is my big brother."

Academically, Pamela was at a second-grade level. We

worked on math and spelling. Never had I met anyone who tried so hard at schoolwork as she did.

"Pamela loves you." Marilyn sent me a grin as we drove home.

"Her family?"

She shook her head. "She's a foster child. With the Reynolds. Do you remember them?"

My face scrunched. "Walter? And Joan?"

She nodded.

"Aren't they, like, in their seventies?"

"Sixties. All their kids and grandkids live far away." She pulled up in front of my house. "They took Pamela into their home when she was ten."

"As a foster child."

"Yep."

"And they don't know anything about her family?"

"I don't know. Maybe. They don't talk about it."

In my mind, I saw Pamela's big smiling eyes, and my heart squeezed.

Marilyn turned to me. "So? Coming back tomorrow?"

Hesitating, I bit my lip. "You think I can help?"

She laughed. "Want me to pick you up again?"

"Please."

∼

"Hallooo," Brenda called out the next morning as the front door banged open.

"What in the world?" She hadn't even called me this time to warn me she was coming.

Pushing my chair back from the kitchen table, I moved into the living room. And stopped. "Oh." My breath caught. "You brought Wayne."

The tall, lanky older brother who'd been like a second father to me.

"Get over here, little bit, and give me a hug."

Wayne wrapped his arms around me and lifted me off my feet. "I have missed you." He swung me around until I was dizzy.

"Put her down, goofhead." Brenda laid her hand on my shoulder. "Remember, she's not been well." She stopped herself, taking back her hand and chewing on a nail.

Wayne put me down, and the room spun.

"Don't let her fall." Brenda slung her arm around my shoulders and hung on until I could stand on my own.

"What are you doing here?" I grabbed Wayne's shirt in both hands. How old was he now, forty-nine? "You've got gray hair."

He pushed his hand on top of my head to hold me still. "I see a couple grays in your lovely locks, too, ma'am."

Brenda slapped his hand away then gave me a hug. "Don't listen to him."

We moved into the kitchen, and Brenda bustled around to get us each a drink. "Wayne brought you some cinnamon rolls."

"You know you're my favorite brother, right?"

He tickled my ribs. "And don't you forget it, lady."

Brenda pushed my computer into the middle of the table and set out some paper plates. "Did we interrupt you working?"

"No, I haven't logged in yet."

Wayne flipped a chair around and straddled it. "Oh please, Miss Nurse. You gotta help me. I've got this pain in my neck I just can't get rid of." He sent a goofy grin at Brenda.

She swatted his back. "I'll tell you who's the pain in the neck."

Once we'd all calmed down a little, I turned my eyes back to Wayne. "Are you still truckin'?"

"Yep. Although mostly around Chicago. We live just outside the city."

I lifted my brows. "We?"

"I told you he done settled down finally." Brenda wagged her head. "Somehow he talked this sweet lady into marrying him."

Yes, she had told me that. I'd missed so much by keeping myself from these precious people.

"I got her with my good looks and charm." Wayne slurped from his coffee cup.

"Huh." Brenda snorted then choked on her glass of milk.

Wayne slapped her back. "You okay there, darlin'?" He turned to me. "She even has a couple kids she's letting me father." His face couldn't have been brighter. "Twins. Boy and a girl, sixteen years old."

"Wow." *God, everybody has kids except me?*

## CHAPTER 21

"I need a flashlight, buddy." I rested my hand on Flash's head, which he'd buried, quivering, in my lap.

Tonight it was a thunderstorm instead of snow, and the lights had gone out.

"I bet there's one in Daddy's room."

Moving with caution across the living room, Flash and I made it to the one door in the house I hadn't opened since I'd been home.

Daddy's desk still sat right inside the door. Just like I remembered, the flashlight nestled in the top drawer, right next to a...

A photo album? Daddy'd never been much on taking pictures.

When I flicked the flashlight on, nothing happened. But batteries were stored as always in the front left corner of the drawer.

As I sat on the floor next to the desk, Flash collapsed onto my legs, still trembling.

Opening the photo album, I turned the light on again.

No, Daddy didn't take pictures. But he saved them.

On the first page was his and my mother's wedding picture,

the same one as on the mantle. Right next to it was my baby picture.

As I turned the pages, I found school photos for me and Danny, graduation pictures, Danny's wedding, with me as groom's woman standing next to Wayne as best man.

Baby pictures of all Danny's kids.

A wedding shot of me and Steven.

My hands stilled. "Daddy, how did you get that?"

Of course. I'd sent a few pictures to Brenda over the years.

The final three pages of the album held more shots of me, my college graduation, Steven and me standing in the empty living room of our first apartment, and...

I clapped my hand over my mouth to hold in a scream.

The last picture was the ultrasound of my baby Alicia, from last September.

"Daddy? Oh Daddy, I miss you. I'm sorry."

Thunder crashed outside the window behind me, and the clock on Daddy's desk flashed on. 9:47 p.m.

∽

DURING MY TEEN YEARS, Daddy and I had fought like wildcats, especially after Danny left for agricultural college.

Standing in this same bedroom, I'd said, "I'm gonna be a nurse, Daddy."

"That's fine. The tech school has a nursing program. I can afford that."

"No." My chin lifted, and I met his eyes straight on. "I'm getting a bachelor's degree. I'm going to be a registered nurse, not an LPN."

"I can't afford that." His cheek twitched.

"I'm applying for scholarships."

"You'd have to be away four years. If you go to tech school, you can live at home, help on the farm." His jaw set firm. "After you graduate, you can work at the clinic in town and still live here and help out around the place."

"Daddy." My voice screeched. "I don't always want to live on the farm."

His face grew red. "Go to your room."

The night of my high school graduation. Jeannie, Daddy, and I sat around the kitchen table with plates of cake in front of us.

"Daddy, I have something to show you."

Slipping my acceptance letter to the university, along with the pages covering my full scholarship out of the envelope, I passed them across to him.

"What is this?"

He read the first few words, then set his hands on the papers to rip them apart.

"Nooo!" I screamed, threw myself across the table, and yanked the papers out of his hands.

"Judy, stop it." Jeannie jumped up to clean the mess I'd made, two spilled glasses of ice water and the cake my elbow had landed in.

Clutching the papers against my belly I faced Daddy. "I'm going to this college. Everything is paid for."

"You are not."

Had he ever yelled at me like that before?

"I am." My voice was a whisper.

And at that moment, so was his. "Then don't ever step back in this house."

A freezing wave washed over me. "That's fine."

## CHAPTER 22

When the storm stopped, I called Brenda. "Can you come over?"

She must have heard something in my voice. "I'll be there in twenty-five minutes."

She unlocked the front door herself as always and found me on the couch, Daddy's photo album open on my lap, and Flash lying at my feet.

Brenda sat beside me. "He was already in the nursing home when you sent that pic from your ultrasound." She touched the page with her fingertip. "You remember how big he could smile."

Closing the book, I set it on the end table and pressed myself into my sister's arms. We cried for I don't know how long.

Sitting up, I dug my fingers into the fabric of the couch. "When I came over to your house the night I graduated, I think that's the only time I remember you not scolding me."

Brenda huffed. "Not like I didn't want to."

"But you let me stay. Helped me get ready to leave for summer school." My throat choked with a laugh. "You made sure my pickup was running right and sent me off two days later with homemade brownies."

"Only because you promised you'd keep in touch with me." She rubbed tears from my cheeks. "I figured otherwise, if I didn't help you, we'd never hear from you again."

I sputtered. "You almost didn't anyway. Please, God, forgive me."

~

THE NEXT MORNING, I managed for two hours to accept phone calls for work.

"No, ma'am. It is not a good idea for you to feed dog food to your baby."

"Yes, sir. You need to hang up and call 911."

"Honey, I'm so sorry your ear hurts so bad. Is your mommy there? Please let me talk to her."

When sunlight streamed through the kitchen window and filled my eyes, I clocked out. Picking up the leash and my mother's journal, I walked with Flash down to the swing.

"Look at that, big guy. Buds on the tree. Spring is really coming."

I flipped the tire swing to empty out the rainwater then climbed inside.

"Mom, I have always been so mad at you. I am such an idiot."

Squeezing my eyes against tears, I opened Mom's journal. Just a few pages into the notebook was this listing.

"Psalm 25:16-18: Turn Thou to me, and be gracious to me; for I am lonely and afflicted. Relieve the troubles of my heart, and bring me out of my distresses. Consider my affliction and my trouble, and forgive all my sins."

Mom's own words followed. "Dear God, forgive me if I'm making a mistake. Hank is such a good man. I don't want to hurt him. But, we're both lonely, and my son needs a daddy."

I closed the book and lifted my face.

"God, forgive me for my anger at her. Forgive me for abandoning my good father. Help me. Help me to stop leaving the people who love me."

∼

THAT NIGHT, I picked up my phone and made the call I'd dreaded. "Steven?"

He stayed quiet.

"Steven?" I moaned. "Please talk to me."

His voice rasped. "Honey." Silence. "I love you."

"Please don't make me cry."

It was too late, and he knew it. Now he laughed. "Oh, Judy."

Flash came over, planted his front feet on my lap, and licked the tears from my face. I had to laugh too.

"What's that noise?"

"You wouldn't believe me." Pushing Flash off my lap, I stood and paced the room. Like Danny had.

"I don't know how to tell you how sorry I am." I took a breath. "I always push away the people who love me."

The refrigerator door back in our apartment banged against the stove, like I'd heard it do a thousand times.

"I wish I was there with you."

"Come home." Steven's words sounded sure.

"I, I can't yet." Flash nudged me to sit on the couch. "I need to heal still. I need to get to know my family again."

"I need you to be with me, so I can heal." His voice softened.

How could I ever have been so angry with this man? "Sweetheart, I'm so sorry." I choked.

Steven dropped a pan on the floor. "Can I come visit you for spring break? It's the first week in April."

"Oh." My face tingled, and my breath rushed out. "Please, please do."

After I hung up, I called Kailey. "Have you been praying for me?"

Her voice was tender. "Always. Every day."

## CHAPTER 23

Sunday morning, Pamela dropped into the seat next to me at church. "Good morning, Ju-dee." Her face flooded with the joy of a cake full of birthday candles.

This child had been my job after school every day last week. She loved me.

"Want a hug?" she asked me now.

Did this scare me? Yes. But I didn't want to hesitate.

Not that I needed to worry about it. Before I could move, her arms wrapped around my neck. She all but climbed onto my lap.

"Hey, cool it, you two." Marilyn plunked into the seat on Pamela's other side. "It's time for church to start. Do I have to separate you?"

Pamela giggled then shushed me with a loud, whistly "shh."

After the last "amen," Danny stood in front of us. "Pamela, want to come to our house for dinner? Mrs. Reynolds said it was okay."

"Yes, yes, yes." She clapped her hands and jumped up. "Where is Aaron?" She hurried off to search for her friend.

"Are you inviting me too?" I grinned at Danny. "Wait, dinner?"

Danny shook his head at me. "You've lived in the city too long, little bit. Out here, dinner is the meal we have at midday."

"Oh yeah." I shrugged. "You're right. Too long."

∾

AFTER DINNER, I helped carry dishes to the sink. "Helen, you are the best cook I've ever met. Such amazing lasagna. Yum, yum." I rubbed my stomach. "Danny does not deserve you."

She gave a shy smile. "That's true. God help him."

"I meant..." I bumped her shoulder. "You know what I meant."

"Scoot." She elbowed me away from the sink. "It's Brett's turn to help with the dishes. I know Danny wants to go for a walk with you. Brett?" She dunked her hands in the dishwater.

As Danny and I walked downhill, we passed Aaron and Pamela as they entered the barn door.

"What are they up to?"

"Kittens." Danny clutched his chest. "Lots and lots of kittens."

"Is Aaron hoping to convince Pamela to take one?"

"I already talked to the Reynolds. Made them promise to take two."

I snorted. "I suppose you want me to take one too."

"I'm gonna move one mama with her kittens up to your barn when the babies are a little older. I've got a cow to move up there soon too."

"Really?" Memories of sitting up with cows when they gave birth flashed through my mind.

"Yep. We've got a new heifer I think may need to be shut up before she calves."

"Nice. Hey, look at you. You've got one of them new fancy tractors with a cab. I bet there's heat and air conditioning in there."

"Mmm, maybe even a computer. Keep looking."

As we moved around the machine shed, I stopped. "My old Case Four Hundred." The tractor Daddy taught me to drive when I was ten years old. Pulled out of the shed, it stood ready for me to climb on.

Circling it, I whistled. "You kept this looking pretty." Fenders desert sunset yellow, wheels fire-boys red, back tires taller than me.

"Sure enough. This is still what I teach the kids to drive first. Hop on. Start her up."

Grabbing the steering wheel, I climbed on and seated myself. "Really?"

"Go."

And I heard Daddy's voice, felt his arms around me. "Pull out this switch. All right. Push that one."

The deep throat of the motor started right up. "Yes." I wanted to clap.

"Push the clutch with your left foot. Get the shift with your right hand. You've got it." Daddy's words held a smile.

Today, Danny stood beside me and gestured with his hand. "Pull up here and drive around in front of the house."

"You are a brave man." The tractor ran smooth, and the years rolled away. "I love this."

As we came round the barn, Aaron and Pamela stepped out, each holding a yellow and white kitten against their cheeks. Helen stood with Elena on the porch, waving at me.

"Brake. Now," Danny yelled.

I did.

Brett had walked out directly in front of me and stood, smiling.

My heart squeezed. *Thank You, God.*

## CHAPTER 24

Pamela met me the minute I stepped into the church building the next afternoon, holding up her hand for a high five.

"Aunt Joan says I can have both kittens." One of her feet always dragged, but she still managed to spin in a circle. "She wants you to come to our house for supper tonight."

The Reynolds's home was on a gravel road just off the highway before my dad's place. Marilyn dropped us off. "Joan said she'd take you home later. See you tomorrow?"

"What else?" My head bobbed from side to side.

The Reynolds were good, friendly neighbors with my dad, so I was familiar with their place. And with them.

"Judy, so good to see you." Joan gave me a hug. No trace of reproach in her face or voice.

"Aunt Joan." Pamela shuffled from foot to foot. "Where's Uncle Walter? Is supper ready? Judy and me got all my homework done."

Joan wrapped an arm around the girl's shoulders. "Supper is nearly ready. Walter is with the chickens. Go help him."

"Goody." Pamela thrust her backpack into my arms. "Thanks. See you soon."

"She loves the chickens." Joan led me around to the back door and into the kitchen. "You picked a good night to come. I made beef roast with potatoes and carrots. It's Walter's and Pamela's favorite."

The room was warm and filled with a rich meaty smell. "It's sure one of mine too." I set the backpack on a chair at the table and turned to Joan. "Can I help?"

"Grab a glass of tea and have a seat. I'm just finishing the salad."

"Pamela calls you Aunt Joan." With a glass of tea in hand, I pulled out a chair.

"We thought Aunt and Uncle would be nicer than Mr. and Mrs. We're no relation."

"Pamela's family?"

"Her mother ran away when she was a baby. Left her with her grandma. When Grandma died three years ago, Pamela went into foster care."

Joan removed plates from the cabinet and set them around the table. "We'd love to adopt her but…" She shrugged one shoulder. "We're nearly seventy. Our health? Our age? Well." She turned to the refrigerator. "We love her so."

The back door banged open, and Pamela came in holding an egg basket in her two hands. "Fresh eggs, Ju-dee. Can she take some home, Uncle Walter?"

"Sure enough, Pammy. Oh sorry, Pam-el-a." Walter Reynolds, large and never hurrying, tapped his knuckles on top of Pamela's head then turned to me with a huge grin. "Look who isn't a little girl anymore." He slapped my back.

"Not by a long sight." I grabbed his strong, rough hand in both of mine.

"We're having some beef from your daddy's herd tonight." He moved to wash his hands at the sink. "Hank always did raise the best beef. Pure angus." He smacked his lips. "Danny does a good job, too, I won't deny."

"And you raise the best chickens and eggs, don't you, Uncle Walt?"

"Sure as shootin', Pam-my-la." He knuckled her on the head again and moved away so she couldn't jab him with her elbow.

∽

"THEY'RE SUCH A SWEET FAMILY." Later that night, I sat on the couch with my phone against my cheek. "I, I don't know. So beautiful." My lips trembled. "Steven?"

"We can still have a family, you know."

"Oh," I breathed. He knew me so well. What could I say?

After a moment of silence, he moved to a different subject. "I am looking so forward to seeing you, baby." His voice held longing? Love? Pain?

"Me too." Mine was a whisper.

∽

"I'M GONNA BE A WHILE," Danny said as he dropped me off at Jeannie's Saturday morning. "I've got a bunch of errands."

Before I sat down on Jeannie's loveseat, I stopped to look at the picture she'd placed atop her small bookcase. "This is your husband. I remember you always had it on your dresser in your bedroom."

He was a boy in a soldier's uniform. So young.

Jeannie set cups of tea on the end table for both of us. "I like seeing him in here when I sit and work on sewing." She eased herself into her rocker. "So. How's your work going? And the after-school program at the church?"

Turning to her, I hesitated again, not ready to sit. "This isn't what I meant my life to be."

## CHAPTER 25

"Sit." Jeannie tapped her knuckles on her knee. "I'll get a crick in my neck looking up at you."

Perching on the edge of the loveseat, I picked up my tea. "All I ever wanted was to be a mom. I even took on a job from home so I could work while taking care of my kids."

She reached for her Bible from the sewing basket on the floor by her chair. "Let me find that verse." After flipping through the pages, she read, "Proverbs 16:9. A man's mind plans his way, but the Lord directs his steps."

She leaned back in her chair and drew in a long breath. "Roy and I got married the day after high school graduation." Her eyes moved to the picture on top of the bookcase. "He left for the army the next week." She held the Bible against her chest. "I got a job at Warmann's Grocery, but I intended to be a housewife as soon as he came home again." Her foot set the rocker moving. "When he went off to Nam, I didn't even tell him I was pregnant. Why worry him?"

My breath caught. I'd never seen such sorrow on her face before.

"I found out he was killed just two weeks after he landed in the country. I lost the baby the same day."

"Jeannie." I moved to kneel in front of her. "You never told me you lost a baby. I'm, I'm so sorry." I clutched her hands in mine.

She squeezed my hands then loosed one to wipe at tears.

Neither of us spoke.

She tapped my wrist. "I'm okay now."

Her voice was rough, and I didn't want to go away from her.

"Sit, Judy girl."

Back on the couch, my hands trembled. How could I show this lady, since I'd kept myself away from her, that I wanted to comfort her? "Why didn't you tell me?"

"Why? And give you something else to be sad about? Besides, I lost my baby nearly twenty years before you were born." She shook her head. "So much time. So much had come and gone."

She started the rocker moving again. "I'd planned to be a wife and mother, but God planned something else. I stayed on at the store. Became assistant manager. I almost got married again, but..." One shoulder lifted. "That never worked out. Then your daddy needed me to come take care of you and Dan. You were my kids. You were God's plan for me."

"Oh, Jeannie, I'm so sorry."

"What for?" She picked up her tea. "You're home again. And Dan's kids are my grandkids." She took a swallow. "Haven't you ever thought of adopting?"

"I was so, so determined to have my own children." My eyes pricked. "Stubborn, you'd say."

"Mm hmm." She smiled at me.

I lowered my eyes. "Steven says we can still have a family."

BRETT SAT beside me in the van on the way to church. "Come to our house for dinner again. I got my pig yesterday."

After dinner, Brett and I walked to the pen they'd set up for his 4-H project, just outside the barn.

"Let me go in first." Brett opened the wooden gate and slipped inside. I saw it then, the small black and white pig huddled in a far corner.

"Come here, sweetie. We won't hurt you." Bret knelt beside the pig, resting his hands on its back. "Come on in now." He glanced over at me. "Slow."

Easing through the gate, I stopped right inside.

"Come on." Brett gestured one hand at me.

The pig squealed and jerked out of his other hand, ran all around inside the pen twice, then stopped right next to Brett and quivered.

He rested two hands on the little animal again. "Come on."

On my knees, I crawled to where they hunched. I lowered my head to get a better look at the black and white bundle. "He looks just like the one I had."

"Her name's Lucy." Brett stroked her back. "Go ahead and touch her."

My fingers rested on the little rubbery, turned-up nose, and the pig snuffled and nuzzled my palm. "She misses her mama."

"Yeah. She just separated from her yesterday." Brett kissed the top of the pig's head.

"Daddy said I shouldn't name mine. Because we had to sell him." I twitched my lips. "I called him Rugger."

Lucy snapped her thin tail against Brett's leg, and he pressed her close to him with both hands. "Dad said maybe I can keep her. Since it's a girl. Maybe I can start my own pig raising business."

"Wow, that's great." I laid my face against Lucy's soft little head. "You are so lucky."

"Yeah, I know."

Peeking up, I caught a smile on Brett's face.

~

THE NEXT AFTERNOON AT CHURCH, Pamela plastered her body against me when she climbed off the bus. She was shaking, she cried so hard.

A pulse pounded in my head. *Lord, what could it be?*

Finding an empty Sunday school classroom, I led her inside and sat us down in the low chairs. "Honey. What is it?"

She rubbed her face against my shoulder and mumbled some words I couldn't catch.

"Pammy?" I tipped her head up so I could meet her gaze. Her eyes were red and her face blotched with tears. "Please, tell me."

"New kids." She gasped and grunted in her throat. "Mean. So mean."

She hid her face against my shoulder again, and I rocked her back and forth.

After a minute, she turned her head to the side, looking away from me. "They pulled my hair. Said I was stupid. Idiot." She shuddered. "Said I had green teeth. My teeth aren't green, are they, Ju-dee?"

"No, no." Joan had told me they had trouble getting Pamela to clean her teeth.

She sat up but wouldn't meet my eyes. "They snapped my bra strap. Said I did, stuff, with all the boys. Bad words."

When I rested my hands under her jaw, she lifted her head. "Jesus loves me, doesn't he, Ju-dee?"

"Yes, sweetheart." I wrapped my arms around her and rested my cheek against her hair. "So do I. I love you, Pamela."

## CHAPTER 26

The family made big plans for the week Steven was coming to be with me.

"Wayne's coming Saturday morning with his wife and kids." Brenda slammed the hood of my car. "When was the last time you changed the oil in this thing?"

My shoulders rose and fell. "I don't know. You're the mechanic. You tell me."

"It's been too long, girl. Good thing I always have supplies with me." She moved toward her pickup.

"How about Darrin?" I trailed after her. "Will he be here?"

"Yes, ma'am." She jumped down from the back of the truck with an oil can and filter in hand. "My man will be here. Has to be something awful special to get two truckers in the same place at the same time and it not be a drop-off."

Brenda met her husband Darrin when he and Wayne were friends in the same truckers' training class.

"My girls are coming too." Brenda wormed her way under the car. "Said you're still their favorite aunt, even if you did leave them in the dust when they were twelve."

My lips twitched. Looking at Brenda's tiny booted feet sticking out from the car, I considered stomping on one.

∽

Friday night I waited up until Steven's car pulled in front of the house.

This time, when I opened the front door, I didn't hold back but moved right into his arms.

Flash tried to push between us.

Steven was gentle but firm. "No, Flash." He pushed Flash's head away from us and moved me inside.

Now I was shy. "Can I take your jacket?" Hanging it in the closet, I waited to turn back to him.

"Judy." Coming up behind me, he pulled me close and laid his cheek against mine.

Whose tears did I feel? Turning, I wrapped my arms around his neck.

"Oh, honey." His voice was a whisper, and surely the tears came from us both. "I've missed you so."

∽

Saturday had been chosen for the cookout.

Yes, cookout. The first weekend of April, my family's tradition was to fire up the grill. They would have even if it snowed.

Steven and I walked to Danny's house an hour or so before anyone else arrived. Brett said he wanted to show Lucy to Steven.

I was proud of my husband, who'd always lived in a city. He sat on the ground in the pigpen and let Brett put Lucy in his lap. Steven cradled her head in his hands. "You can tell just by looking in her face, this is one smart animal."

I'd never seen Brett smile so big.

Later, as I sat surrounded by the other women in the front yard, the sound of a tractor came toward us up the lane.

Wayne's wife Patti stood up beside me. "I am so jealous. Would you look at that? Dan never has let me drive his fancy tractor with all the bells and whistles."

"He looks pretty good in there, doesn't he?" Jeannie sat in the chair next to me, holding Elena on her lap. "He's gotta come back at hay mowin' season. And help."

"Grandma Jeannie?" Elena turned around to study Jeannie's face. "Why you breathing so hard?"

"Ah nothing, sweetie." She hugged the little girl. "You're just getting so big to hold, that's all. Don't matter though. I'll let you sit on my lap for as many years as you want to."

As I studied Jeannie's face, I saw a pinched look take over her eyes and lips. "You sure you feel okay?" I asked.

"Oh sure. Too much apple pie, that's my only problem." She smacked her lips. "Brenda does make the best apple pie."

Steven jumped off the tractor as soon as he'd stopped it in front of the yard. "Judy, Dan said I could come back at hay season and help with the mowing and hauling bales."

Jeannie winked at me. "Sounds like he thinks it's an honor, don't it?"

∼

THE NEXT MORNING, Steven left before me to practice with the band for church. "Dan told them I'm worship leader back home, and they asked if I'd join them this morning with my guitar."

As I sat beside Pamela later and watched the band getting ready to start, she hugged my arm. "Your husband is a cutie."

She was right. Even Irene on the organ shot all her smiles Steven's way.

"I'm glad to see him up there with the band." I met Pamela's eyes. "I've missed him in worship."

When Steven came to sit next to me, I glanced around at those near me.

Pamela on my other side. Marilyn and Kent in the row behind. Danny and his family in front of us.

*This feels so right, God.*

When I brought my attention back to the service, Jon was reading from the Bible. "Hebrews 4:16. Let us then approach God's throne of grace with confidence, so that we may receive mercy and find grace to help us in our time of need."

*Lord? I need You to help me find that confidence again. I need, I need Your grace. Every day.*

## CHAPTER 27

The next afternoon, Pamela and I watched out the window as Steven ran around with the younger kids on the church lawn.

"He's good with kids," she said.

"He's a teacher." Turning her notebook toward me, I glanced at her math work. "A gym teacher. And a math teacher. You should ask him to help you with this. He'd be better at it than me."

A short time later, I watched as Steven sat with Pamela, giving her instructions on her homework. He was as gentle with her as he'd been with the younger kids, and she understood what he told her to do. She beamed under his attention.

*Lord, I do love this man.*

Friday afternoon, Pamela asked me to bring Steven over to her house for supper. "Uncle Walter is bringing home baby chicks today." Her smile was huge.

We stood in front of the chicken house as Walter carried the last crate of chicks from the truck and set them before us.

As I dropped to my knees before the crate, Steven laid a hand on my shoulder. "Did you have baby chickens when you were little?"

"Yes. Ooooh, they're so cute."

Steven knelt with Pamela and me as we examined the fuzzy chicks inside the wooden carrier.

"Reach your finger in and touch them," I told him then stuck my own finger in.

"Cheep, cheep, cheep." It was like long-ago familiar music to me.

"They're so soft." Pamela's voice was full of wonder.

"Hey, that one bit me." Steven lowered his face to frown at the tiny creatures.

"Let's take them inside now." Walter motioned us back so he could lift the crate.

We followed him into the final room full of bouncing chicks, and Walter latched the door. "Okay, pick them up, one at a time, and set them on the floor. Gentle now."

Steven's eyes were bright with discovery as he held the treasures in his hands. "Thank you, Pamela." He smiled at her. "For letting us do this."

Eyes bright, she touched his hand. "I'm glad you like them."

*These two look good together, God.*

∽

STEVEN PLANNED to leave Saturday afternoon. That morning, Jeannie invited us over for breakfast.

"I understand you're a hit with my grandchildren." Jeannie set down a platter of eggs and sausage in front of Steven. "Aaron and Elena talked non-stop last night on the phone about their new Uncle Steven." She quirked her lips. "Even Brett likes you, and that's a grand accomplishment."

"Yeah." I frowned at Steven. "It took me weeks before he didn't scowl every time we met."

Steven grinned and scooped food onto his plate. "I'm a middle school teacher, don't forget. I think like one of them."

Jeannie huffed. "No doubt. Go ahead and pray, and we'll eat."

Scooting back a little from the table, I was fascinated to watch these two people interact. Steven pulled more from Jeannie of her youth and short marriage than I'd ever heard, and she listened with rapt attention to his stories about the kids he worked with.

*God, why can't I draw more depth from people's hearts? Am I so fixed on myself?*

∼

BEFORE STEVEN LEFT, he asked me to take a walk with him.

"It is beautiful here." He linked his fingers with mine. "We should invite Kailey and Ryan and the kids to spend a few days here this summer. They'd love it."

"Steven." I stopped and turned to face him. "I'd really like that."

He grinned. "I'll ask Dan if Kailey could drive the tractor."

We walked on. "What is this field for?"

"Pasture, for the cattle. When the grass is a little taller, Danny will bring a bunch over to graze here." Laughing, I pointed to an apple tree in a far corner. "Let's walk over there. I used to race with the cows to get apples off that tree. From the other side of the fence."

Steven chuckled. When we stood under the tree, he turned me to face him. "I have a couple things I want to talk with you about."

My stomach churned with guilt. "How can I ever—"

"Shh." He laid his finger over my mouth. "Don't apologize again. Come on now. We're past that."

Swallowing, I nodded.

Steven leaned against the tree. "I'm not going to try to convince you to come home yet." He shook his head when I opened my mouth. "Just let me talk, honey. I can see how good it's been for you to be here, in this place you love, with a family who so obviously adores you."

*Yes, God. How could I have kept them away from me for so long?*

Steven tipped his head. "No, I'm not talking about that. Quit looking for things to condemn yourself for."

*He knows what I'm thinking, Lord.*

"The other day when I went to town with Dan, I stopped by the school and filled out an application to teach at their summer school." Taking my hand, he started walking again. "You wouldn't believe how their faces lit up when they heard I was a PE teacher, as well as math." He grinned. "I expect to hear from them any day. Regardless, I'll be here with you this summer."

"But—"

"Wait." He faced me again. "We'll talk about the future later. I'm not done yet."

My stomach quaked. What else?

He wrapped both my hands in his. "I was able to claim Alicia's body from the hospital."

When I flinched, he tightened his grip.

"Wait, honey." His face quivered. "I had her cremated, and I have, I have the urn." He gulped. "We can do whatever you like."

He laid his arms around my shoulders. "We can have a service. Scatter the ashes. Bury them. Maybe right under that apple tree." Tears appeared in his eyes as he gestured back at the tree.

My heart filled with… With what? Sorrow? Comfort? Peace?

"We could have a service right here." He walked back toward the tree. "Put up a little stone, so we'd have somewhere to visit. To pray, to remember our dreams for her."

He turned back and folded his arms around me, pulling me close. "You have to know how much I loved her too. How devastated I've been."

Cradling Steven's face in my hands, I kissed the tear sliding down his cheek. "I love you so."

## CHAPTER 28

"What? What, what is it?"

Flash was on my bed, licking my face.

And someone was pounding on the kitchen door.

"Flash, get off of me. Is something wrong?"

More pounding. "Hey, Jude, wake up."

"Danny?"

Stumbling to the back door, I rubbed my face and shook my head. "What is it?"

Danny stood on the porch, the flashlight in his hand lowered to avoid hitting me in the eyes. "Come on, come on. Ready for fun?"

"It's dark." My voice scraped. "What time is it?"

"Two o'clock. And time for the new baby to be born in your barn. Wanna come?"

My head cleared. "The calf? Are you sure?"

Danny'd brought the small heifer over to my barn a week or so earlier and checked on her often.

"Yep. I thought she might be ready when I looked in on her last evening, so I came back about ten and stayed with her."

He pulled the door a little wider and looked in. "Where's

your shoes? Here, put a jacket on. Come on. You remember how great this is."

I did remember. When I was about six years old, my dad had invited me for the first time to sit with him as he helped a heifer who was having trouble giving birth. After that, I'd gone with him or Danny many times for these amazing events.

"This brings back memories." I grabbed Danny's arm as we walked the path to the barn. The ground was rough, lit only with Danny's flashlight and a sliver of moon.

"It never gets old." Danny entered the barn first and turned on a dim lamp.

"This way." He opened a stall door. "You can go in. She's tame. Sit by her head and talk to her."

Easing into the stall, I breathed in the smell of hay and animal. Another sweet memory.

The black heifer crouched on the floor, her sides heaving with fast breaths.

"She's small." Danny moved to kneel behind her. "I didn't know if I'd have to put her in a head gate and help, or even call the vet. But I think she's gonna be okay. She's a strong girl."

I knelt down, laying my hands on her head and gazing into her soft, scared eyes. "It's gonna be okay, honey. You're gonna be okay."

"All right, the water sack is coming. Not long now." Danny edged closer, his hands on the cow.

As I soothed her, I remembered another time, also at night, in this same stall.

"Isn't it cute?" The calf had lain, quivering, by its mother's side, and Daddy had smiled at me from where he knelt next to them. "Thank God for the miracle of this, Judy."

My face warmed now as I held this young cow's head. "Thank You, God. Help her."

"Here it comes. There's the nose." Danny kept his voice low, but he spoke with excitement.

I scrunched even closer to the mama's face and whispered to her as Danny helped the baby ease out into the world.

"Done. A boy for you, sweet girl."

She and I waited while Danny cleared the calf's nostrils then brought him to lie in front of his mother. A tiny wet, black baby, gasping with new life.

And though she'd never done it before, the mama knew what to do and started licking him dry.

"Let's leave them for a second." Danny slipped out of the stall and I followed.

"The next stall is clean and waiting for them. We'll stay 'til we're sure he can nurse."

A few minutes later, Danny eased the new family into the next stall. I stood and watched as he helped the new calf latch on to his mama and start to suck.

"Lord." I pressed my hands against my cheeks. "I love this. Thank You."

## CHAPTER 29

After a few hours taking work calls the next morning, I walked with Flash down to the tire swing. "Buddy, don't you think we need some hens in our own chicken house?" Grinning, I ruffled Flash's ear. "Some roosters?"

I stepped in the swing with Mom's journal.

I hadn't been able to sleep after Danny left. Sitting at the kitchen table, I'd paged through Mom's notebook, reading entries. My heart was so full of happiness from the calf's birth, and my spirits lifted even more as I read Mom's thoughts and activities.

She said they were surprised to learn she was pregnant, but happy. "Hank has always been close to the other kids, and he's a wonderful daddy to Danny. But, oh my."

The writing became messier, as if she'd been laughing and writing fast. "When he found out we're having a baby, you'd've thought the sun turned on inside his face. He is so excited."

Mom said she was excited too. "I'll be forty when this baby comes. Sure, I was younger, but I've done this before. It'll be all right. And oh my, what if the little one looks like Hank?"

Now as I started the swing moving, I opened to her last entry.

"Lord, how can I thank You enough for this blessing? This beautiful tiny girl You've put in my arms. Such a precious gift, Father. Thank You, thank You."

I hurried to close the book so my tears wouldn't fall on the ink. "Oh, Mom, I'm so sorry I was always mad at you. You missed out on life with me, too, just as much as I did. I, I'm sorry. I wish we could have known each other." My voice choked. "I love you."

∼

THAT AFTERNOON, Marilyn and I stayed behind to clean up after the kids left the church.

"You sure are smiling a lot." She leaned a folded chair against the wall then parked herself in front of me. "What's the deal anyway?"

"Deal?" I widened my eyes.

She nodded and folded her arms, not moving.

"Okay, okay." I laughed. "Danny woke me in the middle of the night to watch a new calf being born. So amazing. I didn't get much sleep, so I'm a little slap-happy. And…"

"And?"

Biting my lip, I reached for another chair to fold. "And, I told my mom I loved her for the first time."

"Judy?" She stepped close to me, her eyes questioning.

"No, no. It's okay. I was reading her journal, and, and I realized how much she really loved me." My eyes teared, and I sucked in a long breath. "And, I knew that I loved her. I wasn't mad at her anymore for leaving me."

Marilyn had never been much of a hugger, but she hugged me now, and dried tears from my face. "Oh, honey. I'm glad."

Her phone rang.

## CHAPTER 30

"We've gotta go." Marilyn grabbed her keys and hurried to lock the door, then ran to her car.

"Mari, what is it?" I tried to keep up. "Who was on the phone? What happened?"

"Jon." She jammed her key into the ignition, whipped her head from side to side to check the road. "He said Joan called him before Pamela ever reached home. She was calling from an ambulance. Walter had a stroke."

"Oh no. What about Pamela?"

"She's in Lorie's van. He called Lorie and told her to keep Pamela 'til she's dropped everybody else off, then meet him at Pamela's house." She turned onto the gravel road leading to the Reynolds's farm. "He and Lorie are foster parents, too, so Pamela can stay with them for now. He wants Lorie to help her pack some things. But he wanted to know if you and I could stay with Pamela for a while this evening. He figured she's going to be upset, and he wants to go to the hospital to be with Joan."

Jon and Angie were already there when we pulled up in front of the house. Marilyn jumped out. "Where's Lorie?"

"She'll be here in a minute." Jon hurried to meet us. "I told her to go ahead and tell Pamela what happened, so she wouldn't be surprised to get here and find everything in an uproar."

"Here they come." Angie spun and smiled. "There's Mama." She was at the van as soon as it stopped, opening the side door and climbing in to help the little boy in back out of his car seat. She'd introduced him to me a couple of weeks earlier as "my baby brother Willie."

Pamela climbed out of the other side and hurried to me. "Ju-dee, what happened? Is Uncle Walter going to die?"

∽

AFTER WE PACKED SOME CLOTHES, Lorie decided to take her kids home. "Thank you for staying here for a while." She leaned out of the van to take the duffle bag. "Pamela depends on you. Where is she anyway?"

"She and Marilyn are feeding the chickens. Don't worry about anything. We'll be fine."

"Okay." Lorie closed the door then yelled over her shoulder at the kids. "Angie, stop tickling Willie. I can't hear myself think over your squealing." She turned back to me. "Pamela will need to sleep at our house. I don't know how long Jon will be at the hospital."

"Go, go." I gestured her to drive on. "We'll be fine."

"Ju-dee, come help feed the chickens."

Waving to Lorie, I walked toward the chicken houses.

As fast as she could on her weak leg, Pamela hurried to hug me again. "I'm so scared. I wish you could be my foster mom."

∽

JON CALLED LATER to tell Pamela that Walter was doing better, then spoke to Marilyn.

"He said it's not as severe as they thought at first, but he's going to wait with Joan at the hospital until her son gets there."

We'd dropped Pamela off with Lorie, and now Marilyn was driving me home.

"You said Pamela can stay with Jon and Lorie? Because they're foster parents?"

"Yes. Willie is in foster care. They're in the process of adopting him, but they can take another child in the home." She drew in a long breath. "Lorie's so busy though. Willie is just two, and Angie is a non-stop bundle to watch. They'll need our help."

"Pamela said she wished I could be her foster mom."

She glanced over at me. "Yeah?"

I clutched my head in my hands. "Yeah."

∼

"We could adopt her." Steven's voice was strong. Serious.

"What?" I almost dropped the phone.

"Maybe. Why not?" Steven ran water in the sink on the other end of the line. "She loves you. And I think she can grow to love me."

"Whoa. Steven?" Flash laid his head in my lap, and I rubbed his nose. "This dog can always tell when I'm upset, or, or… What are you saying?"

"I talked with Jon while I was there. About what they had to do to become foster parents. To adopt." A door opened and closed as he moved into another room. "It might be good for all of us, honey. A new start. A different road."

## CHAPTER 31

April flew by. Spring came alive with scents and colors of beauty, and Pamela and I were together every day.

We took long walks along gravel roads and across fields. Sometimes we enjoyed the sun growing warmer on our skin. Other days we laughed as we dashed to find shelter when a spring shower came from nowhere. We picked daisies and other wildflowers. Even dandelions.

"These are so pretty." She held up a fistful of the yellow fluff to her nose. "Mmm."

"Yes." I smiled at her joy.

"What's that bird? Oh look, there goes a bunny." She clapped her hands and did a little dance.

"My daddy and I used to go for walks like this." I wrapped my arm around Pamela. "He told me the names of all these birds, but I don't remember them now."

He'd also accepted all the dandelion bouquets I picked for him.

"I'm glad you're here with me, Ju-dee," Pamela told me over and over.

"Me, too, sweetie."

A couple of times, Jeannie joined us to look for early mushrooms.

"I'd never trust myself to know which ones are safe to eat." Grabbing Pamela's hand, I turned her around to walk back to Jeannie. "She's a mushroom expert."

"Yeah, you girls just slow yourselves down." Jeannie stooped down and pushed aside some leaves. "I'm not so young and spry as you are. Oh now, here's another one. Come and see, Pamela."

Pamela's eyes grew wide as she examined the bumpy white and tan mushrooms with glints of lilac. "Those don't look like the mushrooms in stores."

"They sure don't." Jeannie added the mushroom to her basket. "Those in the store don't taste as good either. Let's find a few more, and you girls can come for breakfast Saturday morning. I'll cook them for you." She smacked her lips as she moved on, separating clumps of moss and fallen bark to look for more treats. "Along with some farm-fresh fried eggs. Mmm mmm."

∽

STEVEN CAME up for a long weekend, so we could attend the county's Family Services orientation meeting on foster care and adoption. In the evenings, we took online classes together over the phone.

"They need foster parents." His voice sounded thoughtful as he scrolled through the website back in our apartment. "Okay, here's the questions to answer for the first video we watched."

This was all happening so fast. "They need people, sure." I found the questions on my screen. "But they don't just accept anyone. They have to check us out. And..." I stopped, sucked in a shaky breath. "Are we really ready for this?"

Steven's voice came closer to the phone. "I think we are, honey. I have faith in you. In us."

His words warmed me, and what was this sensation rising in my chest? Hope? Joy?

*God, he still trusts me. Oh. Oh. Thank You.*

∽

THE NEXT MORNING, I walked back into Daddy's bedroom and seated myself on his bed. The room hadn't changed much in twelve years. On the wall facing me hung Daddy's gun rack, empty now of the hunting rifles he'd loved.

"Danny must have the guns now. He always hunted with you, Daddy, but I never had the stomach for it."

Farm magazines lay in stacks on the desk. Shoes sat in a neat line inside the closet, which never had a door for as long as I could remember. His clothes still hung there, too, except his one suit.

"I guess he was buried in that." Reaching down, I rested my hand on Flash's back as he lay beside the bed. He slapped the floor with his tail and made a long, sleepy sigh.

I sat back up. "God, I can't thank Daddy for calling me last summer. But thank You. Thank You that he was smart enough to know I'd need to talk to him."

Last July, I'd received a short, clipped call from Brenda one morning. "Your dad is in the hospital. Before he went into surgery, he said to tell you to come here. Now."

Steven came with me. I couldn't have driven alone.

Daddy had a massive heart attack and was taken immediately into surgery. For two days, they weren't sure he would live.

How many hours dragged by as I stayed by Daddy's hospital bed, holding his limp hand and gazing at his pained, white face? "God, what have I done? Daddy, I'm so sorry."

Other members of the family drifted in and out of my fog, but I couldn't force myself to deal with them. My heart gasped for a chance to talk to Daddy.

When the doctors said he was out of danger, at least for the moment, I'd collapsed and wept.

Resting my face in my hands now, I whispered, "Thank You for giving me that gift, God. For the chance to see him again."

## CHAPTER 32

When Daddy woke in the hospital and saw me sitting beside him, his eyes filled with tears. "Little girl. You're here." His voice was a hoarse whisper, from his pain, from not speaking for so long, but he squeezed my hand in his. "Dear God, thank You for giving me the chance to see her again."

Lowering my face close to his, I let my own tears fall. "Oh, Daddy. I'm so sorry. I—"

"Shh." He shook my hand with as much strength as he could. "Just listen to me a little."

I did.

"I was such a fool. An idiot, Judy girl. So sorry." Those were the only words he was able to say that first time.

As the days passed, and he regained a little strength, Daddy kept shushing me and telling me to listen to him.

"I was so scared to have you go away. You wouldn't be where I could keep you safe." Daddy broke down and cried often, something I'd never seen before. He moaned and wept, but he wanted to say more.

"I was the adult back then. You were just a kid. Sure, neither of us should have blown up at each other like that, but for a father to tell his child never to come into her home..." His voice choked. "God forgive me. And I've been so stubborn, never to ask you to come back before this. Never to try to fix things." He rolled his head from side to side on the pillow. "Oh, oh, just a hard, prideful heart I've had."

"I've been pretty stubborn, too, Daddy." I rubbed his rough hand against my wet cheek.

Now he smiled, the all-over-the-face smile I remembered from when I was small. "You come by it naturally."

We spent hours talking, sharing important memories from the years we'd been apart. Steven and I had just learned I was pregnant, and Daddy couldn't stop chuckling. He was so happy for us. One day, Daddy asked me to leave the room so he could have a long talk with Steven.

When I walked into his room the day we were going home, he patted his bed for me to sit beside him.

"I wanted to see you. That's why I asked Brenda to call you to come here. But there was a more important thing I wanted to say to you."

"Daddy?" I held his hand in both of mine.

"We needed things to be right between us. Because..." He turned his head to look straight up at the ceiling, moving his lips, looking for words. "Because I don't want you to carry all this mess with you anymore."

Swallowing, I didn't speak.

He went on. "I don't want you spending your life regretting what happened. Feeling guilty. Keeping yourself apart from your family. We needed to make things right between us, and between us and God." He brought his eyes back to mine. "I'm sorry, little girl, for treating you like I did. For letting it go on so long. And you, you need to ask God to help you put it behind you now."

We'd planned to come visit Daddy again soon, but when I started having trouble with bleeding and my blood pressure, I had to stay in bed. I called him the first night, though. "Daddy, I'm scared."

We talked on the phone often, up to the day before he died. Through those months, Daddy surprised everybody, including himself, and learned how to text.

Sliding off Daddy's bed now, I landed on the floor beside Flash and laid my wet cheek against his warm side. "Thank You, God, for what Daddy tried to teach me then. To not hold onto things. Forgive me that I still didn't let that seep into my heart for the rest of the family, for so long."

Flash washed my tears with his tongue, and I pushed myself up to sit.

"I was so scared, God, that they wouldn't forgive me. And then…" I gulped. "I had so much trouble with the baby."

I pressed my hands against my face. "Oh, Lord, such a mess. Thank You, thank You for not giving up on me. For giving me another chance, with Steven, with my family. With You, dear Lord."

## CHAPTER 33

On May fourth, Pamela and I walked from my house to Danny's for Elena's birthday party. As we climbed the stairs to the front door, I could hear a loud celebration already going on. Or maybe some other kind of ruckus?

"What's all that noise?" Pamela didn't wait to knock but barreled through the door and joined the rest of the kids in the middle of the living room.

"Danny? Helen?" Stepping through the door, I saw them, leaning against the wall, holding onto each other as they gasped with laughter.

Aaron and Bret knelt one on either side of a squirming bundle. For a minute, I wondered if they had a dog or some other animal wrapped in the blanket. But then, through an opening, I caught a quick glimpse of Elena's face. Most of the sound came from her, too, delighted squeals and shrieks. "Stop, stop, stop iiiiit."

Aaron was laughing and wiggling so hard, he could hardly keep from rolling away. He scrunched down and held onto the writhing bundle, while Brett, his face set, grim and serious, wrapped duct tape around his giggling sister.

"Hold on, Aaron." Brett was breathless, and now I saw why. His eyes gleamed with mirth, which he struggled to hold back. "Help him, Pamela. We need to get this birthday present wrapped for Elena."

Brett grabbed at Elena's foot as she popped out of the bundle, and all four kids fell in a heap on the floor.

"No, no, no." Elena wrestled herself free from the others and ran to me. "Aunt Judy, help me." She threw her arms around me. "Don't let them wrap me up like a present."

As I hugged the happy little girl and looked down into her face, I realized I was happy too. *Thank You, God. For allowing me to enjoy closeness to this precious child. Thank You I don't feel lost in grief right now.*

∼

LATER THAT EVENING, I was still laughing over Elena's party when Steven called.

"Judy? Listen." His voice sounded strained.

"Honey? What is it?"

"I told you…" He stopped and drew in a long breath. "Did I tell you the school district here has hired a new superintendent?"

"Yes?" Flopping onto the floor next to Flash, I pulled his big head onto my lap. "You told me. What is it?"

"I don't know if I told you he's decided to join some of the smaller neighborhood schools together. Into fewer, larger schools."

"Okay."

"They're laying off some of the teachers. They told me today. I'm one of…" He choked, coughed. "When school ends, I don't have a job."

I opened my mouth, but something clogged my throat.

*God? How can I help him?*

Words I didn't expect came from me. "Come here. As soon as school is done."

A blanket of peace wrapped around me. This was right.

"You were coming here anyway. You've got the summer school job already."

As I gazed into Flash's smiling eyes, a bubble of joy started in my chest. "I'll start checking the paper here for job openings. Websites for other towns in the area too. There's bound to be an opening for a teaching job near here soon." I hugged Flash. "I'm sure you could work as a sub. Or we'll find another job. It'll be okay, honey. This is a good place to be."

"Judy?" He sounded hesitant, but not so crushed anymore. "Really?"

## CHAPTER 34

On the last day of school, I joined Pamela's class and sat with her through the end-of-year ceremony.

"I'm gonna get an award for perfect attendance," she told me in a loud whisper, squirming with anticipation.

When her name was called, she jogged up to the front to receive her certificate from the principal, smiling big. My eyes burned. *I am so proud of her, Lord.*

After school let out at noon, we went to get ice cream.

"What are we going to do this summer?" She licked ice cream from her cone, bubblegum flavored, and bounced on her seat across the table from me.

Reaching over with a napkin, I wiped the cream dripping down her chin. "Hmm. What should we do?"

"Can I come to your house while you're working? I'll be quiet. I can play in the yard with Flash, and visit the cats in the barn, and swing on the swing, and... When will Steven be here?"

She made me smile. "Yes, you can do that. A lot of days. And when summer school starts, Steven will drive you into town with him. His school ends in a week, then he'll be here."

Gazing at my own bowl of strawberry, I chewed my lip.

Walter Reynolds was home from rehab now, and they'd asked if Pamela could spend time with them. They weren't ready for her to move in. Maybe they never would be. Steven and I hoped we'd be through the foster parent process soon, so she could live with us.

*And maybe, Lord, adoption?*

"Oh goody. I like Steven." She took a big bite of her cone then chewed. "Will he be my teacher at summer school?"

"Maybe. For PE anyway." I grinned at her. "Steven likes you too."

As I gazed at her happy face, I closed my eyes. *Lord, I know it won't be easy to be Pamela's parents.* There'd been a number of days she'd gotten off the bus crying after being picked on by bullies. *But, Lord, we want to be her parents. Help us.*

Pamela reached her foot over to step on mine. "What you thinkin' about? So serious." She tried to get rid of the goofy look on her face, but couldn't help giggling.

I pushed my foot against hers. "Nothing serious. This is a happy day, the first day of our summer together."

∼

THE NIGHT STEVEN planned to arrive, I paced the front porch and threw a ball into the yard for Flash. *Steven sounded so beaten down when he called earlier, Lord. He's always been strong for me. Help me to encourage him now.*

My cell phone rang.

Without looking at caller ID, I answered. "Honey, are you okay?"

"Jude. It's Danny. I'm going to pick you up in a minute. Jeannie's headed to the hospital." His voice rasped. "Her heart."

A rock slammed into my chest. "Wh-what?"

Danny arrived in a minute, barely stopping the truck long enough for me to climb in.

"Tell me what's happening." I fumbled with the seatbelt. "She's going to the hospital in the city? Why not the ER here in town?"

"The EMTs on the ambulance decided that would be best."

"Slow down some, would you? We don't need to end up in the hospital too." We sped around a sharp curve. "Danny. Slow. Down."

With a deep inhale, he eased up on the gas and relaxed his grip on the wheel. "I'm scared, Jude."

"I know. Let's pray." Whoa. How long had it been since I'd made that suggestion? "Father, give us courage. Help Jeannie not to suffer. Give her a safe trip to the hospital, and show the doctors what to do to help her."

We were quiet for a minute then Danny asked, "Is this the night Steven's coming?"

"Oh, thank you. I need to call him."

After making sure Steven would meet us at the hospital, I tried to find other things to talk about to keep Danny's mind calm. "How's Brett's pig? What are the boys going to do this summer? Are they going to summer school?"

By the time we reached the hospital, Danny laughed a little as he told me about Aaron trying to milk their gentle old Guernsey cow. "Elena insisted on helping too." He managed a smile as he turned to me. "I let her stand back and hold onto the tail. She said it was the most important job."

## CHAPTER 35

When Steven stepped into the waiting room, I jumped up and ran to grab his hands. "Tell Danny to sit down. He's making me crazy."

Steven questioned me with his eyes, then squeezed my hand and walked to where Danny had stopped pacing and stood looking out the window into the parking lot. "Dan. Hello." Steven rested his hand on Danny's shoulder.

Danny turned, and I was shaken by the whiteness of his face. His jaw worked, and he struggled to straighten his shoulders.

I watched these two men, the ones who'd always been my strength, and a new realization hit me.

They were just men, human beings who could be weak and scared, battered, shaken.

*God, I want to be strong for them. I need, Lord, I need Your help.*

"How's Jeannie?" Steven asked. He and Danny sat together on a couch.

Stepping out of the room, I looked up and down the halls. No doctors or nurses in sight to give us information. I paced to a window, then turned to the vending machines and surveyed the selections. Nothing looked good.

When I returned to the waiting room, the guys sat with their heads close, talking in low voices. "Danny, you need to stay here in case the doctor comes back. Steven, let's go get coffee and sandwiches. I need to eat."

As soon as we came back with the food, Danny turned from the window to greet us. "The doctor came." His face held color again. "He said Jeannie's doing a lot better. They've given her medication and…" He pressed his hands to his face then shook his head. "She had a heart attack, but not a massive one, not like Dad's." He squeezed his hands together. "They said she's gonna need surgery, probably in a day or two, but angioplasty, not bypass."

He raised his head and met my eyes. "I think I can handle some of that food now."

∽

"Your turn to visit her." Danny's face was white again as he stepped out of Jeannie's hospital room.

Jeannie did not look like the tough woman I'd always known. I sat beside her bed and laid my hand on top of hers.

As she slept, her face sagged, and her eyes were shrunken. Breaths came quick and shallow.

"God, why did I never realize what a treasure You gave me in this woman? This…" I choked. "This mother?"

Brushing my lips against her forehead, I whispered, "Jeannie, don't worry. We're your kids. We'll take care of you."

She was only sixty-seven.

*God, forgive me. Give me the chance to make it up to her.*

Jeannie drew in a deeper breath, and her lips formed a slight smile.

My eyes teared. *Thank You, Lord.*

When I walked out of the room, Danny and Steven waited in the hall.

"Well?" Danny asked.

What, you expect me to know what to do about all this? *God, help us.*

"Come on, guys." I reached out a hand to each of them. "We can do this." We walked back toward the waiting room. "She doesn't have to go into the nursing home. She can come home again."

As they sank into chairs, I stood in front of them. "She can come home. I'm a nurse. Steven will be there. You're so close, Danny. We can take care of her. Drive her to doctor appointments, to cardiac rehab." Warmth filled my chest. "She will feel so much better being home again. She's got a lot of life yet. You'll see. Things are going to be okay."

## CHAPTER 36

On a late June morning, I stood at the tiny gravesite we'd set up by the apple tree. Kneeling, I traced my fingers over the crisp, new letters.

"Baby Alicia, Sweet Daughter, Gift from God."

And below, this:

"Hebrews 4:16: Let us then approach God's throne of grace with confidence, so that we may receive mercy and find grace to help us in our time of need."

In the tree above me, a bird fluttered its wings. A grasshopper rattled nearby.

I blinked at the young rosebush we'd planted at the end of the grave, then spread my hands over the small, flat stone. "I love you, little girl." My heart still hurt, but it didn't sink. A hope rose up inside me. "God, Jeannie's verse, 'A man's mind plans his way, but the Lord directs his steps.' Thank You, God."

When I neared the house, I stopped to watch those gathered there. Brett sat on his heels on the grass next to Jeannie's lawn chair. His smile was wide, his eyes bright, as he gestured and spoke to her with quick words.

In the middle of the yard, Pamela and Aaron sat close together, their heads bent over a kitten.

Not far away, Elena and Flash rolled around, little girl and big dog, kicking and laughing, growling and hugging.

"Thank You so much for this life, Lord. For the family You've given me." My voice scraped in my throat. "So many gifts of grace."

A couple of shouts, then the sound of the tractor and machinery in the nearby field stopped. Danny was teaching Steven how to bail hay. A chuckle bubbled up inside me.

Steven walked up the hill to meet me, his shirt rumpled, pieces of hay sticking out from his hair.

*He looks so happy, Lord.*

"Hey, you." He stopped beside me, panting, laughing, and drew me against his sweaty chest. "You're the prettiest thing I've seen in a month of Sundays." He tipped up my chin and kissed me. "And around here, I've seen an awful lot of pretty."


THE END

# AM I INVISIBLE?

## CHAPTER 1

As I welcomed Cara through the front door, a car horn beeped out on the street. "Mom. Hey, Mom."

I moved onto the porch. "Sonya?"

"I'm going over to Cliff's house for dinner and to study. I'll be home by ten."

"Sony, wait."

But the motor revved, and the tires squealed around the corner.

Inside the house again, I pulled my phone out of my pocket and tapped. "Call Sonya."

It went straight to voicemail.

Three times.

"Iola, that was your daughter?" Cara asked.

I pressed my hands against my cheeks. Take a breath, Yoyo.

*Jesus, help me.*

"Yes. Sonya. Let's go in the kitchen. Coffee's already made."

Cara followed me. "Thanks for agreeing to see me this afternoon. I had a two-hour break between shifts at the library and thought this would be a good use of time."

"No problem. Do you take cream or sugar?"

"A little cream. Can I help with anything?"

"Nope. Have a seat."

Once I'd set the cups and cream on the table, I pulled out the chair across from her. "So, you're new to the area, right? Or just new to the church?"

Her chair squeaked. "To the city. I just finished graduate school last spring, so I've been looking for a job. The library here drew the winning straw."

That was a smile in her voice. Or was she laughing at herself?

"Well, I'm glad you're here."

*Help me focus on this lady, Lord, not my daughter, and how I want to wring her neck.*

"Is this a braille Bible?" The book I'd left on the table creaked as she opened it. "Or part of it anyway. We have a few braille books at the library, and I know this one book won't hold the whole Bible."

I chuckled. "It takes twenty of those volumes to make up the entire Bible."

"I figured." She closed the book. "We only have a few braille books, but I've seen those big volumes before. I'm sure you know, but there's a local library specifically for the blind that handles more braille, as well as large print and talking books."

"Oh yes." I took a swallow of coffee. "I've been getting books from the Library for the Blind since I was a toddler."

A memory flashed. My mother reading the print/braille books to me, laying my hands on the bumps. "You'll learn braille soon, sweetie. Then you'll be reading to me."

That hadn't happened. I'd learned to read braille, yes, but she never had the time to…

Shivering, I shook my head. "Anyway, you said you'd be interested in volunteering for childcare during Hope Group."

"Right. I wanted to find a way to help out in the church. I've worked in the nursery before, but I didn't want to do that just yet." She gulped the coffee, then hurried on. "I want to attend all the worship services right now. I need, I need that encouragement, I guess. I mean, everybody needs that encouragement, of course. Including parents with little kids." She took a breath. "I'll be happy to work in the nursery later, but I just need to settle into the church more, meet a few people." She stopped.

Is she crying?

"Completely understandable." Hurrying to reassure her, I reached out my hand to touch hers.

And knocked her coffee cup over.

"Oh, no. I'm so sorry." I jumped up. "Did it spill all over you?"

"No, not much. I'll rinse it off at the sink."

"Let me get you a clean cloth."

As we rushed for the sink, we slammed into each other, cracking heads.

"Oh."

"Whoa."

I wasn't sure who started laughing first, but soon we clung to each other, giggling.

"Cara, I am so sorry." Drawing in a deep breath, I pulled back. "Such a good first impression as a capable blind person."

"And how about me? I came across as someone you could trust with your children, didn't I? Babbling and crying and, I'm sorry."

Which just started us laughing again.

## CHAPTER 2

❦

After we'd cleaned up, I suggested we move into the living room. "Away from anything I can spill on you." Let's try this again, Yoyo.

"We'll need you to go through a background check, and I'll need two references. It shouldn't take long. For now, just tell me a little about yourself."

"What do you want to know?" She settled back on the couch beside me. "I grew up in a small town in Mississippi. I went to college because that's what my parents always said I would do. No idea what I wanted to study, but I looked forward to going to a large city. Oh, you've got a cat. Will he let me touch him?"

"Her. And that's anybody's guess. Where is she?"

"She looks like she's about to jump—oh."

Esther landed on my lap, all sixteen pounds of her.

"Whoa, Esther." Placing my hands on kitty's back, I turned the furry monster to face Cara. "Meet Esther, queen of the house. You never know when she'll hop up on you and attack. Fortunately, we had her declawed."

"She's beautiful." Cara stroked Esther, and, surprise, my cat purred. "Her name is Esther?"

"Yeah. We didn't give our kids Bible names, but when we decided to have cats, we picked Bible names. Before Esther, we had Jeremiah and Abigail."

"That's funny. Aw, she's purring. How old is she?"

"She just turned two, which hopefully means she's done growing." I pushed the animal to lie on my lap and turned to face Cara. "What did you decide to major in?"

"I didn't decide until I was a sophomore and had to start thinking about something besides the basics. Since middle school, I'd been in love with Irish history, so I thought, why not history?"

"Sounds reasonable."

"Seemed like it, unless I wanted a job."

*Okay, Lord, that's better. She's laughing again.*

"I liked school, but I didn't think I wanted to be a teacher, either in high school or as a professor. So."

Esther curled up into a huge ball on my lap, and I wrapped my arms around her to keep her from rolling off. "So?"

"During my last semester, a visiting professor from another college came to talk to my class about her Library and Information Studies master's program. She said many of the students in their school had bachelor's degrees in history. She talked about all the kinds of jobs her graduates had besides city libraries. In colleges, doing research, with manufacturing companies, law enforcement, museums, I can't remember what all. It sounded interesting." She reached her hand over and patted Esther's head. "I want a cat."

"You want this one?" My fingers brushed the fuzzy lips.

"There are days."

Cara laughed. "I'm pretty sure you're stuck with her. Anyway, library studies sounded interesting, but I wasn't ready to start taking out loans. I'd made it through undergrad school with scholarships and financial aid grants and part-time jobs. I thought I'd better work for a while and save up some money before graduate school. Oh, who plays chess here?"

Cara rose from beside me and walked to the card table along the opposite wall. "It's adapted tactually so you can play. So great."

Scooting kitty onto the couch, I rose to walk to the chess table. "Yes. When I was in high school, I joined the chess club. The other kids and the sponsor made me a chess set with sandpaper on every other square, and by wrapping yarn around the white pieces. Then…" Surprised at the lump that rose to my throat, I pushed on. "Then my mom got me this professionally made one for high school graduation."

"Iola?" Cara rested her hand on my arm. "Are you okay?"

"Yo-la." Breathing through my nose, I stepped back. "Not I-ola, or E-ola. It's Yo-la. Like yoyo."

"I'm sorry. I guess I've never heard anybody say your name. I just saw you on the church's website as the person to call about helping out with the Hope Group."

"No problem." I hurried back to the couch, lifting Esther up and setting her back on my lap as I sat down. "I always explain it to people as yo, like yoyo. So, of course, my husband has always called me Yoyo. I've never let anybody else do that though. Tell me what kind of job you ended up with." No way did I want to talk more about why I'd choked up.

Cara followed my lead and came back to the couch. "The library in the town where I'd grown up. Truthfully, the library where I'd grown up hired me, and I went home." Her sigh was deep. "I moved back in with my parents and worked with the lady who'd checked books out to me since I was six years old. I stayed at that job ten years."

The front door banged open. "Mommy, Mommy, Maaaameeee."

Evan raced across the room, shoved Esther off my lap, and jumped into my arms. "Did you miss me?"

Laughing, I squeezed him tight and kissed his head. "I did. I missed you so much. Do you see we have a guest?"

Evan squirmed to face Cara. "I know you. I've seen you at church. What's your name? I'm Evan. I'm in kindergarten."

"Kindergarten. That's great. I'm Cara, and I think I've seen you at church too. Do you like school?"

"It's okay. I get to take my lunch and have a snack, and we get to work on computers there. Oh, Mommy, let me tell you what I have in my backpack." He jumped off my lap and unzipped his bag.

Cara stood. "It looks like you're about to be really busy. I'll email you my references, and you can let me know what to do about a background check."

"Yes, but we have to finish our conversation. About your life history. And, do you play chess?"

"I do." She stepped toward the front door.

"Let's get together and play." My lips quirked. "I'll even show you I can serve coffee without spilling it on you."

She opened the door. "I'd like that. I'll show you I can have a grownup conversation without crying."

"You can cry if you need to."

Once she was gone, my smile grew huge. *Lord, is this lady going to be my friend?*

## CHAPTER 3

"*D*addy's home." Evan raced down the stairs and to the front door, flinging it open. "Daddy, Daddy, Daaadeee."

Huh? I thought Chris had a meeting tonight. Turning off the stove, I moved into the living room.

"Roar, roar, roar. Where's that little boy who lives here? I'm going to eat him up."

Evan squealed and giggled as his daddy scooped him up and made munching noises.

"Hey, beautiful." Chris leaned in to kiss me and bumped our upside-down son against me.

"Hey, yourself. Why are you home? Didn't you have some kind of committee meeting tonight? Finance committee or youth group helpers or something?"

"Told 'em to do it without me. I needed to see my woman." With a final growl, he dumped a still-laughing Evan on the floor and followed me into the kitchen. "You make enough supper for me?"

"I did. And we're just ready to eat. Evan sweetie, wash your hands."

Chris stopped me as I went to lift the pot from the stove. "Come here a second." He turned me against him and hugged me close. "I'm sorry. I didn't remember what day it was until this afternoon."

September 14. Anniversary of the day my mother died. Alone. In hospice.

∼

WHEN IT WAS time for bed, I opened Evan's door and stuck my head inside. "Evan? Where are you?"

Silence.

"I'm going to find you, you know."

Silence.

Stepping inside, I dropped to my knees. "Hmm. Where could that rascal be?"

A smothered giggle.

"I heard that." I crawled around the room to check for him.

"Of course, you're not in your bed yet, but I'd better make sure."

Pulling back the sheet, I crawled onto the bed to search the whole thing.

"You're not here, but this sure is a comfy bed." I stretched out and laid my head on the pillow. "Oh, this is sooooo nice."

When I made loud, snuffly snores, the giggle grew louder.

"Huh? What was that?" I gave a raucous snort. "Oh yeah, I need to find Evan."

Rolling to the floor, I crawled around some more. "Are you in the toy box? No. Oh wait, I should look under the bed. Ouch, I bumped my head on the frame."

More laughter.

"Maybe in one of the dresser drawers. No. Behind this chair? Sitting on the window? No."

I banged my hands and feet on the floor. "This is not fun anymore. Young man, where are you?"

"I'm scared." A wobbly voice from the closet. "Who are you?"

"Who am I?" As I banged my hands and feet louder, I crawled to the closet door.

"No, no, no. You're scaring me." A long peal of giggles.

"Who am I?" I flung open the door and wrapped him in my arms. "I'm. Your. Mother."

We rolled together across the floor, Evan squealing and me growling. "I'm your mother. I'm your mother. I'm. Your. Mother."

I planted kisses all over his face and prayed he wouldn't tire of this game for a long time.

After teeth were brushed and pajamas on, I knelt beside Evan's bed and we prayed together.

"Sweetie?" I cradled his head in my hands.

"Yes?"

"You're not getting tired of all my mushiness yet, are you? All the kisses and me telling you…you're the joy of my life?"

"Nope. You can still do that for now."

## CHAPTER 4

Chris found me lying on my back in our bed not many minutes later. He stretched out beside me. "This is kind of early for you to go to bed." He clasped my hand in his.

Turning my head to rest on his shoulder, I squeezed his hand. "Thanks for coming home tonight." I blinked my eyes to push at the tears burning behind them. "So silly. It's been such a long time."

He laid his hand on my cheek. "Oh, Yoyo, you're the counselor. Don't you think this is something a person would have to carry their whole lifetime?"

I gulped. "Guess so. Just hold me a minute."

We lay there, quiet, as I allowed the tears to release and roll down my cheeks.

After a while, I pushed myself up to sit against the headboard. "Chris." My throat stuck. Swallowing, I drew in a long breath. "I'm scared."

He pushed up beside me. "Tell me." He took my hand again.

"The older the kids get, especially as Sonya gets closer to the age I was—"

"Iola, no."

I shook my head. "No, listen to me. I mean it. She seems to be growing farther and farther away from me. I know she's not happy. I worry I can't be the mother she needs, like, that I'll fail her like…"

"Stop now." He grasped both my hands. "Sonya is sixteen. Of course, she's unhappy. Of course, she's drawing away from her parents. She's sixteen."

"But—"

He placed his hand over my mouth. "And you are not your mother. You are going to be here for Sony. Besides." He drew me close and laid his cheek against mine. "Don't let go of the good you had with your mother. I wish I'd known her. She and I have a lot in common."

I could hear the smile in his voice. "How do you figure that?"

"We both were, and are, so crazy about you."

∼

"Mom, I'm home. I'm sorry I'm late."

"What? Sony? Where am I?" I rubbed my palms against my eyes, trying to come out of sleep.

"Mom, you're on the couch." A trace of irritation entered Sonya's voice. "I'm sorry. We fell asleep and…"

"You what?" I was wide awake now.

"Please, Mother." Normal, full-blown annoyance now. "Cliff and I were studying on his couch, and we fell asleep. No big deal."

Right. My teeth grinding, I managed to count to ten before speaking again. "Look, Sony, the deal is you're home by ten. What time is it anyway?" I checked my braille watch. Almost midnight. "Sonya."

She must've counted to ten as well. A big sigh. "Okay. I know. I messed up. Again."

I bit my lip not to smirk. "It's best if you don't patronize me right now, honey."

She was silent.

"Go to bed. We'll talk tomorrow. You've got school. Get some sleep." I hesitated then pressed on. "I think you can stay at home this weekend to study. You told me you've got a lot to work on."

"Mom. It helps if I study with—"

"Go on to bed, honey."

She slapped her hands against her legs, sighed again, and dragged her feet up the stairs.

*Oh, God, help me help this child.*

## CHAPTER 5

"Ev, where is your silly sister?" After worship on Sunday, I collected Evan from children's church and stood by the door to the parking lot, bouncing my white cane with oh-so-much patience, waiting for Sonya.

"She's busy talking to all the other silly sixteen-year-olds." Evan giggled and wrapped his arms around my middle.

"Grrrr." I hugged him.

"Iola, hey. Hi, Evan."

I jerked my head toward the voice. Who?

"It's Cara."

"Oh, hey." It was noisy, and I'd only met her once, but I wished I'd recognized her voice. "How are you?"

"Good. You guys waiting for a ride?"

"Yeah. Daddy has to stay and talk to people because he's one of the preachers." Evan's elbows bumped against me as he spun in a circle.

"I could give you guys a ride home. I don't live far from you."

"No, thanks. Evan's big sister Sonya is taking us." I forced a smile. "I waited sixteen years for her to be able to drive so she could take me places. Now I'll wait the rest of my life until she's ready to go."

"I'm here, Mom." Sonya bumped me with her elbow. "You don't have to talk bad about me to people I haven't even met yet." She sighed. "And I only get to drive the car when my mother and brother need a chauffeur."

Wrapping an arm around her shoulders, I gave her a squeeze. "Sony, this is Cara. She's going to be helping out with the Hope Group. Cara, this is my daughter Sonya." I smiled at Sonya. "Now you guys know each other, so I can talk bad about you."

"Good to meet you, Sonya."

"You too. My mother is so funny. Let's go, you guys."

"Real quick." Cara moved a step closer. "I was wondering, Iola, if you'd help me with something."

"Sure. What?"

Sonya huffed. "Now who has to wait?"

"It won't take long." Cara laughed. "After visiting you the other day, I've decided to get a cat. Tomorrow I've got a few hours free between shifts again, and I wondered if you'd go with me to choose one at the shelter."

"Oh, that would be fun. What time?" With one hand, I grasped Sonya's elbow, and with the other, I attempted to stop Evan's spinning.

"I could pick you up about eleven thirty. Maybe we could have lunch at my place after we get the kitty."

"Sounds perfect. I just have to be home by three thirty to welcome Evan off the bus."

"Yeah, so I can tell you all about school." He ducked behind me to slap his sister on the back. "You too. I want you to listen to me talk about school too."

"What a joy." Sonya's voice ached with boredom. "Can we go now?"

"Yes. Cara, eleven thirty sounds great. See you tomorrow."

"Sonya. Come downstairs and have some lunch with us," I called as I set a plate in front of Evan.

"I'm not hungry. I've got to finish my homework."

Except for church, she hadn't been allowed out of the house this weekend. And yet, her homework wasn't done?

"Ev, let's pray." As I leaned over my little boy at the table, I took in a deep breath to keep from screaming at my daughter. "You can eat while I go talk to Sony."

"Okay. Thank You, Jesus, for this food, and please help Mommy not to beat up Sonya." He giggled.

Little rat. I blew a raspberry on his head and hurried up the stairs.

Our kids' bedrooms had no locks, but the door wouldn't open. "Sonya, what on earth? What do you have in front of this door?" I pounded. "Sonya."

Furniture dragged across the floor on the other side, and the door opened. "I want a lock for my room."

I shoved past her and barely stopped my hand from slamming the door. "What are you doing in here?"

"Trying to have a little privacy. As if that's possible in this house."

She piled furniture against the door? Standing with my back against the wall, I dug my nails into my palms. "Why isn't your homework finished?"

"Because I put it off until the last minute. Like usual, right, Mom? I am such a useless, lazy daughter."

*Dear Lord God.*

We always told the kids to count to ten before speaking when they were mad. I counted to thirty.

## CHAPTER 6

"Come on in, Cara. The door's not locked. Esther, seriously, get off my head." As I wrestled the large purring animal down from my shoulders, the front door closed, and footsteps approached me.

"How do you know I'm not a thief? Oh, look." Cara stopped right in front of me. "Are you crocheting?"

"Yes. I'm making an afghan. And I'm foolish enough to do it with the cat hanging around to fight with me over the yarn."

Trying to keep the yarn from unraveling as Esther pawed at it, I stuffed the afghan into a bag and zipped it closed. "The battle really starts when it gets too big for me to close the bag tight. Scoot, cat."

"All right. I'm trying to remember you're just like anyone else. Not act like I'm super impressed when you can do things I've never been able to do. Because I figure you don't want me to do that."

"You figure right."

"But, not only do you have two kids, and you play chess, but you crochet too? What's next?"

"Have you ever driven a motorcycle?" I grabbed my keys and cane.

"I wanna know how to crochet. Wait, what? Don't tell me you've driven a motorcycle blind."

"Yep. Ready to go meet your cat?"

"Yeah. And you can tell me about driving a motorcycle, and I'll tell you about my ex-fiancé calling me out of nowhere last night."

"This does sound like a fun day. Bye, Esther. You're in charge."

∼

"I love this place." How could I not smile? A cacophony of barks and meows greeted Cara and me as we walked inside the animal shelter.

"They do seem awfully welcoming." Cara stopped us in the middle of the noisy room. "Oooohh, I can't take all you guys."

"Can I help you ladies?" A harried-sounding man stood in front of us.

"Yes. I'm not sure where to start." Cara gave a little laugh. "I want to adopt a cat."

"Kitten or adult cat?" He tapped his pencil against what sounded like a clipboard, rustled papers. "The adoption charge goes down once the cats are past six months."

"Oh, well, I don't know."

"The adult kitties are great." I squeezed Cara's arm to encourage her. "We got our delightful girl here when she was just over a year old."

"Really? Okay. I'll be happy to look at adult cats."

"This way."

We jogged to keep up with him as he circled the room.

"All along this wall are the adults. There's only one in each cage, so you can open them to hold the cats if you like." He rattled one of the doors. "Just don't let go of them." And, he was gone.

"There are so many." Cara stood still. "I think I'm a little overwhelmed."

"Hey, they're just cats. You like cats, remember?" I jiggled her elbow. "Take one out. Let's find the one who loves you."

We introduced ourselves to twenty animals, but Cara came back to Teddy. "They have the name Teddy on his cage." She no longer sounded nervous. She was in love. "And I know why. He's a teddy bear. Here. Hold him again."

For the fifth time, I took the soft, affectionate kitty in my arms. "He definitely is a lover," I said, letting Teddy rub my face with his. "I approve. Let's see if we can find that busy man and finalize your adoption."

∽

"I RECOGNIZE THIS STREET." Leaning my head out the window of Cara's car, I inhaled a long sniff. "Is that Russell's Bakery? I know that fresh coffee and cinnamon roll mixture."

"It's three doors down from my apartment building." Cara stopped the car and reached for Teddy's box on my lap. "I told you I live close to you."

"You did tell me that. Let's walk back to the bakery, and I'll buy us cinnamon rolls to go with lunch." Climbing from the car, I moved toward my favorite smell in the whole city. "The kids and I walk here a lot. Once I know how to get to your place from the bakery, I'll drop in on you unexpectedly all the time."

"I'd like that." Her voice was shy, hopeful.

*Thank You, Jesus. This girl and I are going to be friends.*

## CHAPTER 7

"I'm going to show him the litter box in the bathroom first." Cara walked ahead of me into her apartment. "They said I should enclose him in a smaller area before giving him the run of the house, but this is a studio. I can really only shut him up in the bathroom."

I followed her voice, bumping into a few pieces of furniture and hoping she didn't have breakables in my path. "We could sit with him in the bathroom for a while, talk to him, soothe him into his new home."

"Okay, come in. It's tiny." After she closed the door behind me, she set the cat's carrier on the floor. "You can have a seat on the toilet. Nowhere else to sit. I only have a shower, not a tub. Oh hey, Teddy. Don't be scared." Cara knelt on the floor to open the box and crooned at the yowling animal. "It's okay. Come on, let me take you out."

Easing myself to the floor beside her, I reached to pat the quivering feline. "You're going to be okay, little guy. This is home now."

Cara shook beside me.

"What's wrong?" I touched her shoulder. She was... "Are you laughing or crying?"

She gave a big snuff. "I can't believe..." She choked. "I barely know you, and I've got you squashed with me, pressed against my toilet in my cramped bathroom that I haven't cleaned since..." She was absolutely laughing. "I think I've gained a sister."

As we scrunched together giggling, Teddy squirmed away and ran into the shower.

"Poor little guy." Cara drew in a long breath. "He wants to get as far from us as possible." She reached to twist the doorknob. "Let's crawl out of here as quick as we can and try to keep him in here."

~

FOLLOWING CARA TO A BREAKFAST COUNTER, I checked the stool to make sure it was clear, then hopped on. "I don't know about you, but those cinnamon rolls are calling my name. Do we have to eat anything else for lunch?"

Cara laughed as she set a bottle of water in front of me. "I have oranges and chicken salad for sandwiches, but it's okay by me to start with dessert then see if we still want anything else."

"We are truly sisters." I patted the stool beside me. "Now, what about this ex-fiancé?"

"Ooohh." Cara groaned as she passed me a roll. "Wouldn't you rather tell me about driving a motorcycle?"

My breath caught. *Jesus, I think Cara is someone I can trust with this.*

But not today.

Letting out a slow breath, I picked up my roll. "Soon. Maybe when you come over for crocheting lessons. We'll have more time."

"I get crocheting lessons? Sweet. Okay then." She hesitated.

"When he decided to break the engagement, I decided to go to graduate school. It's been more than two years." She took a drink of water. "He called last night and said he wanted to talk."

Be careful, Yoyo. We're just feeling out getting closer. "And, did you? Talk?"

"I said to give me a few days. So I could prepare myself."

We were quiet for a couple minutes, chewing gooey yumminess.

She handed me a napkin. "We knew each other in high school. At least, I knew him. He didn't notice me. He was the star basketball player, surrounded by all the popular girls."

I harrumphed through my bite of roll, and she laughed.

"Yeah. I confess, I was pretty star-struck back then. And very envious." She took a breath. "Then I went to college. He tried that, too, on a basketball scholarship for a couple years. But it didn't work for him. When I moved back, he was working with his dad in their grocery store."

"And when you stopped at the store to pick up a loaf of bread, he suddenly realized how beautiful you'd always been."

She choked, then coughed. "Something like that. Right." She took another drink. "Anyway, we went to the same church. We always had but…"

"I know. I know. Now he actually saw you there."

She laughed a little. "Okay, I'll stop with the self-pity. Anyway, we both joined the singles group, and hung out with that bunch of people for a year or so before he ever asked me on a date.

"And we dated for a few years before we started talking, oh so carefully, about maybe getting married someday. He never actually proposed. We'd driven to the city one day and were walking around the mall, and he stopped in front of a jewelry store."

She slipped off the stool and walked to the refrigerator. "Do you want a sandwich?"

"Half a sandwich. Please."

"I'd never seen this super jock nervous." She opened a drawer, rattled silverware. "I promise you, he broke out in a sweat. He asked if I'd like to look at rings and poof. No drama about it. We were now engaged."

She set a plate in front of me, and we ate in silence for a time.

*What's safe to ask, Lord?*

"And then there were a few more years?"

"You got it. No definite plans about a date. A lot of random talk about a house, and a yard. A dog. Talk about nervous? You should have seen him when I mentioned kids." She hesitated then drew in a breath. "He couldn't have been gentler to me when he said we'd better call it off. He didn't know if he was really the marrying type."

She's definitely crying now.

Wiping my hands, I reached over and found hers then clasped them. "I'm sorry."

"Me too."

The refrigerator turned off. A door closed down the hall.

"Do you still love him?"

"Yeah." She cleared her throat. "Yeah."

## CHAPTER 8

Cara made the bumpy turn into our driveway. "There's a paper or something stuck inside your screen door handle."

"Probably something political." Before stepping out of the car, I turned toward Cara. "Have fun with your kitty. He's a sweetie."

"I will." Her voice held a smile again.

"No, it's not political." The rolled-up sheet of paper I found at the door had one line of braille. "Studying at Cliff's house. Sonya."

Forcing myself to smile, I turned back to wave good-by to Cara then slammed into the house. "Growl, growl, growl." I yanked my phone out of my pocket and slammed my finger on the button. "Call Chris."

"Hey, Babe. Did Cara find just the right cat?"

"You have to talk to your daughter." Whoa, Yoyo, don't scream at him. He's not the one you're mad at.

The phone was quiet.

With a sigh I flopped onto the couch. On top of Esther.

"Yooww."

Jumping up, I growled again. "Crazy cat." I sucked in a breath. "I'm sorry, honey. I know I shouldn't take this out on you."

"Mmm hmm."

"Chris, if you don't say something to me besides that calm, patient…"

"Okay, okay." His desk chair gave a loud screech. "Tell me what Sonya did now."

The front door banged open. "Mommy, mommy, guess what we're doing at school tomorrow." Evan crashed against me.

With a long inhale, I hugged my son. "We'll talk later. Our other little darling is home."

∽

AFTER EVAN WAS ASLEEP, I shut myself up in our bedroom.

*Lord, I don't want to see Sonya when she gets home. I don't want to yell at her. I'm sorry. Why am I so mad at her?*

When Chris came to bed, I sat propped against pillows with a book on my lap.

"Okay, I'm not a good braille reader, but I can see from here you've got that book upside down."

Sticking out my tongue at him, I closed the book and set it on the floor. "So what time did she get home?"

"A couple minutes after nine, declaring loudly that she was home plenty early for a stupid school night curfew, okay?"

With my hands covering my face I gave a long groan.

Chris sat on the bed and pulled my hands to wrap them in his. "Honey, come on."

"Chris?"

He pulled me against his chest. "We had a long talk." He rubbed my hair. "She understands that she is not to pile furniture against her door to keep you out of her room. She will speak to you in person or on the phone when she's not going to be home, not from a car window or with a note stuck in the front door."

I pulled myself up and faced him. "Are you laughing at me?" My voice squeaked, way too loud.

"Shh." He put his fingers on my lips. "No. Maybe a little."

I groaned again.

"Sweetheart, it's normal for a mother and daughter to wrangle when the daughter's a teenager. It doesn't mean anything is seriously wrong with either one. You know that."

"Yeah." Turning away from him, I pounded my pillow into place and flopped down. "I know."

We didn't speak for a few minutes. Chris rustled some papers, and I picked up my book.

"Huh. What do you think of that?"

I rolled toward him. "What?"

"I've got a letter from Stone Valley Church. Pastor Bryan is retiring, and they want to know if I'd like to come back."

I blinked. "Well, huh."

## CHAPTER 9

"Okay, Esther. That's it." Scooping up the cat from where she'd tangled herself in Cara's yarn, I carried her to the bathroom and closed the door.

Cara giggled. "She and I were having fun. I'll have to try crocheting with Teddy."

"Huh. Let's make sure you are confident about how to make a slip knot first."

"Right. I'll try again." Her shopping bag of yarn rattled. "I had fun with the kids last night." She hesitated. "So, Hope Group is not just a women's group, but it's for counseling?"

"Yes. It's open to anyone who might want that kind of support, whether they're already in therapy or not. People share and help each other. And it's safe. Members sign an agreement not to discuss anything outside the group."

"Okay." She handed me her yarn. "Is this right?"

I felt her work. "Perfect." I grinned. "Now you get a crochet hook."

She huffed. "I feel like a preschooler."

"Yes, good girl."

"I want you to know I'm sticking my tongue out at you."

"Bad girl. Now, just calm down and pay attention as I show you how to make a chain stitch."

Cara practiced for a few minutes. "You're a counselor for the church, aren't you?"

"Part-time." I reached over to check her stitches. "Oh, way too loose. Rip it out. Let's start over. Rrrip it out."

"Okay, Yoyo. You're having way too much fun."

"Didn't I tell you this would be fun? Now, watch me."

"You're a professional counselor? I mean, with a license and everything?"

Twitching my lips, I handed the yarn back to her. "Finally. After a lot of years and after the second baby. Try not to pull so much yarn between stitches."

"Right. Like I have any idea what that means."

I patted her knee. "Don't worry, my child. You'll get it with practice."

"Hmph."

"I'm serious. Work hard, and I'll even buy you your own cloth crocheting bag."

"Aww, so sweet."

*Father, this is becoming an important friendship.*

"Like many counselors, I think, I chose the job because a counselor helped me." I hesitated then went on. "I've needed that help several times over the years."

Cara squeezed my arm. "Thanks for trusting me with that." Her crochet hook clanged on the floor, and I giggled. She leaned to pick it up. "I'm not going to give up on this. Laugh at me all you want."

"Sorry." I smothered a laugh.

"Right." She elbowed me. "Did you wait to go back to school until after the kids were born?"

"Huh, no way would Chris ever let me do that." I checked her work again. "That looks better. Good job.

"When Chris graduated, he was offered a ministry in a small-town church." I shifted on the couch. "I still had two years of school left, but I didn't want to wait to get married. Chris said okay, but he insisted I continue school immediately, with distance ed. A few times he drove me to night classes several hours away from where we lived. Hey, listen." I snorted. "That's Esther banging against the bathroom door."

"Aw, poor kitty. Let her out."

Scrunching my face at her, I went on. "One class at a time, it took me years to finish. And I had to wait till we moved here to be able to do an internship at a hospital. My degree is in social work."

The front door opened.

"Okay, Mom. Here I am, reporting in to my parole officer. Oh, hey, Cara." Sonya's voice lost some of the sarcasm for the last sentence.

"Good to see you. Your mom is teaching me to crochet."

"Nice. She wants to teach me, but I'm not sure we could keep from chewing off each other's heads long enough for me to learn."

Don't react, Yoyo. "How was school?"

"Glorious, as always. Have fun crocheting, Cara. I'm going up to my room now, Mother, to work obediently on my homework."

Count to ten. "Good. Please finish it before you call Cliff."

No reply. Her bedroom door snapped closed, but gentler than usual.

"If you weren't here, that would have been a slam."

"Aww." Cara laid her hand on mine. "You're a good mother."

I closed my eyes. *Please, God.*

∽

"Mama, Mama." Evan squeezed me in a hug then circled around me. "Here comes Sonya. And Cara-ie." He giggled after the last word.

How does he always keep so happy?

Among the other voices leaving the worship service, I heard them then, Cara and Sonya laughing together as they neared Evan and me waiting by the side door.

"Hey, Iola, Evan." Cara gave me a quick hug. "Do you guys need a ride home?"

"Mom?" Sonya stood in front of me.

I thought of asking if she wanted a favor, since her voice wasn't rude. Like usual. But, remembering Cara saying I was a good mother, I resisted. "Yes."

"Since Cara can give you guys a ride home, I'd like to go to Cliff's house. He invited me for lunch and studying."

"You already brought your schoolwork?"

"I brought my computer. He's got paper. That's all we'll need."

"Right. Who uses textbooks anymore?" I shrugged. "Okay. Call me if you're staying later than six."

When we reached home, Evan hopped out of Cara's car and dashed to the front door.

"Ma-ma, hurry. I gotta go-o-oo."

Oh, Iola, you are slipping. Why didn't you ask if he needed to go before you left church? Hurrying after him to the front porch, I called over my shoulder to Cara. "Thank you so much. Do you want to stay? Have lunch with Ev and me?"

Cara closed her car door and walked up beside us. "I would but, mmm, I've kinda got something planned."

"Mom-mee!"

Unlocking the door, I patted Evan's back and gave him a little push. "Go, go, go. Hurry." I turned back to Cara. "Yeah? That sounds interesting."

"Alan's going to call."

"Alan? Oh, is that the ex-fiancé?"

"Yes. He said he wanted to talk. He wanted, he wanted to come here, but I said we should start with a phone call." Cara was always shy, but just then, an extra bit of uncertainty tinged her voice.

With both arms around her shoulders, I squeezed. "Go, go, go. Hurry."

"You're a goof, Yoyo." She was smiling now.

## CHAPTER 10

"See you next time." Waving goodbye to Lucy, my favorite Uber driver, I hurried through the rain to the front door and inside. "Hey, Esther. I'm home. What's for supper tonight?"

Thoughts ran through my mind of the lady I'd counseled this morning, what we had in the freezer, and whether or not Evan had worn a jacket today. I was almost to the kitchen before I was stopped by the sound.

"What? Who?"

From upstairs, it sounded like? Muffled crying?

"Evan?" He couldn't be home. "Sonya?" She better not be home.

I hurried up the stairs but stopped before I opened her door.

Yes. She was trying to bury the sound, but she was sobbing.

"Sony?" With a gentle push, I opened her door and moved to kneel by her bed. "Honey. What is it? Are you sick?"

She lay on her stomach with her pillow over her head. Under my hands, her shoulders clenched, and the sobs grew louder.

"Oh, baby." My heart squeezed for this child who was such a struggle for me. Lying beside her, I pressed her close to me.

"Sony, sweetheart. Shh. Don't cry so hard. You're going to make yourself sick."

She turned to face me, and her wet cheek touched mine. "Mom, Mom, I can't. Mom, please."

*Dear Jesus, what can I do for this child?*

With her head cradled against my shoulder, I stroked my hand up and down her back. "Take a breath. Easy. Easy."

Once she quieted, she pulled away from me. "Please don't make me go back to that school. I can't stand it."

"Sure, Sony, you don't have to go back today. Did you check out at the office? Why didn't they call me?"

"No." She sat up on the bed. "I didn't check out. And I don't mean just today. I don't want to ever go back to that school."

∼

"WHAT DID YOU TELL HER?" Chris asked as we loaded the dishwasher after dinner.

"What do you think? My usual pep talk. Of course, she had to go back to school. She had to hold up her head and face her problems. Rah rah rah." I handed him some silverware. "I am such a dunce. I didn't even ask her what happened, why she was so upset. What kind of mother…" I inhaled a long breath. "Let's start over. What did the school counselor say?"

Chris closed the dishwasher. "Let's sit down. Are both kids in their rooms?"

"Evan fell asleep as soon as the kitty snuggled in beside him. Sonya's been in her room ever since she got home this morning. She wouldn't say one more word…"

"Okay. Okay." He wrapped an arm around my shoulders and walked me to the couch. "The counselor said Sony ran out of her geometry exam crying. When she tried to come back quietly a few minutes later, six girls in the class met her with sniffs and boo-hoos, then giggles."

I jumped from the couch. "What? Did they get—"

He pulled me back down. "They were all sent to the principal's office and given several hours of detention. But Sony ran away from school without checking out."

"She'll probably get in more trouble than they did." My fists clenched. "What did Sony tell you?"

Chris smoothed out my hands and held them in his. "She said she studied for the test. Hard. But she just didn't understand it." He sighed. "She looked at the test paper, and none of it made sense to her."

"Why hasn't she talked to her teacher if she doesn't understand what's going on? Why didn't she—"

"Honey." He rested a hand against my cheek. "The counselor said it's not just geometry. Sony is failing all of her classes."

"Chris?"

"We're going to have to go with her to meet with all her teachers. Probably get some tutoring. But let's not talk to her anymore about it tonight."

"No." Rubbing my face with my hands, I sucked back tears. "No. Tonight, I need to try to break a chunk out of the wall between us."

~

"Sonya, I've got laundry." I knocked on her door. "Honey?"

The door opened, and Sonya grabbed the basket from my hands. "Thanks."

Before she could close the door again, I pushed inside. "I have a question."

She didn't respond.

"Nothing to do with school." I swallowed. "It's your clothes. I noticed some rips. And some stuff has shrunk."

She slapped her leg. "Mom, please. What do you think—"

"No, listen." How I hated the fact I couldn't help her shop for clothes. Maybe I could offer something better. "How would you like to go shopping with Cara? I bet she'd go, and she's younger than me you know. She'd probably be a lot of fun."

"Cara?"

*Oh, Jesus, is that a touch of hope I hear in her voice?*

Sonya didn't have girlfriends to go shopping with either. But Cara?

"Okay. But let me ask her myself." She tried to sound bored, but yes, there was hope in her voice.

## CHAPTER 11

"Mom. You can't move your pawn two spaces again." Evan was frustrated with me.

"Sorry, sweetie." I scooted my chess piece back in its proper place. "Your turn."

*Jesus, help Cara and Sonya to have a good shopping trip. Let them be friends. Lord, Sony needs a friend.*

"You're in checkmate, Mommy."

"What? No."

Evan gave a big sigh and slid down from his chair. "You're not paying any attention to the game."

"Sure I am." He was right. My five-year-old beat me again. "You're just getting too good for me."

Reaching out to grab him before he slipped away, I pulled him onto my lap. "I'm sorry, buddy. I am paying attention. I want to play with you. Here, watch." Lifting his shirt, I blew a raspberry on his stomach.

"Stop, stop." He screeched and wriggled. "Okay. Okay. Let's play something else. It's no fun beating you at chess so fast."

"I'll bet." I let him drop to the floor. "What should we play?"

"Let's play cat and mouse. I'm the mouse. You can't catch me."

This led to ten minutes of us crawling around the house. Through the living room and kitchen, up the stairs and down again, him jerking out of my hands any time I caught hold of his foot, and off again.

"You'll never catch meeeee. No, no, noooo."

Both arms around him, I pinned him to the floor, crouched over him, and covered his face with sloppy kisses.

"Mom-meee, stop. Yuck, stop."

He wrapped his arms around his head, so I switched to tickling him.

The cat jumped on my back. "Whoa. Esther, no."

"Yay, my good friend Esther." Evan wriggled away from me, jumped up, and plucked the traitor off me. "You're the mouse, Mommy, not me. The cat got you." His giggles muffled as he buried his face in the kitty's fur.

The front door opened, followed by Cara's and Sonya's laughter.

"Sony, your turn now." Evan's voice sang with glee. "Esther and I just beat Mommy in the cat and mouse game."

"No way, buddy. That is not my game tonight." Rattling shopping bags, Sonya jogged up the stairs. "Bye, Cara. Thanks so much."

"Wait. Wait." Cara moved to the bottom of the stairs. "Let's show your stuff to your mom."

"Not now. I'll show her later." Sonya's voice was already all the way down the hall. "You guys can visit." Her room door closed.

"Cara, visit me." Evan dumped the cat back on me and ran to Cara. "Visit me now."

She grunted as he slammed his body against her. "Uh, sure."

"Ev, slow down." Dragging myself to my feet, I hurried to

unwrap my son from around my friend. "Let's not overwhelm Cara."

I plastered another kiss on his face. "Go pick up the chess pieces, would you?" I turned to Cara. "Want some coffee?"

"Sure. That'd be nice. Evan, would you play chess with me next time I come?"

"Okay. Can you play better than my mom? I need a challenge."

I tweaked his chin. "I'm sure she does, buddy. Thanks a lot."

Cara and I walked into the kitchen. "You're being awfully nice to my kids today."

"I had a fun time with Sonya, and I don't want Evan to feel left out." She pulled a chair from the table. "Honestly, I'd love to play chess with him."

I poured the coffee and set the cups on the table. "He's actually a great chess player. Chris has been teaching him the game since he was a toddler."

"That's amazing."

Flopping into a chair, I wrapped my hands around my mug. "He's amazing all right. Beating me at chess one minute, crawling around the house giggling the next."

"Iola?"

"Hmmm?"

"I really did have a nice time with Sonya. She's a fun girl. But…"

Uh-oh. "But?"

She sighed. "I don't want to come between you guys. I mean, I don't mind being her friend, but she asked if I'd go with her to get a haircut." She tapped her fingers on the table. "You're her mom. I don't want, I don't want to seem like I'm taking your place. Or like I don't think you can do these things because you're blind. Or, Oh." She huffed out another breath. "Am I making any sense?"

I laughed. "If I weren't afraid of knocking over your coffee,

I'd reach over and squeeze your hand. It does make sense. Thank you, Cara." I chewed my tongue. "What did you tell her? About going with her to the beauty salon."

"I wanted to say we should ask you. But that sounded like I was treating her like a kid. I said maybe the three of us could go together."

Coffee spewed from my mouth into my cup. "I bet that went over well."

"Not so much. She said never mind if I didn't want to go."

"Oh boy. I'm sorry."

"No. It's okay. I think I rescued her honor. I laughed and said no, no, I'd love to go with her. I said I needed a cut anyway. But, seriously, it wouldn't bother you?"

With my elbows on the table, I set my chin in my hands. "No. If I'm able to give her somebody fun to go with her to get her hair cut, I'll feel like I've done something good as a mom. I do feel bad that I can't help her much with clothes, and how her hair looks, and, Sony and me, we have an awkward relationship." I paused. "Look, I'm not trying to be a burden."

"Yoyo." Cara's chair scraped, and she circled the table to stand beside me. "Stop it now." She shook my shoulder. "I like Sonya. I want to help if I can." She clapped her hands together. "Let's both stop apologizing to each other." She sniffed. "What do you have cooking in the crockpot that smells so good? Did you want to invite me to dinner?"

I covered my face with my hands and laughed. "Yes, I do. I mean, if you're not tired of my family..."

Cara growled. "Iola?"

"Wait. That's not what I meant to say. Stop pulling my hair. Ow. Stop already."

## CHAPTER 12

"Chris, honey, where have you hidden yourself?"

Friday night. Evan was asleep, and Sonya had gone to Cliff's house to, hopefully, study. Chris was home, no meetings at church, and I looked forward to alone time with him.

"Chris?"

"In the office."

Picking up speed, I moved to the tiny room off the kitchen where we'd both crammed our desks. "What are you doing?"

"Looking at Sony's history essay." He scraped the chair from my desk closer to his. "Come sit by me."

Air puffed from my lips as I collapsed in the chair. "She won't send me any of her homework to look at. I've got a college degree, too, you know."

"Yes, ma'am." He rubbed my knee. "I tried to talk you into going through the graduation ceremony, remember? But you—"

"Yeah, yeah, yeah." I rested my head on his shoulder. "How does her essay look?"

"Mmm, okay. I've got a few suggestions."

"A few, huh?" I giggled. "Have you talked to them at the tutoring center about how she's doing with science and math?"

He scooted his chair around and pulled me onto his lap. "I have."

"That's a big sigh." I snuggled close to him. "That bad?"

"She's having a lot of trouble. You know that." He rubbed my arms. "I guess we haven't paid enough attention to her learning disability lately. It seemed like..."

"Honey, stop. Don't do that. We had good reason to believe she was getting along okay. Her teachers have been encouraging."

"Yeah, but..."

"It doesn't help to blame ourselves." My fingers trailed along the edge of his desk, finding an open envelope. "What's this?"

"It's that letter I got from Stone Valley." He paused. "I was going to reply to them. I'm not sure what to say."

"Honey?" I turned to face him. "What? Are, are things okay at work?"

He sighed and rubbed my face with his hand. "Things are good. I guess." He gave me a gentle push off his lap and stood up with me. "Let's go get a cup of coffee."

In the kitchen I started a new pot. "Sorry. I drank the last of what was already there." I pulled out his chair. "Sit. Talk to me."

He sat and bowed his head as I stood behind him, rubbing his shoulders.

"Baby, what is it?"

"I don't know." He kept his head bowed. "Nothing bad has happened at the church. I'm just not sure anymore. Is this big church really my dream?"

My hands rested against his shoulders, then I wrapped my arms around him. "Well, let's figure out your dream together. I'm beside you all the way."

He turned his chair and pulled me onto his lap again. "Do you remember after I graduated? When we first got married?"

A giggle erupted. "I remember many things about that time. To which are you referring?"

He laid his head against my shoulder. "I said I'd never expect you to be a traditional pastor's wife. I didn't want you to feel like you had to involve yourself with all the busyness of the church."

"Yeah?"

He lifted his head and laid his rough cheek against mine. "Maybe my understanding of my calling has changed. Do you think your calling might have changed?"

"My calling?" I bit my lip. "It, it could. If it needed to."

What is my calling anyway?

My hands held his cheeks. "What do you think about all this?"

He sat up, laid his arms on my shoulders, and rested his forehead against mine. "I was reminded of a Bible verse from Psalm 62. I wait quietly before God, for my victory comes from Him. I guess, I guess I need to take any changes slow."

## CHAPTER 13

"Let me take a look at your scarf." Settling next to Cara on the couch, I reached for the crocheting in her hands. "Has Teddy been helping you with it at home?"

She laughed. "He hasn't bothered me much, but Esther is headed this way. Here, you take my scarf, and I'll try to contain your cat."

"Good luck with that. Ooohh, nice. Your stitches are getting to be pretty even. And the length is almost good enough for a finished scarf. Do you have any certain, mmm, man in mind to gift with this?" I elbowed her.

"You're trouble, Yoyo. Esther, sit. Give me your paws. You do not get to play with that. What makes you think it's for a man?"

"Oh, I just thought—what on earth was that?"

Without realizing I'd left the couch, I was up the stairs and stopped outside Sonya's door. "Sony, what happened?"

It had sounded like a choked-off cry of pain, but no sound came from her room now.

I knocked. No answer. Pushing the door open, I stepped inside. "Sony."

"She's not in here, Iola." Only then did I notice Cara had followed me up and into the room.

I turned to her. "Did you, didn't you hear?"

"Yes." She rested a hand on my wrist. "Shh. Listen."

This time it was just a muffled groan. A whimper?

Banging my shoulder against the door, I rushed out of the room and down the hall to the bathroom. "Sony. Open the door." I rattled the doorknob.

Silence.

My heart pounded in my ears. "Sonya."

"No, Mom." Pause. "Cara can come in."

What?

"Just Cara. I mean it, or I won't open the door."

Sonya was sixteen, but tonight, she sounded about six. Crying, mad, ready to stomp her foot. Scared?

I let go of the doorknob. "Okay, honey."

The door opened an inch, and Cara pushed inside.

"Jesus?" My lips were cold.

Muffled voices sounded on the other side of the door.

"What's going on with my child? Lord, help her. Help me."

Moments later, the door opened, and Cara came out. She moved me away from the bathroom.

"Iola. Let's go sit down." She scooted us into my room to sit on the bed. "She's, she's okay. She's going to be okay."

Cara's normal way of speaking was calm. Now she sounded scared.

"What's wrong?" I pulled away from her.

She gulped. "She's cut herself. Not a dangerous cut, but I think she'll need a couple stitches. We need to take her to the emergency room."

"What?" My voice screeched, and I jumped up, heading for the door.

"No, wait." She stopped me at the door. "Wait please. I'm, I'm so not a parent, but you need to be careful with her." She puffed out a long breath. "Iola, she's, she's got a lot of scars. She's been cutting herself for a long time."

The front door closed, and Chris's steps mounted the stairs. "Honey?" Not too loud, so he wouldn't wake Evan. "Yoyo, where are you?"

The room spun round me, and I braced myself against the wall. "In here." I choked, cleared my throat. "Come here please."

## CHAPTER 14

"Okay. I got the largest coffee I could find." Cara wrapped my hands around the paper cup then sat next to me in the emergency room waiting area. "If you're sure that's what you should have."

My hands shook, but I raised the cup to my lips and sipped the hot liquid. "Why didn't Sony want me to stay in the room with her? She must be scared."

"She's so embarrassed." Cara handed me napkins. "Wrap these around the cup. It's really hot. Why did they say they were calling a psychiatrist? She didn't try to kill herself."

"It's standard procedure. With cases of self-harm." My teeth chattered, and I took another sip. "God, help me. This isn't a case. It's my daughter."

Cara laid a gentle hand on my arm and didn't say anything.

A baby cried somewhere in the waiting room. Someone moaned, and someone else coughed.

"Cara?"

"Yes."

"What kind of a mother am I?"

"Oh, Iola." She took the coffee cup from my hand then wrapped me in a hug.

Laying my head against her shoulder, I whimpered and gasped and snuffed tears.

"Shh, shh, shh." Cara rubbed my back. "Shhh."

After a pause, I pulled back. "Where's my coffee? Where's the napkin?"

"Here." She handed me the napkin. "Wipe your face. I'll give you the coffee if you promise not to squeeze it too hard and spill the whole cup." There was a smile in her voice.

I giggled then choked and sniffed and wiped my face. "You're a goofhead."

"That's better."

*Jesus, thank You for giving me this quiet, soothing lady to be with tonight.*

"I should call Chris."

"Umm, okay, but you just called him five minutes ago, and we don't know anything else yet."

My eyes squeezed, and I took a sip of coffee. "You're right." I shifted on the chair. "He should be here. He was being kind, to stay home with Evan and let me come, but Sonya would feel more comfortable with him here."

"Yoyo, you're her mom. She loves you."

My face trembled. "I've never felt like I could be a daughter's mother."

"Okay, that's it." Cara took the cup out of my hand and stood up. "Come on. Let's walk."

"But we have to wait to talk to the doctor."

She took hold of my arm. "Just out in the hall. I'll tell them at the desk where we'll be."

For several minutes we paced the length of the corridor in silence. In and out, I took long breaths. When I heard traffic outside a window, I stopped and leaned against the sill. "Cara? Thank you for being here with me."

She parked herself beside me. Someone passed by us pushing a rattling cart. Probably cleaning staff.

"I never did tell you about driving the motorcycle, did I?"

"No." She chuckled. "Now's a good time."

## CHAPTER 15

"*L*et's walk some more." Taking hold of Cara's arm, I started us pacing the hall outside the ER again. "My mom was an alcoholic."

As we passed an open door, a TV comedy show played. Must be another waiting room. "Did I tell you my dad died when I was a baby?"

"Yes." She turned us around to head down the hall the opposite way.

"He and I were in a car accident. He died, and I was barely hurt, except for a very focused brain injury, which destroyed my sight.

"Mom said I was her miracle baby. First, God finally gave me to them after she and Daddy had been trying for a child for years. Then, she lost Daddy, but God saved my life in that accident. He didn't leave her alone." I gulped. "They named me Iola, Welsh for 'valued by the Lord.'"

*Why must I still cry, Lord, when I tell this story?*

Cara pressed tissue into my hand. "I'm so sorry, Iola."

After swiping at my face with the tissue, I went on. "My mom was great, a single parent, raising me as a blind child. From preschool on, she made sure I received all the rehabilitation training available and that the school did everything they were supposed to do for me. She got me signed up for sports, clubs, whatever she could think of to keep me involved with other kids, to make friends.

"She took me to church." I shook my head. "She loved God, told me Jesus loved me, but she was so lonely. Without Dad, with no family nearby, no close friends. She worked full time and made sure I had everything I needed." I hesitated. "And she was so alone."

People passed us in the hall, talking in low voices.

"She drank by herself, after I went to bed. But I knew. And as I grew older, she knew I knew. She was so sorry, but…"

We stopped by a window again, and I turned my face outward, pressing my hands against the glass. "You didn't bring my cup of coffee with you by any chance, did you?"

Cara pressed the cooled cup into my hands. "What kind of a friend do you think I am?"

"You're the best." Coughing and laughing, I took a long drink.

"And oh, how Mom made sure I kept up with my studies. I was able to get scholarships and grants for college, so I didn't need loans." I took another drink. "Less than a month after I left for college, Mom died of cancer." I choked. "I hadn't known anything about her being sick."

Cara wrapped an arm around my shoulders, but she didn't try to stop me from going on.

"She left me a very sweet braille note." Outside the window, a loud ambulance siren stopped at the hospital. Drawing in a long breath, I turned to face Cara. "She said she'd found out a few months back that she had stage four liver cancer. She hadn't told me, because she wanted me to go on with my life. She decided not to have treatment. There was little hope it would help, and she didn't want to put me and herself through a prolonged, painful death. She died in a hospice facility."

Cara eased me to a bench just outside the ER waiting room. She wrapped her arms around me, and I rested my head on her shoulder and wept.

## CHAPTER 16

The door to the waiting room clicked open. "Mrs. Frazier?"

I straightened on the bench.

"Are you Sonya Frazier's mother?"

Scrubbing at my eyes, I stood and turned toward the man's voice. "I'm Iola Frazier. You're Dr., um, Randolph?" I held out my hand toward him.

"Dr. Randall, yes." He grasped my hand.

Cara stood beside me, bumped my shoulder.

Be a grown-up, Yoyo. "How's she doing, Doctor?"

"She's resting. We put in five stitches and gave her a tetanus shot." He moved to stand on my other side. "Dr. Chang, our on-call psychiatrist, will be in to see her in a moment. I'd like Sonya to stay overnight. You said Sonya's father wasn't able to come tonight? I'd like you both to meet with some of our staff in the morning, to discuss the therapy program we have for teens."

"What?"

Stay overnight? Therapy program?

Calm down, Iola. Take a breath.

"Can I see her?"

"Yes. I'll let you know when Dr. Chang has finished."

As his footsteps moved away, I searched for my phone. "I have to call Chris. Where's my phone? Cara? Are you here?" Why am I screeching?

"Iola." Cara wrapped an arm around my shoulders. "I'm right here. You left your phone on the bench." She nudged me around until my legs bumped the bench.

Plopping down, I squeezed my arms around my middle. "I'm sorry. I'm, oh, I feel…"

She sat down beside me. "Take a breath maybe?"

"Are you? You are laughing at me."

"No, I'm not." She had a rich bubbly laugh, and she couldn't hold it in. "Okay. I am a little. Sorry." She cleared her throat. "But I've never seen you like this. So, so out of control. Take a breath. Call Chris. Let's think about next steps."

∽

"By the time I got to see her, she was almost asleep." Collapsing onto the couch beside Chris, I hugged his hand with both of mine. "They'd given her something to calm her down. I couldn't talk to her."

Chris pulled me close and squeezed my shoulders. "We'll see her in the morning. We can talk to her then." He rubbed my back. "It's going to be okay."

"I don't know. Why would she do this? Cara said she has lots of little cuts. How long has this been going on? Why didn't we know?"

"Shh." He pressed my head against his shoulder. "I don't know, honey."

We were silent.

I pushed myself upright. "Is Evan okay? Did he wake up?"

"Nope. Sound asleep. Not a twitch."

Esther rubbed against my leg, and I reached to pick her up. "It must be nice to be five."

"Yeah."

The refrigerator turned on in the next room. A car drove by outside.

"We need to get some sleep." Chris bumped Esther off my lap and took hold of my hands. "Father God." His voice scraped. "We know You love Sony even more than we do. Teach us how to help her." He paused. "Lord, please help our little girl."

## CHAPTER 17

"Look at you, Cricket. You're already eating breakfast." As soon as we moved into Sonya's hospital room, Chris tried to make her laugh. "You don't have a roommate? Why? Did they figure out you snore?"

"Oh, Daddy." Her voice was full of tears, but she managed a laugh as Chris pulled her against him.

My throat filled. *Lord, why...*

I shook myself. *Lord, thank You they are so close.*

I moved around to the other side of the bed and sat on the edge. "Good morning, sweetie." Oh, what can I say? "I love you so."

Easing down next to her, I scooted close and pressed my face against hers. "I love you, baby."

Her voice croaked. "Mom, I'm sorry. I, I'm, oh..." She shook in my arms.

"Shh, shh. It's okay. Shh."

My body pulsed with tension as Chris and I paced the corridor outside Sony's hospital room. "Why is it taking so long? Why'd they make us leave?"

Chris laid his hand on my arm and pulled me to a stop. "They have to talk to her alone. You're a counselor. You know that."

*Lord, I wish I was Evan's age so I could scream and kick and have a real tantrum.*

"I don't want to be a counselor. I want to be a mom. What? You think they suspect us of abusing her?"

"If you were the therapist in the case, would you have to check out that possibility?"

"Oh, oh, oh." I spun away from him. "Don't mention me being a counselor again."

*Lord, I know exactly what kind of questions they're asking her. What have they noticed in me that could lead to them seeing me as an abusive parent? A neglectful mother?*

An elevator door jangled open. Announcements sounded over the loudspeaker.

"Mr. and Mrs. Frazier?" It was Sonya's psychiatrist's voice.

Chris gave me his elbow, and we walked to meet her.

"Doctor, tell us what's going on with our daughter." My voice rose toward hysteria.

Chris pressed my hand against his side. "Can we go in to see her now?" He sounded scared.

"Let's go into an office, where we can talk in private." Her feet clicked down the hall, and we followed her into a room. She closed the door. "Please have a seat."

As I sat, I clutched my arms against me. *Let Chris talk, Yoyo. Calm yourself a little.*

A desk chair squeaked. "I'm Dr. Chang. I just spoke with Sonya."

"Yes, we've met." I sucked in a long breath. *Why am I shivering?* "You were the on-call doctor last night."

"Yes, Mrs. Frazier, I remember speaking with you. You weren't able to come in last night, Mr. Frazier."

"I stayed at home with our five-year-old son."

Chris sounded defensive. Was she trying to find faults with our parenting?

"We're both here now, Dr. Chang. Please tell us what's going on with our daughter." My teeth chattered.

Chris closed his hand over mine. "Yes, Doctor, please."

"Physically, she'll be fine. As we told you, Mrs. Frazier, we stitched the wound and gave her a tetanus shot." Papers rattled. "Did either of you know your daughter was harming herself?"

"No." I scooted to stand up. "I told you last night—"

"Iola." Chris's hand on my shoulder pressed me to stay in the chair. "Sonya has had no marks of hurting herself that I've seen. She's sixteen, and so, of course, we don't help her bathe." He drew in a breath.

"I understand." Her chair squeaked again. "All of the scars are on her abdomen. She has…" She hesitated. "She has many scars. This has been going on for a long time."

## CHAPTER 18

As soon as the office door closed behind the doctor, I jumped up. "I can't stand this. She's treating us like it's our fault. And what did she mean about it going on for a long time? If I wasn't blind, I would have known?"

"Honey, sit down." Chris pulled on my hand. "We have to stay calm. Let's see what the social worker has to say."

The door opened and closed. "Hi, Mr. and Mrs. Frazier. I'm Kendy Marlin, the social worker in Sonya's case. Nice to meet you both."

Okay, she sounds like she's barely twenty and a little too chipper. What kind of a name is Kendy anyway? I kept my mouth shut.

"It's good to meet you, Ms. Marlin." Chris's hand pressed against my knee. "We want to know what we need to do for our daughter."

"Sure." She grasped my hand and shook it. "And please call me Kendy."

Breathe, Yoyo. Don't talk yet.

The chair across the desk squeaked and papers rattled. "So,

Dr. Chang recommends that Sonya stay in the hospital for a few days."

"Tell us about that." Chris wrapped my hand in his.

"Sure. I checked with your insurance company, and they will allow Sonya to stay in the hospital three nights. That means she could be in for three days of therapy."

"What kind of therapy?" Chris's voice quivered.

"She would meet with Dr. Chang, who is a psychiatrist, as well as Dr. Brozowski, one of the psychologists who work with the teens. Having her stay in the hospital for a while will help work the idea of security into her plan for the future. We know you will remove any sharp objects from where she can reach them at home, but we understand that's hard to do entirely."

Sharp objects? *Oh, dear God.* My stomach clenched.

"Okay." Chris drew in a long breath.

"Of course, here at the hospital, we can keep her from unsafe objects, while we teach her to want to protect herself." She paused. "Even from herself. It's important that she accept the notion of wanting to guard herself, to understand her value as a person."

*Jesus, didn't we teach her that?* My eyes pricked, and I clamped my jaw.

"We have a day program here for teens with different needs, which Sonya can continue to attend after she goes home. There are also meetings which you two can attend with her and ones for just the two of you, so we can work on methods the whole family can use to help Sonya." Her chair scooted. "I know you want to help her. I know you're scared, and we want to help you too."

My eyes flooded in spite of all efforts to control them. *Lord God, please...*

∽

"Why wouldn't they let us see her again today?" Kicking off my shoes, I slammed the front door closed. "And why didn't you argue about it?"

"They recommended this as a good way to start her therapy. They do this thing on a daily basis." Chris dropped his keys on the end table. "I didn't see any good reason to set us up as adversaries. We want them to help Sony." As he walked toward the stairs he added, "At least I do."

My jaw dropped, and I squeaked, "And just what does that mean?"

"Nothing." His voice muffled, and he groaned. "I have to get to work. I have several meetings I should be at today. Don't forget, we asked for Evan to get off the bus at Zack's, in case we weren't home by bus time."

"Yes, thank you." A little too much sarcastic politeness, Yoyo? "I do remember, and I will get him home. Don't worry."

"Yoyo, wait." He moved back toward me.

"You've got to get to work, remember?" I turned my back to him and headed for the kitchen. "Better not be late."

## CHAPTER 19

As soon as the front door closed behind Chris, I called Cara. "Did you say you have a few hours off between shifts today?"

"Yes." She paused. "Do you need company?"

*Jesus, thank You so much for this precious friend.*

"I do." I scrunched my face to hold back tears.

"Perfect. I was looking for an excuse not to use my break to do laundry. How about I bring lunch by? Any preference?"

"Surprise me." I hiccupped. "I don't have the brainpower to make a decision."

Letting the phone drop to the kitchen table, I rested my face in my hands. "Okay, Lord, I need Your help here. I don't need to slide into self-pity."

～

CARA SET carry-out sacks on the table, then gave me a quick hug. "I couldn't decide on healthy or yummy, so I got both."

"Yeah?" I brought our coffee to the table. "Sounds smart."

"I picked up chef salads from the deli and shakes from my

new favorite ice cream shop." Bags rattled as she emptied them onto the table. "I remember you said your favorite ice cream is peanut butter-chocolate."

"Oh, my goodness, I owe you so many favors."

"You're teaching me to crochet, remember?" She plunked food cartons in front of me then scooted out the chair across the table. "Come on now, tell me what's happening with Sonya."

Collapsing onto my own chair, I wrapped one hand around the shake and the other around my coffee. "We saw her at breakfast but…" Yoyo, don't start crying already. "In the end, I made Chris mad at me."

∼

AFTER I EXPLAINED what all happened at the hospital and before Chris left for work, Cara stuffed a napkin under my hand. "Wipe your face."

Laughter bubbled out of my mouth, and I had to use the napkin to wipe my nose from crying as well as the ice cream on my lips. "You are such a goof."

"Mmm hmm." She stood. "I'm getting more coffee. You?"

"Please."

After setting the refilled cups on the table, she rubbed my shoulder before taking her seat again. "Sounds to me like you guys are just under a truck-load of stress, more than Chris being mad at you."

"Probably so."

We didn't speak for a couple minutes as we ate our salads.

"How did you and Chris meet anyway?"

"Oh." I swallowed a bite of boiled egg. "My motorcycle story."

"He taught you to drive a motorcycle?"

"No. No, no. Chris has never been interested in riding a motorcycle. Let's back up."

Scrubbing my mouth with a napkin, I scooted back from the table. "After Mom died, I went a little crazy. I've never drank alcohol. For as far back as I can remember I'd promised myself I wasn't going to let that ruin my life like it had Mom's. But my dorm roommate partied a whole lot more than she studied. I kept on studying. I wanted to do that much for Mom. But I started hanging out with Kayla and her friends."

Cara let me talk.

"We had a lot of interesting Friday night parties. They took me into the country and let me drive their car along an empty road. We went hiking and got lost in the woods during a thunderstorm. In the middle of the night."

I reached for my coffee. "One Friday, Jassen, Kayla's boyfriend, decided we should repaint his entire apartment. His roommate was out of town, so he figured this would be a perfect time, and a fun surprise, for the roommate."

"Did the painting include the roommate's bedroom?"

"Yes. I painted it, actually. By myself. Jassen gave me a can of purple paint, a brush, and a stool to stand on to reach high. 'Have a blast,' he told me and left me alone in the room." I took a sip of coffee. "He didn't give me any sheets or anything to cover furniture."

"Oooohh. Oh my."

"Anyway." I rested my chin in my hand. "One night after the gang was pretty sloppy, not roaring drunk you know, just sloppy, they decided to ride their motorcycles. Jassen said since I hadn't drunk anything, I should be his designated driver."

"O-kay."

"He sat behind me and gave me instructions." My lips twitched. "It was December, and we did some cool skidding. Eventually, we ran into a snow pile and landed on our sides. Jassen wasn't hurt, but I, I not only broke my shoulder, but I really messed it up."

"Tell me you wore helmets."

"Of course. These were smart, reasonable college students."

"Mmm."

"Anyway, I spent most of the winter break in rehab, and that's where I met Chris. He was there after surgery for his broken ankle."

"How did he break his ankle?"

"He was taking out the garbage, and he slipped at the top of his front porch stairs. It was icy, and he fell down all nine steps."

She giggled. "Not as fun a story as yours."

## CHAPTER 20

When I heard the school bus turn onto our road, I walked next door to Zack's house to meet Evan. I didn't want to arrive with enough time for Zack's mom to ask questions about Sonya.

"Mommy, you're home." Evan didn't sound as exuberant as usual as he walked to meet me. "How's Sony?"

I raised my hand to wave at Zack and his mom when I caught their voices. "Thanks, you guys. Hey, little man. Let me give you a three-armed hug."

This was what Evan called it when I wrapped both arms around him and pressed my cane along his spine.

Today he didn't laugh. "Mama, you said Sony hurt herself. What's wrong? Is she home?"

With one arm around him, I walked us into the house and to the couch. "Jump up here, buddy."

He scrambled onto my lap and buried his face against my chest.

"Hey, baby." Lifting his head, I peppered his face with kisses. "It's okay, honey. She's okay." My hands moved to his sides. "Maybe a little tickling would help."

"No, no, nooo." He giggled and writhed but didn't get down. "You sure, Mama? Sony's okay?"

I drew him close again. "I'm sure. She hurt herself a little, and…" I gulped. "She's very sad. She's going to be in the hospital for a couple of days, but when she comes home, it'll be our job to help her be happy."

Evan was quiet.

When I tipped his face up again, I found tears on his cheeks. "I promise, buddy. She'll be okay." *Lord, please make it true.* "Trust me, Ev. I'm your mother."

Rocking him from side to side, I sang our lullaby from First John chapter three. "God calls you His son, and that's who you are. He loves you so much, and that's who you are."

∽

THROUGHOUT OUR MARRIAGE, Chris claimed the words from Ephesians chapter four about not letting the sun go down on your anger. Maybe Cara was right. Maybe we were just stressed, and he wasn't mad at me. But I stayed up until he came home that night.

"Hey." He dropped his keys on the end table and sat on the other end of the couch.

"Hey." My lips were dry. "So, what happened with the pipes? Why did you have to stay so late?"

"The pipes in the kitchen burst." His voice sounded weary. "We had a flood all the way into the fellowship hall before anyone realized, because nobody had been in there all day. I took our coffee pot down to wash it out, and whoa." He cleared his throat. "Anyway, it took a while to find a plumber to come in the evening. Then somebody, meaning me, had to stay there while they did the work."

"Sorry."

"It's okay."

We were quiet, then, "Are you mad at me?" popped out of my mouth.

Silence.

Chris stood up. "I'm not mad at you, honey, but..."

My stomach flopped. "But?"

He walked toward the kitchen, then stopped and turned back. "This isn't about you, Yoyo." Once they started, his words spurted out. "Not about you not being able to be a good mother to a teenage girl because you're blind. Because your mom was an alcoholic, or because she died without letting you in on her sickness." He slapped his hands against his legs. "This is about Sony. Not you."

"Whoa." I jumped to my feet. "How many days have you let the sun go down on all this?"

"What?"

My cheeks were hot with a flush. I didn't know what else to say.

"Oh, Yoyo." He hesitated. "I'm tired. I need to go to bed."

He stepped toward me, but I moved away from him.

"Okay." He let out a deep sigh. "I'm getting up early and going to the hospital before work. Maybe you can spend some time with Sony, too, while Evan's at school."

"At least you're allowing me to try to be her parent," were the words that tried to force themselves out of my mouth, but somehow I kept them in.

## CHAPTER 21

Next morning, I climbed on the bus and headed to the hospital. *Lord, help this to be a better day.*

The bus door closed as I took my seat. "All right, listen up." The driver stood at the front and called back to us. "Trivia question of the day."

A few people around me moaned, but others shushed them. "Quiet. I wanna hear."

"Give me one name of a bird that sticks it out in the winter in Alaska."

More grumbling. "Not fair." "Make it multiple choice." "True or false, true or false."

"Nope. You know the rules." He sat and started the bus moving. "For anybody new, winners get to choose one lollipop from my basket. You're allowed to bring me an answer another day."

*Jesus, help me to control my tongue today with Sony.* My fingers twisted the handle on my purse. *Help me to be the mother she needs.*

"You look familiar to me." The older lady escorting me to Sonya's room patted my fingers where they rested on her arm. "Did you used to work here in the hospital?"

"No, but if you've been volunteering here for six years, you may have walked with me before. I did an internship here about that long ago."

"Hmm. Maybe. It's hard to remember how many years." We entered the elevator. "Are you an intern again, or do you have a job here now?"

"I'm visiting my daughter." I thanked God she didn't ask any more questions as she walked with me to the room.

As I sat next to Sony's bed, waiting for her to come back for lunch, I practiced what to say to her.

What is wrong with you, Sonya?

Why didn't you talk to us?

What is it you want from this?

Fortunately, none of these were spoken out loud, because in a few minutes, Sony was there, plopping a lunch container in my lap.

"You could have come to have lunch with all of us, but I figured you wanted to drill me full of questions." She plunked down on the side of the bed and peeled open her own lunch.

Take a breath, Yoyo. Remember, your daughter is hurting.

"What's for lunch today? How's the food?" Opening my own lunch, I picked up the wrapped sandwich.

"It's all right, I guess. I got you chicken salad."

"Thanks. Smells good."

We were quiet, forcing ourselves to chew. A cart rolled by the open door. Down the hall, a phone rang.

"Sony, please tell me what's going on." *Lord, why do I have to cry?*

"Ah, Mom, don't do that." She shoved napkins into my hand. "That just makes it worse."

Of course. That's what I can do for her. Make it worse.

"I'm sorry. I didn't mean that." Sony set her food aside and took hold of my hands. "I'm sorry, Mama. So sorry."

Pull yourself together, Iola. Oh, woman, sometimes you drive me crazy.

Taking my hands from Sony, I laid them against her cheeks. "No, baby. Don't tell me you're sorry. I won't tell you I'm sorry either. What good will any of that do?" With tears dripping down my face, I leaned over and kissed the top of her head. "You and I know best how to fight. So, we may do it kicking and screaming, but somehow, I'm going to help you through this. I'm your mother. I love you."

## CHAPTER 22

"Mommy, can I pleeeease go over to Zack's house to play? Pleeeease." Evan grabbed my hands and bounced on the porch in front of me. "You can come get me when Daddy and Sony are home. I don't want to wait anymore."

*Thank You, God, that at least someone is back to normal.*

"Ev." With my hands on his shoulders, I stopped his bouncing. "Okay. You can go over now. But don't make Zack's mom crazy."

"Huh? Why would I do that?" He jiggled under my hands.

"Right." I gave him a kiss. "Be good. Daddy will come get you in a little while."

I slumped back in the porch swing.

"I'll pick Sonya up on my way home from work." Chris's voice on the phone had sounded tired, defeated.

"Okay." We hadn't talked much the last couple of days.

*Lord, this family needs Your help.*

I swiped at tears. No more crying, Yoyo. This wasn't like me.

Our car bumped up into the driveway and stopped. The front passenger door opened, and Sony hurried up the steps. "I'm going to bed, Mom. Please just leave me alone for now. Dad told me you guys hid every possible sharp object you could find in the house. I won't hurt myself."

My eyes and mouth popped open, but before I could speak, the front door banged behind her.

Chris took slower steps onto the porch then sat down beside me. "Can I hold your hand?" His voice quivered.

"Please."

He wrapped his hand around mine, and we sat, leaning against each other. A car passed on the street. An owl hooted.

*Lord, we need each other's support. Help us.*

"Where's Evan?"

"He's at Zack's. I told him you'd come get him soon."

Chris started the swing moving. "They suggested at the hospital that I bring Sony in for an early-morning counseling session tomorrow." He rubbed the back of my hand with his thumb. "Then they said she should participate every day, in the same activities she's been doing, for the next two weeks, then knock it down to three times a week for a while."

"What kind of activities?"

"Individual counseling, group sessions, different kinds of therapy, music, crafts, exercise. Hours for homework with some tutoring assistance available."

"Okay." I linked my fingers with his. "So, we'll keep her out of school for now?"

"Yeah. Maybe we should even talk about homeschool for a while." He rubbed my arms. "It's getting chilly. Why don't you go inside? I'll get Evan."

∼

After Evan was asleep, I paused outside Sony's door. Should I tell her good night? She'd said to leave her alone for a while.

Pressing my lips together, I tapped my fingers against my chin. *Jesus?*

All right. I'll leave her alone tonight. She probably won't mind Chris checking on her later on.

Chris was in our office, but I didn't hear any noises from the computer. I pulled up a chair and sat beside him.

"Honey." He turned to me and took hold of my hands. "I'm sorry about the other night."

"Me too."

Don't cry.

"You know I believe you're a wonderful mom." He traced circles on my palms.

"And we both know I don't think so. I'm as aware as you are that I've had problems with my own mental health." Raising my chin, I stiffened myself to push back tears. "I've always struggled with being a mother, especially to Sony, because of my mom, because of my blindness. Because—"

"Shh." He scooted even closer and pushed my head against his shoulder. "And you know I think the problems between you and Sony aren't that much different than between many moms and teenage daughters." He kissed the top of my head. "We're not going to solve all that tonight. Take a breath." He rubbed my back. "You know I'll support you whatever you want to do. If you decide you need counseling again, that's certainly okay with me. But..."

I pushed myself up to a sitting position. "But right now, we need to help Sony. Not focus on, on all the problems I want to drag up about myself."

"I think you have fewer problems than you think you do." He drew his finger along my lips. "We're both feeling pretty stressed right now."

Squeezing my eyes together, I let out a long breath. "I love you."

"I know. I love you too."

## CHAPTER 23

As soon as the house was empty the next morning, I climbed on the treadmill. "No music today, God. No audio books. I need to talk to You."

Once my feet were moving, I searched for what to say next.

"Jesus? Father? Lord? I don't know where to start."

My fingers hovered over the controls. If I set it on running, I wouldn't have to think. No, walking is a healthy exercise. And you need to think.

"Father?" I didn't call God "Father" often, but today, I needed a father.

"I am such a mess. You know that even better than I do. Mom taught me that Jesus loves me, but it wasn't until I met Chris that I finally let You take a major part in my life."

Today, no one around but me and God, it was an okay time to let tears flow.

"Chris always says he fell in love with me as soon as he met me in the hospital rehab department."

We'd spent hours just talking back then, both of us taking the opportunity to spill out all that mattered to us to a complete stranger.

"Jesus loves people so much." I could still hear the tears in Chris's voice. "I want to spend my life helping lonely people understand this."

After days of listening to him talk like that, I began to believe what Mom had always told me.

Chris was the first person I told, "I was able to do so many things, even though I was blind, when Mom was beside me. Now that she's gone, I'm not sure I have the courage to try to do all this by myself." And after a minute, "I'm so mad at her. I thought we were close. Why didn't she let me share her dying? Didn't she trust me?"

"I know you're really hurting," Chris had told me. "I believe, I believe you are going to be important in my life, Iola. Please let me help you."

"And he did, God." Holding on with one hand, I swiped tears with the other. "He connected me with a Christian counselor and psychiatrist. They helped me deal with the sickness I was hiding, and…" My face quivered, and my throat clogged.

Take a deep breath, Iola.

"And I finally understood what Mom had been trying to tell me. That You loved me. That You could use me."

Chris encouraged me when I decided to become a social worker. I wanted to help other people the way Miranda, the counselor he'd introduced me to, had helped me.

"But, God, it's Sony I need to help now."

A thought struck me. "Lord, You trusted me with her. Oh." My heart skipped a beat with that realization. "Whoa." My feet moved, and I drew in deep breaths. "Father? You trusted her to me." After more deep breaths, I could only whisper. "I need to be strong for her, and I can't without You. She's my baby, Lord. Please, help me."

When Chris dropped Sonya off a couple of hours later, she again went straight to her room. But I followed right after her.

"Good, Mom. Make it in quick so I don't have time to push any furniture in front of the door."

Hold your tongue, Iola. Remember you're the adult here.

"Did you and Daddy get anything for lunch?"

She flopped onto her bed. "No. I wasn't hungry."

Before she could tell me not to, I nudged her over and sat beside her. "I was planning to have ice cream for lunch. Wanna join me?"

"Oh good, Mom. Way to help out your fat daughter."

"Sony." I stopped. She was not fat, but probably over her recommended body weight. She'd always called herself fat though. Was bulimia part of her troubles?

"Don't worry, Yoyo. I haven't been forcing myself to throw up." She turned onto her back. "Wanna see my scars?"

"What?"

"Here." She took hold of my hand and placed it on her abdomen under her shirt.

Biting my tongue to keep from jerking, I let my hand rest for a minute. As I began to trace my fingers along the skin right above her pants, I wanted to sob.

They'd told me she'd been doing this for a long time. Besides the new stitches, I felt dozens of thin, smooth lines.

Oh, my baby.

*What should I say, Lord?*

"Pretty crazy, huh, Mom?" Now, her voice held tears. She never cried in front of me. We fought instead.

Nudging her over a little more, I lay beside her and wrapped her in my arms.

## CHAPTER 24

Sunday night, Cara invited me to go out for ice cream.

"Oh sure, leave me like this." Chris's voice was muffled by Evan, who was sprawled across him on the couch.

"Ev? Are you sure Daddy can breathe?" I gave him a sloppy kiss.

"Mama, Mama, noooo." He squealed and wriggled and bounced on Chris.

"Be gentle with Daddy, sweetie." I gave Chris a kiss, too, then moved to the front porch.

Cara's horn honked. "Ready?"

"So ready." I clicked the passenger door shut. "Let's go, chicky."

"Are you up for sitting outside?" Cara eased her small car out of our bumpy drive. "It's getting colder, and this may be about the last time this fall we'll be able to enjoy being outdoors."

"Sure. I'm not a freeze baby."

"Good. Then you'll join me in a double scoop." Definitely a smile in her voice.

We found a park bench and settled down for some serious

frozen therapy. "Was this the weekend Alan was coming to visit?"

She groaned. "Yes. He came. He just left an hour ago."

"Uh-oh, was it bad? Is that why you needed a double scoop?"

"Yes, it is why I needed the ice cream, but no, it wasn't bad." She paused. "We actually had a really nice time."

"Mmm hmm." I took a large bite of caramel fudge to stop myself from saying anything else.

"Yes." Her mouth sounded full, too, but she went on. "He wants to get back together."

"Uh-huh." Taking another big bite, I shivered and hunched my shoulders.

"He said he realized as soon as I left for grad school that he'd made a big mistake." She chewed in silence, but when I didn't respond, she went on. "He started taking classes online, and he'll finish his business degree in December."

"Okay."

"He said he's been looking for jobs here in the city. He wants to move here, spend some time with me, and convince me he's ready to get married this time."

"Whoa. He came right out with all of that, huh?"

"Yep."

We munched without talking for a minute. Geese flew by overhead. A dog barked in the distance.

"That's really all I want to say about that right now." Cara sat up a little taller. "How's Sonya?"

"I see." I kicked both feet on the grass in front of us. "She's okay, I guess. Cliff is over tonight visiting with her."

"I know Cliff from church. Is he her boyfriend?"

"Nooo, just friends. Good friends. Best friends since we moved here, and I found them huddled together in a corner of the kindergarten Sunday school classroom."

"Huddled together?"

"Yes. Sony was new and shy, so she escaped to the corner.

Apparently, that was Cliff's normal seat, since he never felt comfortable with the other kids. They've stuck it out together for more than ten years, both of them kind of misfits."

"Do they call themselves misfits?"

"Yes."

"And there's never been anything romantic?" She took my napkins. "There's a trash can right over here. I'll be right back."

As I lifted my face, I could smell the sweet scent of fall flowers in the park, smoke from a fireplace in a house nearby. *Thank You, Jesus. This is lovely.*

Instead of sitting down again, Cara clapped her hands. "Now I'm needing some coffee therapy. Some nice, warm coffee."

Laughter bubbled out of me, and I stood up. "You are a trip, Miss Cara."

Once we'd picked up the coffee, Cara took a couple sips and sighed. "That's better. Now let's just drive around for a while. I can't think of anywhere else to go."

"You're the boss."

"Yes. And, I believe I asked about the romance between Cliff and Sonya."

"Mmm." I took a careful drink. "I think Cliff might have had that idea a year or so ago, but Sonya just shook her head and said he was her best buddy. So Cliff had another girlfriend for a while, but that didn't work out. Sony's been kind of comforting him like a little brother ever since."

"Poor Cliff."

"Yeah." I tapped my fingers on my cup. "Of course, all of this is secondhand knowledge from Chris. Sonya doesn't share with me."

"Sorry, Iola."

"Me too." I took another sip. "However, what Sony doesn't know is that most days, I'm going to be accompanying her to the program at the hospital."

## CHAPTER 25

"Why didn't Daddy give me a ride to the hospital?" Sony dragged her feet as I tried to hurry her out the front door.

"Because he needed to be at work earlier than you needed to leave. And since Evan just left for school, I'm free to go with you now."

"Are we taking Uber?"

"Nope. The bus trip to the hospital is an easy route, and I'm hoping to find another fun driver like I had last week."

"Beautiful."

That ended our conversation as we walked to the bus stop. And, yay, it was the same trivia-happy bus driver.

"All right people, listen up."

"Is this your friend, Mom?"

"Yes, shh. I want to hear." I tapped her knee.

"I had toast very early for breakfast this morning." Over conversation and groans, the driver raised his voice. "Any of you have the same?"

"Yeah." "Yes." "Absolutely." "French toast, does that count?"

"No, no, no. That's not the question you get the lollipop for. The question is…" He waited for silence. "Toast was a popular breakfast food in the stone age. They mixed two grains together with a little water and set it on top of a fire. What were the two grains they used?"

Louder groans. The driver seated himself and drove on.

"What a joy." Sony squirmed beside me. "So, are you going to hang around me all day? I thought this therapy was supposed to be for me. How can I pay attention to it with you looking over my shoulder?"

"No worries, my love." I tapped her knee again. "I'm going to meet with the social worker for a while, but then I'm going home. Daddy will pick you up after work."

"Why can't I just take the bus by myself?"

"Because the directions for the program are that a parent accompanies you, at first anyway."

"Huh," she grumbled. "They don't trust me either."

*Lord, does she sound a little relieved?*

∼

THAT EVENING, after I'd chased Evan around his room growling, "I'm your mother," I made my way to Sonya's room. The door was open. "Can I come in?"

"Sure. Why not?" Her voice was less than happy, but I figured I wouldn't get a better invitation.

Sonya sat at her desk, so I plopped on the bed near her. "What are you doing?"

"Writing in my journal."

"You have a journal?" Wait. I hesitated. "Is that something they suggested in therapy?"

"Brilliant, Mom. Aren't you a true social worker slash counselor?"

*God, I am not going to let this child get me mad.*

"I'm also your mother."

Her pen scraped across the paper.

"Sony, please tell me what's going on. Why do you hurt yourself?"

*Lord, it's past time I ask her.*

No response.

When I laid my hand on her arm, she slammed her pen on the desk and pulled away, jumping to her feet. "No, Mom. Go away."

I stood up. "I'm not going away, honey."

Sony flung herself onto the bed. "Go. Just go."

Sitting again, I rested my hand on her back. "No."

Sony tensed, and I rubbed her shoulders with both hands. "Please talk to me, sweetheart."

She gasped, moaned, then turned her face toward me. "I wanted to scream. I needed to, to get everything out." She drew in ragged breaths. "When I cut myself, it hurt. I was so glad. I could cry. It feels, it felt so good."

"Oh, baby." I lowered my face to rest on hers. "Lord, help my… Please help Your precious child."

## CHAPTER 26

Chris gave Sony a ride both ways for her therapy the next day, but as soon as she was home, I forced my feet to take me into her room. "Hey. Can I come in?"

"Come."

Sonya sat at her desk again, so I took the bed. "How was your day today?"

"Okay."

Great. "Tell me what you did."

She tapped her pen on the desk. "They had an arts and crafts time. Some of the kids are really into art. I guess they can express some of their feelings that way, painting, drawing, clay." She sighed. "I've never been good at art. Or anything else either." The last words she muttered with her face turned from me.

Gripping my hands together, I refused to reach out and touch her. I didn't want to push her away. She needed to talk to me. Keep your mouth shut for a little, Yoyo.

"They have a piano in the room where we were working. I played on that a little." She turned toward me. "Remember how I used to clunk around on the piano in our old church, when I was little?"

My mouth fell open. Be careful, Iola.

"I remember. Then you started playing whole songs, after you'd listened for a while, when Mrs. Grafton came to practice for the worship services."

Sonya had only been two when she started with the piano. I brought her over to play in the nursery while I studied on the computer in the church office.

Sonya's chair squeaked. "Yeah. You used to tell people how surprised you were when you came in the sanctuary and thought it was Mrs. Grafton playing 'Ode to Joy,' and you found me sitting on the piano bench playing."

"I did used to say that." Why had I stopped?

"Mrs. Grafton started giving me piano lessons before I was three." There was a smile in her voice.

"Why didn't we continue that when we moved here?"

She turned back to the desk and picked up the pen. Tap, tap, tap, fast taps. "I don't know. We kind of forgot about it, I guess. Such a big move."

"Yeah."

Chris got the offer to work as family minister for the larger church. An older nearby pastor, Pastor Bryan, was looking for a small church to serve for ten years or so before he retired, and the congregation at Stone Valley welcomed him.

My throat was dry. "We thought it'd be better for me to move to a larger city. For transportation, to finish school, easier to find a place for an internship. Work eventually."

"Yes." Her voice was soft. "Of course, we didn't really expect Evan."

"No." We laughed together.

We'd thought I wasn't able to have more children. But Evan surprised us when Sony was almost eleven.

"Honey?" Memories pushed into my mind, Sony playing the

piano, running around laughing with the kids in the small town church.

Chris loved that church.

"Mom?"

"You were really happy back in Stone Valley, weren't you? You had friends." A heavy rock dropped in my belly.

And Chris loved it there.

"Mom?" Sony laid her hand on mine. "Are you okay?"

Pull yourself together, Yoyo. "Sure." I gave myself a mental shake then squeezed Sony's hand. "So, did you like being back on a piano today? Can you still read the music?"

She took her hand away. "I could." I hadn't heard her voice sound so bright since? I didn't know how long.

"Well then." As I stood, I rubbed my hands on her shoulders. "I'm going to talk to Dad about getting you a piano. Or at least an electric keyboard. What foolishness that we've let this go so long."

"Really?" She reached a hand and touched mine, then drew back. "Maybe. I don't know. One of the therapists at the hospital plays. She said she could work with me a little. Let's wait and see how it goes."

"Okay."

*Lord, this child is afraid to have hope. Forgive me. Help her.*

## CHAPTER 27

"Chris? Are you already asleep?" Closing the door, I walked to the bed.

Chris still sat up, his hands lying on a closed book in his lap.

"What's up?" I sat beside him and took his hand in mine.

"Nothing. Just reading a little. Thinking."

"Honey?"

"Hmm?"

Resting my chin in my hand, I drew in a deep breath. "Sony and I were just talking about how much she loved playing the piano back at Stone Valley. Remember?"

"Yeah." He paused. "Why didn't we pick up her piano lessons again once we got settled in here?"

"I was wondering that too."

I chewed my lip then turned to face him. "She was really happy back there. She had friends. She loved playing the piano with Mrs. Grafton."

"Mmm hmm."

"And you loved it there too." My lips trembled. "There was a lot of work, and just you. Preaching, visiting people in hospitals and nursing homes. Manual labor around the building. People helped, but…"

"I remember. It was great." There was a smile in his voice.

"We shouldn't have moved here, should we?"

"Iola, what are you talking about?"

"We moved here for me."

He took hold of my hands. "Honey, no. It was a family decision. We thought the schools in a larger city would probably have better programs for Sony's disability. It looked like a good career move for me."

"And how has all that worked out?" My throat clogged, and I shook my head. "You and Sony were so much happier there. Have you gotten back with them, since they asked you about returning?"

"Yes. I told them…" He shifted on the bed. "I said we were still praying about it."

I rubbed my eyes and squeezed my cheeks. "I guess I'd better start doing that, huh?"

∾

"A CROCHETING LESSON sounds like a wonderful relief." I flopped onto the couch. "Thanks for coming over today."

"You bet." Cara sat beside me. "Let Esther stay today. Teddy and I have come to an understanding about my crocheting at home."

"All right." I grabbed up my cat before she could stick her nose in Cara's bag. "Teddy seems like a more reasonable animal to me, though. Let me see what you're working on right now."

"I'm working on a granny square, like you taught me." She handed me the small square. "You'll be proud of me. This is how far I've gotten after ripping it out three times."

"Good girl. Ooohh, so soft. Is this baby yarn?"

"Yes. My brother and his wife are having another baby. I decided to risk it and try to do a blanket with this delicate stuff."

"You are brave." I captured Esther's paw before she could stick it in the soft piece.

"Is Sonya at the hospital today?"

"Yes. She's doing the program there three days a week now. The other two she usually spends with Chris at the church, going over her schoolwork with him and practicing the piano."

"That is so great, she's playing the piano again. I heard her the other night, from the nursery during the Hope Group."

"She's good. She started out playing by ear, but she actually picked up reading music really quick. Learning disabilities are weird. Reading regular text has always been a struggle for her, but music was easy."

"It's sure a gift from God. I need a sip of coffee. Hey, what's this?" She handed me the sheet of braille I'd left on the end table.

"Bible verses." I laid the page on top of Esther, who'd stretched out asleep on my lap. "I copied down some of the verses my counselor gave me when I was wondering how I could continue to be a capable blind person without my mom to help me."

Running my fingers across lines, I whispered parts of these favorites I'd treasured for years. "From 2 Peter 1, His divine power has given us everything we need for a godly life. Philippians 4, I can do all this through him who gives me strength. From Ephesians 3, Now to him who is able to do immeasurably more than all we ask or imagine, according to his power that is at work within us. And 2 Corinthians 12, But he said to me, 'My grace is sufficient for you, for my power is made perfect in weakness.'"

My eyes squeezed to hold in tears. "I can feel Esther purring through the paper." I handed it back to Cara. "You'd better put it back on the table before she wakes up and decides to tear it."

Esther purred in her sleep and covered her face with her paws.

"I'll need all of those verses if we move back to Stone Valley."

"Are you seriously thinking about that?"

"Maybe. You won't miss me anyway, since you'll be moving back home to marry Alan."

"Huh. Not hardly. He said he'd move here to be with me, remember?" She hesitated. "I am taking a few extra days off next week, for my visit home at Thanksgiving, though. So we can have more time together, to talk, to try to figure this all out."

"Good." I rested my hand on her shoulder. "Are you happy about all this?"

"Maybe." She paused. "Yes."

## CHAPTER 28

"What do you think, Esther? Are Sony and I going to make it through a whole day alone together without arguing?" The cat growled and grumbled as I reached under her to pull out the laptop I'd left on the couch. "You're right. We haven't started with schoolwork yet."

"Mama!"

When Sony screamed, I left the computer and ran up the stairs. "Honey?"

Pushing open her door, I hurried to her bed. "Sony?"

She sat on the bed, hunched over, shaking and dragging in sobbing breaths.

I sat beside her and pulled her close. "Sweetie. Shh, shh, shh. Breathe easy, honey."

She took hold of my hand and dropped something inside, then squeezed my hand shut. "Help me, Mama. Help me."

As we rocked and cried, I whispered, "Jesus, help us. Help us, Jesus."

Finally, Sonya pulled away and lay back on the bed, burying her face in the pillow. When I opened my hand, I found a staple.

"Sony?"

Her voice muffled in the pillow. "I crawled all over the floor, looking. I found it stuck in the carpet under my bed and yanked it out."

*Please, God.*

"Honey? Did you cut yourself?"

"Not much." She turned to face me and took hold of my hand, laying it on her belly. "It's really tiny. It doesn't need stitches this time."

My fingers trembled as I felt wetness on her skin. "Let me get a washcloth, sweetie. Stay here."

When I returned with a warm cloth, she took it and cleaned herself.

"Sony?" I sat beside her again. "Can you talk to me about this?"

She sat up beside me, resting her elbows on her knees, her face in her hands. "I hate myself, Mama."

*Lord, help me keep my mouth shut.*

"I'm ugly. Too heavy. My glasses are too thick, my hair is thin and straggly. Cliff is the only boy who ever takes a second look at me, and that's just because he doesn't have any other friends either."

Stay quiet, Yoyo.

"And I'm dumb." She slapped her hands on her knees. "I still have to struggle when I read. You say it's a learning disability, but truly, I'm just dumb. I'm lucky to get Cs in school. I've never done anything to make you proud, like other kids do their parents, no academic awards or club or athletic prizes."

"Sony—"

"No, Mom. Just don't. No. And you know what the worse thing is?"

I clamped my teeth on my lip.

"The kids at school aren't mean to me usually. I see other kids being bullied, and that's not what happens to me. They just ignore me. It's like I'm invisible." She rocked from front to back.

"That time when those girls laughed at me when I cried? In a way, I was glad. At least I knew I was really there, that they could really see me."

*Lord, can I hug her yet?*

"I want to make sure I'm not invisible. I like pain, because then at least I know there's something to me."

Yes. It was definitely time to hug her.

With my face pressed to Sony's, I sang our lullaby. "God calls you His daughter, and that's who you are. He loves you so much, and that's who you are."

## CHAPTER 29

"Oh, Mom, you're gonna be so happy." Sony flopped onto the bus seat and scooted over for me to sit beside her. "We've got your favorite driver again today."

"Oh, goody. I'm starting a list of trivia facts to research online when I have time."

"Maybe you can help me do that for an English essay." Her voice sounded hesitant.

I squeezed her hand. "I will."

"All right, ladies and gents." Everyone quieted as soon as the driver stood and spoke. "Did I tell you my daughter's getting married this weekend?"

"Yes," a woman yelled from the back. "Do I get a lollipop for that answer?"

"No, ma'am, but I applaud your courage. Nope, that's not the question of the day. I've been learning an awful lot about wedding history and customs. Tell me this. Where did the tradition of a white wedding dress come from?"

As he started the bus, murmurs and groans arose, just like every day. I smiled.

Sony's hand still lay under mine, and hers began to shake. "Mom?"

"Hmmm?"

"You've told me that when you and Daddy met, you were having trouble with depression and anxiety."

Grinning, I winked at her. "Not because of meeting Daddy."

"No, I didn't mean…"

"I know, honey." I shifted in the seat to face her better and took hold of both her hands. "I'd probably had that problem for a long time. Daddy asked me to see a counselor and a psychiatrist. I've done it a couple more times over the years."

"And it helped you?"

*Lord, give me the right words.*

"Yes. It helped a lot. That's why I decided to become a counselor."

The bus stopped and started again. The overhead speaker which announced the stops wasn't working today.

*I hope one of us notices when it's our stop.*

"Medicine helped. Counselors have given me reasonable ideas, even if sometimes it was stuff I already knew. It always helps to hear it again, from more than one person. Christian counselors have introduced me to comforting, smart Bible verses."

"This is our stop. What Bible verses helped you most?"

When we'd stepped onto the sidewalk and moved away from the bus door, I stopped and faced her. "I can give you a list sometime if you like. My favorite is Psalm 34:18: 'The Lord is close to the brokenhearted and saves those who are crushed in spirit.'"

~

"Are you guys going to use all this stuff to decorate for Christmas?" Cara had agreed to help me bring our Christmas supplies from the attic.

"No." Setting the last box on the living room floor, I rubbed the dust from my hands. "My hope is actually to weed through it and throw a lot away. Besides all the stuff we've collected since we've been married, there's boxes of junk Chris's parents gifted us with when they cleaned out their attic."

"Oh, joy."

"Tell me about it." I knelt down and pulled open a lid. "Let's start a keep pile and a throw-away pile. Are you going home to visit your parents again for Christmas?"

"The library doesn't close until six o'clock Christmas Eve, and I drew the winning straw for working that final shift. Alan's coming up to go to church with me that evening, then we're driving home to his parents' house that night. I'm staying over and spending Christmas day with them."

"Whoa. Not even engaged yet, and already you're dividing up holidays with in-laws. Now, this definitely goes in the keep pile." I held up the glittery ball with the date, which I was still able to feel, of the year Chris and I got married.

"For sure." She hesitated. "Actually, we're having Christmas evening dinner with both sets of parents. And the engagement is being announced."

"Seriously?" Dropping the ornament back in the box, I crawled over to give her a hug. "It's decided?"

"Mmm hmm. I'm getting an engagement ring for my Christmas present." Her voice took on shyness, but I could hear her happiness.

"That is so great." I bounced up and down on my knees. "And we'll finally get to meet him on Christmas Eve at church."

"Yep. How about this fluffy Christmas stocking?"

"Let me see it."

She handed it to me.

"No way. This is so old, it has to be from when Chris was a kid."

"You're not going to ask Chris?"

"Nope. He said, 'Do as you will.' He's ready to clean things out as much as I am."

We worked for a few minutes to untangle a string of lights.

"Iola?"

"Hmmm?"

"Would you be my matron of honor?"

My hands stopped. "Really? You don't have a high school or college friend to ask?"

"Not anybody as special." Shy Cara again.

"Oh, honey." I dropped the lights and hugged her. "I'd love to. You are so special to me too."

My heart squeezed. *Lord, thank You for this lovely friend.*

As we untangled more lights, the furnace turned on. Esther bumped against the bathroom door, where I'd shut her up to protect the open boxes.

I gulped. "I'm really gonna miss you. If we move to Stone Valley."

"Tell me about that."

"Chris has been talking to people in the church there. About the schools. He's found nearby counseling programs for Sony, a psychiatrist only a twenty-mile drive away."

"That, that's good." She laid her hands on top of mine. "I'll miss you too. If that happens."

The front door banged open. "Mama, Cara. Look what we made in art today. For the Christmas tree." Evan banged through the boxes on the floor until he reached us and draped the construction paper chain around my neck. "Isn't it beautiful?"

"It is." As I ran my fingers over the bumpy links of different shapes and sizes, I leaned to give my son a kiss. "This stays in the keep pile for the next fifty years or more."

## CHAPTER 30

"All right, family." Chris clapped his hands. "Let's get this tree decorating party going." He pulled the lid off a box. "Here, we have a plethora of stars to choose from to shine at the top."

"A plethora, huh?" I wound my way through the clutter on the floor to join him. "That means we probably have some that'll go in the throw-away pile too. Evan, go tell Sony to come down and join the party."

Esther screeched.

"Oh no, I stepped on the kitty's tail." Stooping, I grabbed her up and gave her a squeeze. "It's your own fault, cat. You know better than to get in the way of my feet."

"Here's something that'll cheer the kitty up, a whole chain of bells." The ringing concoction sailed across the room as Chris tossed it, and Esther hurried to jump out of my arms.

"I hope it wasn't something we wanted to keep." I grinned. "We'll never see it in one piece again."

"Mama? Daddy?" Evan's feet raced down the stairs. "Sony's not here."

"What? Of course, she's here. I just saw her half an hour ago." I scrunched my nose. "Maybe an hour."

"Check in the basement." Chris made his way to the tree. "I've found the perfect star. Ev, she's probably doing laundry."

"Sony, Sony, Sony." Evan screeched his way down the basement stairs.

"I didn't hear her go down." A prickle of fear touched the back of my neck.

"She's not there." Evan slammed the basement door. "Sony, where are you?"

"Chris?"

"I'll check her room."

He was back in an instant. "Her wallet's gone. Her keys. The shoes she wore today."

God is so good. Only a minute passed, as we stood silent, my heart throbbing so loud the others could surely hear it, before Chris's phone rang.

"We're on our way." He laid his hand on my shoulder but spoke to Evan. "Buddy, get your coat and shoes. You're going to Zack's house." He turned back to me. "She's at the hospital. She sounds, she sounds okay. Do you know their phone number next door?"

Evan didn't ask questions. Or waste time. Scooping him up at the front door, I squeezed him tight. "It's gonna be okay, sweetheart. I love you."

*God, let it be okay.*

~

Sony sat with Cliff's parents when we hurried into the waiting room. Kneeling in front of her, I wrapped her in a hug. "Honey. Are you okay?"

"Mama." She sobbed and pressed her face against my shoulder, trembling.

"Jeff?" Chris walked to Cliff's dad. "What's going on?"

"Sonya called us." The man's voice grated. "Cliff tried to kill himself."

Sonya shook in my arms. In the chair next to her, Cliff's mom wept.

∼

AFTER THE DOCTORS assured Cliff's parents he would live, we drove Sonya home. I sat in the back seat beside her, snuggling her close to me.

Before Evan would go to bed, he climbed into Sonya's lap on the couch. "Are you okay? Are you gonna stay home now?"

"Yes, buddy." Her voice was full of tears. "I'm not going anywhere. I promise."

## CHAPTER 31

"I need coffee." Chris headed for the kitchen. "Sony, hot chocolate? Yoyo?"

"Hot chocolate for both of us." If I'd thought Sony would agree to it, I'd have pulled her onto my lap. Trying not to scare her off, I pressed close to her on the couch and took one of her hands in mine. Neither of us spoke.

"Drinks for all." Chris set a tray on the end table then sat on the floor in front of Sony. "Honey, talk to us."

"Here, sweetie." I placed a cup of cocoa into her hands and laid my hand on her knee.

"Esther, no." Sonya passed the cocoa back to me and wrapped her arms around the cat, who'd jumped onto her lap. "No cocoa for you, bad kitty." From her muffled voice, I knew she had her face pressed into the cat's fur.

Setting Sony's cocoa back on the table, I picked up my own mug and clutched it tight in my shaking hands.

"Cliff called me tonight right after supper." She'd raised her head, and her voice trembled. "He said he was down the street a few houses and asked me to come out to him and not tell anyone."

I set down my cup before it spilled then squeezed my fingers tight together.

"As soon as I got in the car, he took off, before I could get my seatbelt on. He drove fast, squealing around corners and talking loud and crying. He said he'd decided to kill himself."

Her body jerked next to me, and she gasped but went on. "He'd been collecting sleeping pills a few at a time from his parents' medicine cabinet for months, and he talked his cousin into buying some whiskey for him. He said—" She gulped. "He said we could drink and take the pills and just fall asleep, and put an end to, to everything and everybody who hurt us."

She was sobbing, squeezing Esther so hard she growled.

Chris took the kitty and set her on the floor then sat on the couch on Sony's other side. When both of us were clasping her hands, she went on.

"I wanted to." It came out an angry shout. "I wanted to." A pleading whisper.

*Dear Lord, no.* I clamped my teeth on my lower lip to hold back words.

"We parked at the river, and Cliff started drinking the whiskey. I tried to take a drink, but it just made me gag. I couldn't take any more of it. Then he opened the bottle of pills and offered it to me."

She stopped. I held my body still.

"I didn't take any, so he took the bottle back and swallowed a bunch of them. He drank more whiskey and laughed and cried and kept telling me it would just be like falling asleep. After a while, he didn't talk as much. He sounded sleepier, and I got scared. I yelled at him and shook him. He rested his head on my shoulder and handed me the bottle again. He said, he said he loved me, then he didn't say anything else."

When I rested my face against hers, I felt wetness on her cheeks.

"I wanted to take the pills, Daddy, Mama. I didn't want to be alone, without Cliff. I wanted to, to stop fighting inside myself all the time. But I couldn't do it."

Pulling her hands free, she turned and wrapped her arms around my neck. "I thought about you, Mama. How sad you've always been that your mom died without talking to you, without telling you she was going to die. I didn't want to do that to you again."

She pulled back. "So I called 911 and Cliff's parents. I kept slapping Cliff and shaking him until the ambulance came. I screamed at him not to leave me."

Stroking her back, I strained to calm her trembling. *Father, sixteen years ago, You gifted me with this beautiful child. Tonight, You gave her to me again. Thank You. Thank You.*

An overwhelming sense of peace settled over me, took my breath away. *Lord, You make all things new.*

~

That night I tucked Sony into bed just like I did Evan. With my face pressed against her hair, I whispered, "The Lord is close to the brokenhearted and saves those who are crushed in spirit."

When I walked into our bedroom, I found Chris sitting on the side of the bed, his head bowed. He pulled me down beside him. "Is she asleep?"

"Almost. I stayed until her breathing calmed." I rested my head on his shoulder. "Put in your resignation. Tell Stone Valley we're coming. We need to go soon."

He turned toward me and cupped my face in gentle hands. "Are you sure?"

"Yes. She needs a drastic change to begin healing. And for now, my most important job is to mother her."

## CHAPTER 32

After the Christmas Eve service, Cara, Alan, and Cliff came back to our house for cookies and cider.

"I want to show Cliff the new electric keyboard I got from the grandparents," Sony'd told me before church. "It's okay if I ask him over, isn't it?"

As Cara followed me into the kitchen, I said, "A month ago, I would have said no way."

"But now?"

After flicking on the coffeepot, I turned to her. "God has shown me what a peace that passes understanding can really mean. It's not a struggle for me to forgive Cliff. He's still important to Sony, and I don't mind that." Resting my hands on the table, I shook my head and smiled. "Cliff is a hurting person who Jesus loves and, I love him too. The night God saved Sony's life, it changed me inside."

I opened a container of homemade cookies. "You know me. Always jumping to speak before I listen. Miss Foot-in-Mouth. I'm slowing down a lot these days."

"What about finding a job?"

"I was silly to think I had to move to a big city to find a job.

My first counselor would have pointed me to Ephesians 3 and asked why I thought I could limit God." I popped a piece of fudge into my mouth. "Mmm, yummy. And for the next few years, I have the job of being whatever I need to be for Sony. Counselor, coach, teacher." My hands hovered over another container of goodies. "God, help us teach her the wonder she really is." I shook my head. "Not to mention, mothering my little rascal Evan." My lips twitched. "Plus, maybe God's calling me to be a preacher's wife. Whatever I can do to help Chris in the church."

"I'm gonna miss you." Her voice trembled.

"Oh no. None of that. We'll get busy planning all the girl time we'll do, trips between here and Stone Valley." I shook her shoulder. "Don't even start that missing stuff."

Cara chuckled. "What does Evan think about moving?"

"He's a little sad about leaving his friends. But, he's a social flutter-by." I grinned. "That boy has no doubts about himself. Try this cookie with dried fruit. So great." I handed her one. "Anyway, Ev'll have no trouble making new friends."

"Come on. What's keeping you guys in here?" Alan, a big man with a voice full of laughter, walked into the kitchen. "You gotta join us in the living room. Sonya says it's time to sing Christmas carols."

And we did. "Silent Night," "O Holy Night," "Joy to the World."

Sony and Cliff led us. Cliff sat beside Sonya as she played the songs on her new keyboard, and after a few shaky words, his rich bass voice joined with her sweet soprano.

*Lord, thank You for being the source where these two can find hope.*

"Mommy, Sony was laughing tonight." Evan scrunched into a ball under his blankets. "She's gonna be okay, isn't she?"

"Yes. How about you? You going to be okay, with a new home, new school, new church?"

"Yeah." He yawned. "I'm gonna miss Zack. We're taking Esther, aren't we?"

A chuckle worked up from inside me. "Of course, we are." I ruffled the kitty through the blankets where she snuggled against Evan. "What would she do without us?"

"Mama?" His voice fought against sleep. "Can we still play the 'I'm your mother' game in the new house?"

THE END

ABOUT THE AUTHOR

Kathy McKinsey grew up on a pig farm in Missouri, and although she's lived in cities for more than 40 years, she still considers herself a farm girl.

She's been married to Murray for 33 years, and they have five adult children.

She's had two careers before writing —stay-at-home-Mom and rehabilitation teacher for the blind.

Now she lives in Lakewood, Ohio with her husband and two of her children. Besides writing, she enjoys activities with her church, editing for other writers, braille transcribing, crocheting, knitting, and playing with the cat and dogs.

http://www.kathymckinsey.com

ALSO BY KATHY MCKINSEY

ALL MY TEARS

We all face challenges, and this book is a combination of challenges which people encountered.

In ALL MY TEARS, Beth fights to recover from alcoholism and to mend her relationships with her family.

In FORGIVEN, Ann doesn't believe God can forgive her.

In I BELIEVE IT'S TRUE, Kathleen wrestles with a years-old fear and with saving her marriage.

In GIFTS FROM MY BROTHER, Cassie needs to learn to deal with chronic depression.

In MY FAMILY, Martie finds herself the single parent of the eight-year-old niece she barely knows when the child's parents die in a car wreck.

## MILLIE'S CHRISTMAS

Millie, an orange kitten, shares about her first Christmas. Her best friend Ruthie, six years old, teaches Millie about Christmas—food, decorations, music, presents, and Jesus!

Millie's friend Bruce, the family dog, also helps her celebrate Christmas, and sometimes gets her in trouble.

When Ruthie's big brother Jake breaks his ankle, Millie learns about sad things, like divorce, when Jake can't visit his mommy for Christmas. Millie watches Ruthie's family love each other through the sadness, and find joy in Christmas.

Share this story with a child you love, struggling with sadness at Christmas. Jesus' love and truth remain solid.

ALSO FROM SCRIVENINGS PRESS

***Beneath the Seams***

*by Peyton H. Roberts*

**A Social Impact Novel**

Fashion designer Shelby Lawrence is launching her mother-daughter dresses nationwide when she receives a photo of the girl who will change her life forever. Runa, the family's newly sponsored child, is a clever student growing up near Dhaka, Bangladesh. Shelby's daughter Paisley is instantly captivated by their faraway friend. As the girls exchange heartwarming messages, Shelby has no idea that a tragedy in Runa's life is about to upend her own.

Dresses are flying off clothing racks when a horrifying scene unfolds in Dhaka that threatens to destroy Shelby's pristine reputation. Even worse—it sends Runa's life spiraling down a terrifying path. Shelby must decide how far she's willing to go to right a tragic wrong.

Both a gripping exposé of fashion industry secrets and a heartwarming mother-daughter tale, *Beneath the Seams* explores love, conscience, hope, and the common threads connecting humanity.

### *Rainstorm*

### by Cindy Bonds

### Romantic Suspense

Laurel Ashburn has a scarred past, filled with corruption and pain. After an injury overseas sends her home, she moves back in with her foster mother and to a town that hates her. Being home puts her on a path to find a missing friend. But when she's attacked over and over, who will be willing to help?

Detective Dev Hollister traded in the big city for a slower pace and less crime in rural Arkansas. After rescuing Laurel from an attempted kidnapping, he finds himself intrigued with this headstrong and stubborn woman.

While Dev's job is to protect Laurel, he wants much more than to solve the case. He wants to give her a new life and reason to stay.

Laurel will have to push beyond her dark past to trust Dev with her life. But after losing so much, can Laurel survive one more storm?

∽

***Blue Plate Special***

*by Award-winning Author Susan Page Davis*

## Book One of the True Blue Mysteries Series

Campbell McBride drives to her father's house in Murray, Kentucky, dreading telling him she's lost her job as an English professor. Her father, private investigator Bill McBride, isn't there or at his office in town. His brash young employee, Nick Emerson, says Bill hasn't come in this morning, but he did call the night before with news that he had a new case.

When her dad doesn't show up by late afternoon, Campbell and Nick decide to follow up on a phone number he'd jotted on a memo sheet. They learn who last spoke to her father, but they also find a dead body. The next day, Campbell files a missing persons report. When Bill's car is found, locked and empty in a secluded spot, she and Nick must get past their differences and work together to find him.

Scrivenings
PRESS
Quench your thirst for story.
www.ScriveningsPress.com

*Stay up-to-date on your favorite books and authors with our free e-newsletters.*

ScriveningsPress.com